THE HUACA

PRAISE FOR

THE HUACA

"*The Huaca* has just the right amount of magic, a perfect dash of romance, and a mystery that will satisfy readers from beginning to end. A breathless read!"

ELANA JOHNSON,
Author of the Possession series

"Mickelson skillfully brings an ancient artifact into a contemporary setting. She opens the door to a place where the living and the dead can reunite, and, more important, to the secrets of friendship, love, and trust."

DIANA LOPEZ
Author of *Confetti Girl* and *Choke*

"Marcia Mickelson's *The Huaca* is original and captivating, combining all the elements of a great read with a touch of *Raiders of the Lost Ark* mystery and magic. I couldn't put it down 'til the last page, and when I did, the story remained in the forefront of my mind for days."

TAMRA TORERO
Author of *Shayla Witherwood: A Half-Faerie Tale*

A NOVEL

MARCIA MICKELSON

SWEETWATER BOOKS
AN IMPRINT OF CEDAR FORT, INC.
SPRINGVILLE, UTAH

ISBN 13: 978-1-4621-1190-9

Published by Sweetwater Books, an imprint of Cedar Fort, Inc.
2373 W. 700 S., Springville, UT 84663
Distributed by Cedar Fort, Inc., www.cedarfort.com

LIBRARY OF CONGRESS CATALOGING-IN-PUBLICATION DATA

Mickelson, Marcia Argueta, author.
The huaca / Marcia Mickelson.
pages cm
Summary: Ellie struggles with normal high school life after the death of her mother, until the day loner Gabe de la Cruz shows what his sacred Incan huaca can do.
ISBN 978-1-4621-1190-9 (alk. paper)
[1. Death--Fiction. 2. Mothers and daughters--Fiction. 3. Future life--Fiction. 4. Inca mythology--Fiction. 5. Religious articles--Fiction. 6. High schools--Fiction.] I. Title.
PZ7.M581924Hu 2013
[Fic]--dc23

2013001816

Cover design by Angela D. Olsen
Cover design © 2013 by Lyle Mortimer
Edited and typeset by Melissa J. Caldwell

Printed in the United States of America

10 9 8 7 6 5 4 3 2 1

FOR MY MOTHER,
CORINA ARGUETA

Other books by Marcia Mickelson

Star Shining Brightly
Reasonable Doubt
Pickup Games

ONE

THE SNOW MAKES EVERYTHING clean again. That was what my mom said once when we were looking out the window at a fresh snowfall. I, in my wide-eyed optimism, believed her. It had been an evening snowfall where the snow covered our lawn, the driveway, streets, cars—everything within sight. The next morning, the serene, dream-like quality of the snow had been replaced by a murky, gray slush. Car tires had sullied their way over the fresh snow, leaving in their wake a trampled, dirty mess—nothing like the pure, flawless blanket of snow from the night before. So I stopped believing that snow makes everything clean again. It may last for a few hours at best, but in the end, everything seems dirtier.

That conclusion was especially evident when I woke up to melting snow and my scum-covered car. I did have one resolve as I got dressed. I kept telling myself, *I don't care what Sarah thinks of me.*

I kicked my UGG boots under the bed, knowing Sarah

would be wearing hers. Instead, I wore my black Chuck Taylors and the brown hoodie Sarah had been telling me to throw out. I didn't even brush my hair; I just pulled it up with a rubber band. I wasn't going to dress up for her—now that she was planning on shunning me. She'd made that clear to me through several text messages and emails. I understood why she was so angry at what I'd done, but it had been the right thing to do, despite whatever consequence I was going to face.

I used the sleeve of my hoodie to wipe the remaining snow off the windshield of my red Honda. As I slid around in the snow, trying to get in, I realized I should have opted for the boots. And a proper winter coat would have been a better option as well. New Jersey winters called for a bit more than Converse and a hoodie, but such trivialities were low on the list of what I cared about at the moment.

Despite the cynicism regarding my mom's snow observation, I really missed her on days like these. The snowfall reminded me of her optimism, and I wished she were still alive. Currently, my optimism was at an all-time low. I really needed and wanted her in my life.

By the time I got to school, I was ten minutes late. In history, Sarah walked past me to her seat. I couldn't recall a time all year long when Sarah didn't stop at my desk to say, "Time to make history, El." The scent of her cucumber melon shampoo wafted past me, but I refused to turn around or catch her eye.

I knew to expect this and had prepared for it on some level, but now that it hit me square in the stomach, I couldn't breathe. I just sat in my desk, still, unmoving, even after Mr. Zetlin directed us to start copying his notes. The side of his hand and the back of his white button-down shirt were smeared with green ink from the dry erase markers. I took a deep breath and mechanically copied the notes, not thinking about the Maya civilization or caring about its impact on our present day.

After the notes and boring lecture, we started the part of history class that I could actually stand—the oral presentations. Mine was coming up in two weeks, but I hadn't even started on the research yet, and I was beginning to freak out. Zetlin had randomly assigned each of us a civilization. I was assigned the Inca civilization. The only fact I knew about them so far was that the Incas were from Peru. Gabe de la Cruz was up first, and I could almost hear the collective groan spread through the class. I didn't fully understand why, but most of the junior class steered clear of him. Maybe it was the ever-present hoodie that covered his head, even in the summertime. It could have been his way of shutting everyone out, telling them not to talk to him. They didn't. Or maybe it was the brooding look permanently on his face. I didn't think I'd ever seen the guy smile.

Gabe pulled his hoodie up over his head, leaving a tuft of brown, wavy hair sticking straight up in the back. I heard a snicker behind me, and then Gabe patted down the back of his head. He stood up, extending to his full six-foot height, and then walked to the front of the room. I heard a slight whisper behind me, and I knew what they were talking about without even turning around: Gabe's arms.

My eyes rose to his arms as he held the index cards in front of him. His naturally tanned skin and the dark arm hair did little to hide the tiny scars if you were looking for them, which I was. The scars were on his inner arms, spreading up the length of his forearms. Everyone said that he was a user or a cutter. I supposed either one of those could be true, but for some reason I couldn't even explain, I thought neither one of them was true. There was no logic behind my assumption. I just didn't believe it.

Gabe looked down at his index cards and started. "At first, I was disappointed that Mr. Zetlin assigned me the Maya civilization. I'd been hoping for the Incas. My great-grandfather is full-blooded Inca, and I know everything there is to know about their civilization."

The collective groan returned, this time more audible. Mr. Zetlin cleared his throat as Gabe paused for an instant before continuing. I sat forward a little more, my attention caught by what he just said. He knew everything there was to know about the Inca civilization. I silently wished for just a fraction of that knowledge.

Gabe looked down at his index cards and then shoved them in his back pocket. "But, in a way, I'm glad that I was able to spend so much time researching the Mayas. Their civilization is one of the most dominant indigenous societies of Mesoamerica. Some of their settlements date back to 1800 BC."

Without ever referring back to his index cards, Gabe went on to tell us about the temples and palaces they built, the religious influences, the development of the calendar system, and the great Maya contributions that were still evident in our lives today.

After history, Sarah walked past me without saying anything. Trina was at her side, in UGG boots and perfectly straight hair. Jenna followed a step behind and half a foot below them. She shot me an apologetic look that was half sincere. Everything she did was always halfway: she only halfway dyed her hair, halfway made good grades, and only halfway fit in with the others. She was just trying to keep up with a duo that only halfway let her in, so she had no real sympathy for me. My being on the outs only let her in more.

Maybe it was some misguided sense of sentimentality that made me believe Sarah would still be my friend despite what I'd done. After all, we were best friends—the kind you cut your finger for. We were ten when we did the whole blood sister thing with her brother's Swiss army knife.

I carried my lunch to the first empty table I found. Dad had made zucchini bread the night before and had slipped a piece into my backpack. I unzipped the ziplock plastic bag.

"You're sitting by yourself because of me." It was Gabe. His dark brown eyes looked down at me.

"What?"

"Thank you, by the way. And I'm sorry." He grabbed a green apple from his wrinkled brown lunch bag and sat down across from me.

I looked up at him; it was the first time I'd looked straight into Gabe de la Cruz's eyes. Yeah, everyone knew him, but did anyone really *know* him?

"Okay," I said.

"I know it was you, Ellie," he said. He spread one hand out on the table between us. My eyes sunk down, focused on his long, tanned fingers.

I put down the zucchini bread. One bite and I didn't want anymore.

"Thank you for going to the police, telling them who did it. I know that there are a lot more people who knew what happened." He tipped his head toward Sarah's table. "And you're the only one who came forward."

I nodded, unable to face him despite my complete innocence. I'd been at home that night. Mischief Night—that was what we called it in Jersey. It was the night before Halloween when groups of jerks banded together to pull stupid pranks. Most were innocuous—toilet papering and egging houses, door ditching, and writing on cars with bars of soap. But sometimes, arrogant jerks like Bradley Mason set out to do more. Bradley and two of his friends hit Gabe's house that night. They broke in, carried his couch to the front yard, and set it on fire. They would have gotten away with it too. None of his friends would have turned him in. He'd told Sarah—maybe he thought it would impress her somehow. She'd sworn Trina, Jenna, and me to secrecy. I'd consented at first, until I had really thought about it. In the end, I couldn't keep the secret. Knowing there had been a crime, a victim . . .

"Well, I just wanted to say thank you. And I'm sorry your friends are mad at you." He held the apple between his thumb and middle finger. His other hand was still on the table between us.

"I guess they're not really my friends then," I said, looking up at him.

"I think you deserve better friends." Gabe stood up and stretched. Giving me one more look that was neither a smile nor a frown, he picked up his wrinkled paper bag and shuffled his black Chuck Taylors toward the door.

I turned to glance at Sarah's table. She was laughing and stopped suddenly when she caught me watching her. She pressed her lips into a thin line—the closest she'd ever come to an apology. She combed her fingers through her perfectly straight black hair. It was a nervous habit—one I know that she hated. I used to correct her every time she did it, just like she'd nudge me when I'd bite my nails. I chewed my fingernails until they bled, and she had been trying to get me to stop ever since she decided girls should have nice nails. This was right after fifth grade, right when everything started to change.

It was easy when we were little. We lived by our own rules, no social standards to follow. Stuff like that didn't matter then. The ultimate goal had been fun, trumping our previous day's enjoyment. I wasn't sure what my ultimate goal was anymore. I knew it didn't have anything to do with stupid high school stuff like social standing. Even the importance of friends seemed questionable. What was so great about friends if they turned their back on you for doing the right thing? I guessed Sarah felt betrayed because I hadn't kept her secret, but how did anyone expect someone to keep that type of secret? Friends didn't ask friends to do that.

I finished my dad's zucchini bread and the turkey sandwich I'd made that morning. I tried to focus on things of actual importance, like my Spanish test later in the day or the essay I had due tomorrow. I didn't want to think about Sarah and how we used to be friends.

After school, I lingered by my locker, not wanting to face the after-school craze where everyone analyzed how you walked and who you walked with. I dug out some old tests from the bottom of my locker and stuffed them into my backpack. The sound of laughter rolled down the hall behind me, and I tried not to let it bother me. Stupid high school stuff. Why couldn't I be done with it already? Next year, I'd be a senior, and I could spend my days fantasizing about how it would be to be done with this place—away at college, where everything really mattered.

"El." The sound of my name snapped me out of the only comforting thought I'd had all day. It was Sarah, and the way she said my name felt familiar yet far away. It was the way she used to say it before high school—and all the junk that came with it—became so important to her.

I closed my locker and turned toward her. "Hey."

Sarah looked down both ends of the hall. "Look, El. I'm sorry I was so harsh in my texts, but I can't believe you blabbed. After you promised."

"I'm sorry, but it was the right thing to do." I looked down at our feet—my Chuck Taylors next to her three-hundred-dollar UGG boots.

She growled. "Why does it always have to be about the right thing with you?"

My eyes shot up from the ground. "Seriously? You're asking me that?"

"You know that I like Bradley. And he trusted me with this, and I trusted you. You're my best friend and I can't trust you?"

"Why are you protecting him? He committed a crime."

Sarah threw her hand in the air. "It was a prank! And that guy, Gabe, is a jerk. He's trying to take over Bradley's spot on the track team. Bradley is a senior. He deserves that spot."

"Sarah, I didn't do this to hurt you. I did it because Bradley did something wrong, and I can't just stay quiet about it. They have to know who did it. Bradley should face the consequences."

Sarah sighed and leaned back against the locker next to mine. "It's Mischief Night. That's what happens on Mischief Night."

"He set Gabe's couch on fire!"

"He's going to pay for a new couch—a nicer one probably. And he'll do some community service. He does that anyway—he's a member of the National Honor Society, you know."

I took a step away from my locker. "National Honor Society. What a joke."

"Friends stick together. That's what I'm trying to say. I just don't know if you get that."

Her devotion to Bradley seemed to override any loyalty that near-lifelong friends should have. With her last statement, she walked away. How had it come to this point when seven-year-old Sarah and Ellie had been inseparable? Peas from two different pods, but always together.

As I watched her walk away, her perfectly straight black hair splayed down her back, moving only when she wanted it to, I felt like I did that day she'd left me behind in the three-foot section of the pool—all alone, out of my element, and unsure what to do without her presence.

Sarah had always had a confidence I lacked. It's what compelled her to jump off the high dive when she was six, swimming a perfect breaststroke to the shallow end where I predictably was. I would stay in the three feet, pinching my nose as I tentatively slid my face into the water. Sometimes, I would follow Sarah to the deep end, one hand gripping the edge, the whole way into the ten feet and the whole way back. It's how I lived: holding onto the side as I watched Sarah dominate the center. Her confidence and complete control of the elements around her fascinated me. They are what induced me to follow her, hoping that in the process I would gain a semblance of that confidence, that control.

When we were nine, I finally laid my fears aside enough to let Sarah walk with me to the edge of the diving board. She jumped in first and waited for me below, swimming to me as I flailed my arms after surfacing from the jump. She grabbed my arm and helped me swim to the side. As I clutched the edge, I felt both the shock of hitting the water and the exhilaration that I'd accomplished a Sarah-like feat.

It was through my friendship with Sarah that I'd gained enough confidence in subsequent years to ride the train into the city without parents, to get my ears pierced, to kiss Joey Peters behind the gym when I was twelve. But all of those successes and accomplishments seemed inconsequential now, as she walked away from me to find her next high dive while I remained behind in the shallow end.

•••••

At home, I finished up the rest of dad's zucchini bread while I read through my chemistry notes. The aroma of roast cooking in the Crock-Pot wafted through the kitchen, and I couldn't wait for Dad to get home so we could tear into it. After finishing my assignment, I unloaded the dishwasher and set the table.

"Hi, El. How was school today?" my dad asked as he came into the kitchen. He squeezed my shoulder and set his laptop case on the counter.

"Okay. How was work?"

He rolled up the sleeves of his charcoal button-down shirt and ran a hand through his graying blond hair. After he washed his hands in the sink, he lifted the lid of the Crock-Pot and speared the roast with a sharp knife. "Just fine. This looks like it's ready. You hungry?"

I walked over and peered around his shoulder, my stomach tightening with anticipation as the smell filled the room. "I'm starving."

He unplugged the blue ceramic Crock-Pot and carried it to the table. He scooped out the carrots and potatoes and placed them on our plates. The steam rose from the neat piles and billowed, covering the space between us as he carved large pieces of roast.

I forked a potato and blew on it, willing it to cool off so I could take a bite. I should have blown longer. My first bite was too hot, and I swallowed fast, burning my throat as it went down. I quickly followed it with a drink of cold water.

"How were things with Sarah today? I know you were worried."

I shrugged, not wanting to talk about it, and stuffed my mouth with a bite of roast.

"That bad?"

"I don't think she'll ever forgive me."

"You did the right thing, El. You always do." He leaned back in his chair, stroking his neatly trimmed beard. "You wouldn't have been able to live with yourself, holding that secret. Some people can . . . just hold something to themselves forever, and you can't see through them to know what they're hiding. But that's not you. You're so good, so pure, El. That's why I knew you would make that decision—to tell the police."

We'd spent all weekend talking about it, and Dad had left it up to me. He said I could choose whether I wanted to keep Sarah's secret or go down to the police station to report it. He'd gone with me once I'd decided. I'd even called Sarah to give her a warning about it, and that's when all the angry texts began. I'd had a whole weekend full of them. Some of them I hadn't read yet. I knew that Bradley and his friends had been questioned, arrested, bailed out, and would probably receive only a small sentence or fine.

Bradley Mason and his pack ran Westfield High, just as their fathers ran Westfield, New Jersey. They were the tall, pretty boys of our town, headed right to East Coast colleges and then on to Wall Street jobs. They probably thought nothing would stop them. The pranks they pulled, the people they hurt, were merely small obstacles to be hurdled over, just like the ones they left far behind them in track meets.

Dad put his fork down and crossed his arms over his chest. "I know she's been your friend for a long time, but it sounds to me as though she's not really acting like your friend. Friends don't treat each other like that. And she doesn't have to forgive you for anything. You didn't do anything wrong."

"I know." I pierced another piece of roast and brought it to my mouth. "I hope she gets over it, but she really likes this Bradley guy, and he probably hates me."

"I'm sorry, El. Having a friend shouldn't be so painful. Sometimes, even though you love someone, it's best to cut her out of your life. If Sarah's going to keep treating you like that, she's not a good friend to have."

I shook my head and pushed a few potatoes around on my plate. Sarah had been my best friend for so long. How do you just stop being friends with your best friend? "I don't think I can do that."

"I know you'll do what's right, El. You always do. Why don't you spend a few days hanging around with other friends? Maybe you'll see that your life would be better off without Sarah."

I couldn't imagine my life without Sarah; it was like she'd always been there. A few recent events couldn't eradicate the shared memories formed over a decade. I shook my head involuntarily at Dad's suggestion. I couldn't cut Sarah out of my life. Not now. Not after losing my mom. I had to cling to the small shred of friendship left with Sarah. I didn't have much in my life anymore—just Dad and Sarah.

"I think Mom would have liked your pot roast," I said, taking another small bite.

He reached for his glass of water. "Yeah, but she hated the Crock-Pot."

"She would have been happy that you tried making something new. She would have loved it."

"So, do you think you'll do winter track again this season?"

He always did that—changed the subject. It was just too

painful for him to talk about her. I liked talking about her, keeping those memories alive. I wished he would indulge me sometimes.

"Yeah, I guess," I said, knowing he really wanted me to. Running was more his thing, so I did it, but I didn't love it. I knew how important it was to him, how he'd lost thirty pounds over the last two years due to running and had gotten the super expensive weight system in our basement.

"Good," he said. "You need to keep up with it in the winter so you can stay in shape for spring track."

I nodded and went back to my roast. As we finished eating, there was no more mention of Sarah, track, or Mom. Unfortunately, those were three topics that Dad and I couldn't completely agree on.

COME ON, CUMMINGS· YOU REMEMber how this is done. Get going!" Coach Dennis yelling at me did little to motivate me to finish my mile run. Despite my dad's insistence that I sign up, I'd almost abandoned winter track this year. I'd just about told Coach Dennis that I wouldn't do it, but memories of my mother bundled up in her red chenille stocking cap propelled me to show up today. I glanced at the stands as I neared the end of my lap. She had been a constant in that stand. She'd been at every meet, and many practices, in her cap and long, matching scarf. That is why I did winter track this year: I hoped to feel her presence as I ran through the chilly air.

I tried to fall into a good rhythm, remember to keep pace and not get overly enthusiastic at the start. The other milers kept passing me. First it was Gerald King—it wasn't unexpected and neither was it a blow to my ego. He was quickly followed by Gabe, Thomas from biology, and even that freshman, Lizzie. That one stung a little. I couldn't let a freshman beat me. After Gabe lapped me, I began to ask myself again why I even signed up for track this year. I had sworn at the end of last season that I wouldn't do it, but here I was.

Noticeably absent from track practice were Bradley Mason and his buddies. They'd been suspended for two weeks. I almost felt like everyone was staring at me, faulting me for that suspension.

After practice, Coach Dennis critiqued our performance and tried to get us geared up for the next practice. I wondered how many people would drop out between now and then. I sat on the field as the group dispersed. My calves were aching, and I spent a few minutes stretching, berating myself for not keeping up with running in the off-season.

I watched the track clear out slowly, the cooled-off bodies beginning to feel the icy chill in the air. I felt the frosty lawn beneath me, cool moisture penetrating the thick black fabric of my Lycra running pants. I didn't care, though. It felt good. The cold feeling was numbing, and I just wanted to stay on the frosty lawn enclosed by the track.

Just ahead of me, Gabe de la Cruz was walking around the track, cooling off. Despite the frigid weather, he had worked up a sweat, evident by the wet trail that ran down the course of his back. He stretched his arms over his head, and the muscles in his back rippled under his white T-shirt. He turned around quickly and caught my eyes just before I could turn my head away. I looked out into the bleacher stands and then toward the parking lot, but my eyes were automatically drawn back to Gabe as I sensed him walking toward me.

This time, his eyes held mine as he closed the distance between us. He stopped just short of reaching me and bent down to pick up a gray hooded sweatshirt just a few feet from where I sat. Turning his eyes away from me, he pulled the sweatshirt over his head. I took the opportunity to look away from him and focus on the poor movements I was attempting to pass off as stretching.

Despite my focused attempt to look nowhere near his direction, I saw him continue toward me. He dropped down to the ground beside me, draping his arms over his lanky bent legs.

"Feels good, right? A run like that?" he said.

Nothing about running on this wintry day felt good, and the thought made me question myself for doing winter track for about the twentieth time that day. "I guess," I said.

He looked at me, running a hand through his brown, wavy hair. I pulled my eyes away from his hair, and they inadvertently traveled down his arm to his hand, which moved to the grass between us. He ran his fingers through the cold grass, plucking up small bunches and letting the short brown blades fall back to the ground. He repeated the action—grabbing and tossing small bits of grass—over and over, and he shifted his eyes from me to the grass between us. Maybe he was thinking of something to say. Maybe he was nervous.

"You going to do hurdles again this year?"

Hurdles? I tried hurdles once last year, at the insistence of Coach Dennis, who'd wanted me to give them a try. It had been one lucky practice, followed by one terribly demoralizing meet, in which I'd tripped twice over the hurdles and had come in last place.

"No," I said. "I doubt Coach Dennis wants me anywhere near the hurdles. I suck."

"You weren't that bad," he said, his hands still plucking grass, his eyes still on me. A slight smile came to his lips.

"You don't have to say that."

"You could do it," he said. "You have the leg strength.

You just need to work on your rhythm a little."

My eyes went instinctively to my legs, wondering how he would be able to gauge my leg strength. I looked back at him, and he flinched, probably realizing how awkward that had sounded.

His eyes were now on his hand working in the grass. He pulled what was left of the dried patch on the withered lawn between us.

"Hurdles are more for sprinters. I'd better just stick to distance," I said, taking my legs out of the stretching position they were in. I pulled myself up and reached for my backpack, catching Gabe's eyes as they traveled up the length of my legs. He saw that I'd caught him looking and quickly turned his head toward the end of the track.

"Guess I'd better go," I said, pulling my backpack onto my shoulder.

He jumped to his feet and pushed his hands into the front pocket of his hoodie. "Bye, Ellie. See you later."

"Bye." I turned to walk toward the student parking lot where I'd parked my Honda. It was three years old and had been my dad's car before he bought the Lexus last year. The Honda had collected over a hundred thousand miles. It had been his commuting car—drove it to New York City and back every day before he decided to go green and start taking the train. Now, the Lexus stayed parked at the train station just three miles from our house. Once in a while, he'd still drive in if he had a meeting and the train schedule didn't correlate, or if he had a business dinner after work.

I loved the Honda, though. It was the perfect car for me, and I was thankful my dad had kept it for me instead of trading it in. The independence of a driver's license and a car made me feel grown up. I took good care of it too, with regular oil changes. The guys at the lube place already knew me and knew exactly when I'd be in. Plus, I vacuumed and washed it every week.

I opened the door and slid my backpack inside. As I looked down, I groaned. My front tire was flat. I knelt down to get a better look. Wedged between the tread was a thick screw. "Man!" I said as I stood up and walked to the trunk. I took each step gingerly, since my calves still ached. When my dad turned over the keys to the Honda, he'd gone over car care, quizzing me and making sure I knew how to take care of it. He'd shown me how to change a tire and watched me as I did it by myself. So I knew how to change tires. It was not my favorite thing to do nor was I particularly good at it, but I could do it.

I pulled out the jack and lug nut wrench, grateful that at least it was light out and I wasn't stranded on some highway somewhere. I started loosening the lug nuts and was able to get three loosened. The fourth one did not want to budge, and seemed to sense that my muscles were already wasted for the day. I tried several times to push on the wrench and pulled on it, and I even put one foot on it to force it loose. But it remained glued, cemented, and unwilling to give.

I sunk to the ground and sighed, breathing heavily. I sat there for a few minutes, my shoulders heaving and my lungs gasping for air in the cool afternoon. After garnering enough strength to just stand up, I looked around the parking lot. Maybe I could get a ride with someone and have my dad come back with me later. But I didn't recognize any of the stray cars left in the parking lot, so I abandoned that idea. It was only a four-mile walk; I could do it. I'd done it before, but the one-mile run had already taken its toll on my increasingly exhausted body.

As I was reaching for my backpack, consigned to the idea

of walking, an old, yellow Volvo station wagon pulled up next to me. I knew the owner—everyone knew the owner. Gabe had been driving that old station wagon since he got his driver's license. Everyone called it the banana boat.

He got out of the car and came around to where I was standing. "Need some help?"

I shrugged. "I have a flat. I know how to change it, but I just can't get this lug nut loose."

"Let me try," he said, picking up the lug nut wrench. He squatted down and grimaced as he applied pressure. It took him a couple of pushes, but he was able to get it loose.

"Thanks. I just couldn't do it." I reached out for the wrench. "I can finish doing it now, but thank you for stopping to help."

He gave me the wrench and stood up. "Let me put the spare on for you."

"You don't have to. I can do it."

"It's okay," he said as he bent down to jack up the car. Then he pulled off the lug nuts and the tire, more quickly than I would have been able to. The rest of his movements were much the same way.

"You do this a lot?" I asked.

"Not a lot. Just enough." He rolled the flat tire toward the trunk. "Is your spare in here?"

I walked over to him and pulled the spare tire out. He took it from my hands and, in less than five minutes, he had it mounted and was tightening the lug nuts.

"Thank you. Thanks so much," I said as Gabe stood up and stretched out. "You really saved me."

His hands were dirty with grime from the tires. He rubbed them on his sweats and then picked at the dirt under one of his fingernails. "I'm really sorry about your mom."

"My mom?" The mere mention of my mother tensed

my stomach. I felt as though my chest was being squeezed. Thoughts of her were never far away, but hearing someone outside my family mention her brought back that panic I'd felt when I first heard of her murder. It was like that small measure of peace I'd found those months ago was taken away because someone mentioned her. It made the hurt start all over again. I looked away from his dirty hands, at the empty parking lot.

"Yeah, when she died. I'm sorry about that. I never got a chance to tell you. I always wanted to."

"That was a long time ago." The words were so trite, but I couldn't think of what to say. Thank you? Nothing seemed appropriate, probably because Gabe mentioning her wasn't appropriate to begin with. But, then again, he wasn't exactly the epitome of appropriateness.

"I know. I know. I just remember when it happened. I felt so bad for you, and I always wished I could come tell you, or do something for you."

"Well, you changed my tire. So, there. You did something for me." I was hoping that comment, however ridiculous, would lighten the mood.

He bent down and picked up the jack. "Right. Well, I'd like to do more. Can you come over some time?"

"Things are really busy right now, with school and everything." What did he have in mind? I didn't want to find out. I reached for the jack. He hesitated before giving it to me.

"There's something I can show you . . . it's the thing you dream about, maybe. What you most wish for." He shook his head and frowned, dipping his hands deep into the front of his hoodie. "I know that sounds stupid, but it's something like that."

I opened the trunk and threw in the jack, backing away from him, toward the driver's seat. "That's a terrible line. Go with you and my wildest dream will come true?"

He dropped his head and kicked a pebble, shooting it across the parking lot. "That's not what I'm saying. It's not that."

"I'd better go. Thanks for helping me."

"Ellie, wait." He pulled one hand out of his pocket and reached for me but didn't touch me. "I wasn't saying that. I was just talking about your mom."

"Don't use my mom to get to me. What's wrong with you?"

"I'm not trying to get to you. I wish I could explain, but it's complicated. I just have to show you."

"No. No, I have to go." I backed into the seat and shut the door, locking it as soon as I was inside. He didn't make a move toward me. He slid his hand back into his pocket and looked at me for only an instant before shifting his eyes to the ground.

I pulled away and watched him in my rearview mirror as I drove. He stood in the same spot, kicking pebbles, looking up occasionally to watch me drive away.

I always knew he was strange; everyone said that. But sometimes you wonder when people say that. Perhaps the person they're talking about is actually normal—shy or maybe just a loner. And besides, everyone makes that stuff up. That's what I thought about Gabe. They talked about how his parents were crazy, how his house was haunted, and how he was schizophrenic or something. That all seemed exaggerated—mean stuff that everyone makes up just to have someone to pick on.

But maybe they're right. Maybe he is a bit crazy. Why would he go on about my mom? Saying he was sorry? That he wanted to show me something?

As I replayed the conversation, anxiety pricked my

senses, making me sweat, causing a chill to come over me. I tried to shrug off the sensation, but it stayed with me and made me shiver all over. Why would he bring up my mother? Why did he say he was sorry?

When I got home, I dead-bolted the front door and went up to my room. I locked my door and leaned back against it. I was breathing heavily. Was I scared of him? I didn't believe he had anything to do with my mother, but why did he bring her up?

I walked over to my computer and did a Google search for "Gabe de la Cruz." I didn't find him on Twitter or Facebook, but he was mentioned in an obituary for his father. I didn't know his father was dead. Actually, I didn't really know anything about his family. The obituary mentioned Gabe and his mother; he appeared to be the only child. It didn't say how his father died, and I wondered if it was an illness. Maybe his father's death made Gabe think we had something in common, a link of some kind.

The thought sobered my frantic thoughts, and I closed the search window on my computer. Gabe was probably just weird and couldn't think of a proper way to ask a girl out. Despite this thought, I didn't look forward to seeing him at school the next day.

I lay on my bed and looked across my room to a half-finished quilt draped over a recliner. My mom had started it months before she died. After she was laid off from her job at a marketing firm, she started quilting. She was no quilter. Her stitches were uneven and the squares were crooked, but I loved the quilt. It represented who she was shortly before she died. Sometimes, if I was having a hard time sleeping, I would sit in the recliner and cover myself with it, wishing it were her arms around me instead.

I planned on finishing it one day as soon as I learned how to sew. In the meantime, I kept it on my recliner so I could see it when I lay in bed.

It happened last summer. I was staying at Sarah's house that night. My dad was on an overnight trip in the city, preparing for a presentation the next day. I'd wanted to cancel my sleepover with Sarah and had told my mom I would stay with her so she wouldn't be alone. But she said she was going to stay up late quilting and listening to the *Les Miserables* sound track.

The next morning, our neighbor, Lisa, came over to meet my mom so they could go to the gym. That's when she found her. The door's lock had been broken, so Lisa went inside. She found my mom on the bed. Lisa said that, at first, she thought my mom was sleeping, but she wasn't. Someone had broken into the house the night before. She'd been strangled and stabbed. Several things had been stolen—some jewelry, her laptop. I couldn't even remember what else. None of that mattered.

My mom had been taken from me. They never found the killer. I suppose the investigation was still open and ongoing, but I didn't think they were really looking for anyone.

At dinner, I thought about telling Dad what had happened with Gabe, but I stopped with explaining the flat tire and only mentioned that a boy at school had helped me.

"Next time that happens, call me. I could have called someone to come pick you up."

"That's okay," I said, biting into a meatball. "I got home okay."

"Good. I'm sorry. Is that why you seem upset today?"

How could he tell? I hadn't said or done anything that would show I was upset. He just knew me so well. "Yeah, I guess. I'll be fine."

I didn't feel like rehashing all my emotions of the day. I was tired and wanted to forget some of the thoughts that had rolled through my head. Besides, Dad was uncomfortable talking about my mom. I didn't think he'd even reached the first part of the mourning process. Anytime I tried to talk about her, he just clammed up and shut me out. Right after it happened, it seemed like he was in shock, unable to process what had happened.

I suppose he felt responsible for it in a way, as though, if he'd been home, it wouldn't have happened and she would still be here. I wondered about that sometimes. He doesn't go out of town often; most of his work is in the city. He and his colleague, Simon, were meeting with new clients and had spent that night dining with them. They spent the night in a hotel, preparing for the presentation they were giving to the board of directors the next day. The police had even questioned my dad. I guess they always suspect the husband. But Simon said they'd spent all night working on the presentation.

"Do you want some more salad?" Dad asked, holding the bowl toward me.

"That's okay. I'm not that hungry today."

"How was your first day of track?" he asked, dishing out more salad onto his own plate.

"Okay. I'm sore already, though."

"Don't forget you have to stretch out really good before and after."

"I know," I said. I took one last bite of meatball and then stood up. "I'm going to take a bath and then go to bed. I'm really tired."

"Okay, El. Good night. I'll be down in the basement if you need anything."

Down in the basement—it's where he spent most nights.

I blamed late-night TV infomercials. It had been one of those infomercials that had sold him on the idea of buying the home gym and weight system. He spent almost two hours every night down there, lifting weights. I leaned over and kissed his forehead. "Good night."

THREE

MONDAY MORNING, I FELT LIKE I wanted a new start. Friday afternoon's run-in with Gabe was still fresh on my mind, and I realized I didn't really want to face the awkwardness that would come when I saw him. I wished I could go back to before Mischief Night, when Sarah was still my best friend and I didn't have to worry about facing banana boat guy. I wanted to mend the rift with Sarah, to feel like I could talk to her the way I used to, when I could tell her anything. She would have been the first person I called to recount the strange encounter with Gabe.

I wore the two layered shirts Sarah bought me for my birthday last year. I didn't wear them often—maybe just once. I pulled out the skinny jeans Sarah and I bought together with our Christmas money last year. She'd worn hers many times, but I never had. Skinny jeans looked way better on Sarah than they did on me. I tore the tag off and threw it in the garbage.

I went to the bathroom and pulled out my makeup case. I usually wore only mascara every day. Although my hair was dark brown, that color didn't make it to my lashes, and they're so light and thin that mascara was a necessity. I never did lipstick and only sometimes wore blush, but I ripped open an unopened eye shadow and dabbed some on my eyelids—a smoky charcoal.

My red Chuck Taylors were by my bed and I wanted to put them on, but instead I kicked them under the bed and walked to my closet. I really didn't know why ballet flats were in again. I seemed to remember my mom telling me she used to wear them in college. But here they were again with their circular toes and big bows. I had half a dozen pairs. They were all mall trip finds. When Sarah would spend hours looking at clothes, I would just buy another pair of ballet flats—a small token to show for the day.

I put on the silver pair without bows. Bows would be too much.

•••••

"You look cute today," Sarah said to me when she slid in the desk behind me in history.

"Thanks." The words should have been comforting, pleasing—it's what I'd been hoping for when I got dressed that morning. But they seemed empty and filled me with shame instead. I suddenly wished I were wearing anything but the layered tops and skinny jeans. My feet felt tight and sweaty inside the silver ballet flats. As I turned around to face the front, I saw Gabe watching me across the room. Not that I'd ever seen the guy smile, but his frown looked more pronounced than usual. I turned from his disapproving stare to Mr. Zetlin's notes on the white board and started writing down each word.

"Hey, El." Sarah poked me with her pen and I turned back to her. "Let's get together this week. What are you doing Friday?"

"Nothing, I guess."

"Well, I'll come over. We can talk about my birthday party plans."

I guessed we were friends again. It only took a pair of skinny jeans and ugly silver shoes to get me back to friend status. I suddenly wasn't sure if I even wanted to be there.

The thought stayed with me as I drove home. It was the same drive home of the last three years—down the oak tree–lined street behind the school toward the Catholic Church, past the teahouse and the tiny playground where Sarah and I had spent most days the summer after fifth grade. Sometimes, we'd ridden our bikes down to the teahouse and peeked through the burgundy drapes to try to find Sarah's mother, Mrs. Winter. It's where Mrs. Winter spent many lunch hours planning events or conferences. Mrs. Winter would spot us through the window and shoo us away, a rigid smile pasted to her face.

We would pedal down the street to the tiny playground hidden in an alcove of trees. It was our place. It was where Sarah first told me about her crush on Todd Gunderson and where she'd first called me her best friend. June twenty-third—the date I'd kept as close to my heart as the "best friends" half-heart pendant Sarah had given me that day. But it was also the place she'd deserted me that same June day when Todd Gunderson showed up and asked her to bike down to the Rialto. She hadn't even looked back at me as she pedaled to keep up with his two-thousand-dollar Cannondale.

It was Sarah's way—a loyal best friend one day and a fierce deserter the next. She would cling to me until the next best opportunity presented itself. Those opportunities usually came in the form of boys. I was pretty used to it. Her present opportunity seemed to be Bradley, and I guessed it was up to me if I wanted to stay in the background until she was ready for me again.

Driving past the playground today didn't bring the usual string of nostalgic feelings, just empty ones—empty as that hidden-away playground. The text I received as soon as I pulled into the driveway didn't do anything to remedy the lack of nostalgia I was feeling about my friendship with Sarah.

I wasn't surprised by her words, but they stung just the same as always. *I want to hang out on Friday, but let's just play it cool at school. Bradley's still not over what you did.*

Play it cool. I knew what that meant. I was still on the outs, taking a backseat to whatever she wanted at the moment. Currently, that was still Bradley, so just as she'd left me behind to go after Todd Gunderson, I was being left behind now. Only this time, she was more blatant about it. After all, Bradley was not over what I'd done.

That last line hit a nerve, the one nerve that I usually allowed to go untouched by Sarah and whatever she did. But not tonight. I couldn't believe she was still blaming me for the aftermath of Bradley's prank. He was the one who'd done something terrible and had lied about it. Yet I was the one being punished, forced to hang out with my best friend only when he was not around to see it.

It was all I could think about throughout the night and into the next morning. Dad had left my dry cleaning draped over my computer chair. I picked it up and stared at the cashmere sweater I'd begged Dad to buy me at the start of the school year. Sarah and I had gone clothes shopping at the mall, and she'd bought the same one. She'd convinced me to put one on hold and bring him back later to buy it. I didn't love it—I knew that right away. It wasn't something I would have picked on my own, but I'd lied to him and told him how much I loved it and wanted it. I stared at the plum-colored sweater and wished I had his three hundred bucks back. At the time, I had thought the sweater would somehow bring Sarah and me closer, help our friendship be what it was once. But it wasn't a sweater made of magic. Now it was merely a reminder of how hard I had tried to keep the friendship. I should have known then that our friendship was unraveling, but it took what happened with Bradley and Gabe to make me really see it.

I opened the closet, slid all my clothes to one side, then hung the sweater up against the wall and pushed back the other clothes to hide it. I pulled out my brown hoodie and black Chuck Taylors. I didn't want to lose Sarah as a friend, but I also didn't want to lose myself. Sarah would just have to accept me. If she didn't, I would face the consequences. I just didn't want to play that game anymore.

I thought about what Dad had said about cutting her off, being better off without her, but it wasn't that easy. She was a part of me, and I was a part of her. Cutting her off would be like cutting off a piece of myself. I'd already lost an important part of myself when Mom died. I didn't know if I could stand losing any more, but I had to face Sarah. She would have to concede.

She didn't show any sign of conceding when she blocked me out at lunch again. I sat at a table alone again and wondered if getting together on Friday was out. Maybe I should consider making new friends. A school of two thousand surely had other girls I could hang out with. But staring at my peanut butter sandwich alone at a table meant for eight didn't give me incentive to go out and meet new friends. It didn't even seem worth it at this point. School would be over in a few months, and next year would be senior year, and then college.

I often thought about college—what it would be like. I really wanted to go away, live in a dorm or apartment, have a part-time job, and stay busy all the time. I would walk across a crowded campus, stand in long lines to buy textbooks, stay in the library until late in the night, sit on the lawn with my laptop to write papers while artsy guys with long hair and glasses waved to me as they walked by.

That was my goal—what I really wanted in life. The here and now, the temporary aches and pains of high school, didn't matter to me. It was all just paying my dues, putting in my time until my real life began.

I looked over at Sarah with her friends, the ones that dressed and flirted like her. She glanced my way and shrugged with a sad look on her face. Her forehead creased and she wrinkled her nose. She wasn't doing it to be mean; she was just protecting herself, trying to make a place for herself. *This* is what mattered to her, what her goal was, and she had to sacrifice me to achieve it.

I wasn't mad at her. I felt sorry for her, mostly because I didn't think that, in the end, she would find what she wanted or be happy with what she had. I turned back to my sandwich and tried to go back to my daydream about college life.

I caught myself watching Gabe as he came into the cafeteria a few minutes later. I tried to look away quickly, before he saw me, but it was too late. He caught me looking and smiled as he walked past the cafeteria line. I quickly looked down at my sandwich.

I had never thought of him *that* way. He was always just the freak kid that everyone in class avoided. We could always expect the same thing from him. Brown corduroy pants, black Chuck Taylors, and a hooded sweatshirt—pick your color, he had them all. He wouldn't wear his hood inside the school—it was against the dress code, but as soon as he was outside the door, he'd throw it on over his curly brown hair, no matter the weather. I wasn't sure why I knew so much about his wardrobe. I liked to watch people and know their habits—where they hang and who they hang with. So I guess I had watched Gabe before and noticed his quirks and style. I had ignored him most of the time, though, and not paid much attention past the surface.

"I'm sorry about Friday." Gabe appeared on my right and slid down into a chair. "I didn't mean to freak you out."

I forced a smile and shrugged. "It's okay."

He held a brown paper bag in his fist and laid it down in front of him. He pulled out an apple and took a bite. "I thought about it later and how weird everything sounded."

"No big deal. Thanks again for helping me out."

"Right. Well, I hope we can be friends."

His offer of friendship didn't exactly correlate with what I had been thinking earlier. Yes, it had occurred to me that I needed to make new friends, but Gabe wasn't really who I'd had in mind. I took a bite of my sandwich and smiled.

"So you're not interested in staying Sarah's friend?" He motioned over to her table. "You're sitting over here again."

"I guess she's not the kind of friend she used to be."

"Good for you."

Although I agreed with his statement, I didn't want him telling me that. It wasn't his place, and he was a little too frank for just having become my friend—if I could call him that already.

"If you know so much about friends, why aren't you sitting with any?"

He gave a small laugh and grabbed his crinkled lunch

bag. "Are you trying to say you don't want me to sit here?"

"Just asking a question. Where are *your* friends?" I looked around the cafeteria, emphasizing my point.

"Friends are okay, I guess, but most of the ones you find around here are fake. You know, they just want to be your friend if there's something in it for them. I'm pretty sure you know what I mean."

I opened my water bottle and took a small sip, replacing the lid and letting my eyes trail over to Sarah's table.

"I'm sorry," he said. "I'm not trying to be mean. I know that good friends are hard to come by. The ones who use you or are only there when it's convenient—there's a lot of those. Who needs them? I don't. Sometimes it takes a long time to find the right one. The one who'll be there when it's not easy, when you really need them. Those are the ones you can count on, the ones you can let see the real you."

"That's what I thought Sarah was."

He turned to look over his shoulder, where she sat with Trina and Jenna. "What about the other two? Aren't they your friends too?"

I shrugged. "They sort of used to be, but now they just follow Sarah. They transitioned more easily into the whole high school image thing. You know, sort of breezed through the awkward stage. I just sort of stayed in the awkward stage, and they're not really wanting to wait for me to catch up. And I'm not sure I really want to."

"I don't think you're awkward." Gabe said the words quickly and then looked down at his lunch bag. He pulled out a bag of chips and a sandwich and then crumpled up the bag.

"Not sure that means much, coming from probably the most awkward kid in our junior class."

A smile spread across his face, and he laughed quietly

for a few seconds. "None of that really matters to me. I am who I am, and whoever doesn't like me just stays away. I'm fine with that. You're still here, so I guess that's something."

"I guess I have nowhere else to go. That doesn't mean I like you."

"Well, do you like passing history?" he asked.

"I need to pass history."

"Maybe you should start taking notes."

"Yeah, right. Like you ever take notes. Besides, I can barely read Zetlin's chicken scratch. What is it with males and messy writing?"

"You can't blame the seventy you got on our last pop quiz on Zetlin's writing."

I unscrewed the lid on my water bottle and then screwed it back in, repeating the action over and over. Finally, I pushed it away. "How do you know what I got on the last pop quiz?"

He shrugged. "You don't sit that far away."

"It's all these civilizations; I just can't keep them straight. Give me a chemistry problem, a quadratic equation, and I can solve that, no prob. But how do you make heads or tails of all these different civilizations?"

"It's not that hard. I can help you."

I wasn't sure if he could be of any help. He never did take any of Zetlin's notes, but somehow he seemed to know everything. My thoughts went back to his almost flawless presentation on the Mayas and his statement that he knew everything there was to know about the Incas. But I didn't know if I wanted Gabe de la Cruz as my study partner. "I don't know."

"Think about it. I know your presentation on the Incas is coming up. I can help you with that," he said. He shoved the plastic covering of his sandwich against the crumpled paper bag and balled them into his hand. "I'll see you later."

"Bye," I said, not looking up to see him go.

A minute later, I turned around and he was standing by the cafeteria entrance. He quickly looked in my direction before going into the hall. I hazarded a glance toward Sarah's table. Bradley was sitting next to her, ignoring her. He was gesturing and explaining something to the jock next to him. Sarah looked right in my direction, her lips pursed and eyebrows drawn together. She mouthed the word, "What?" I didn't need to see the rest of her mouthing to know she wasn't happy with me, probably annoyed I was talking to Gabe.

•••••

After I finished my math test, I pulled out the meager research I'd scraped together on the Incas. The math test was supposed to take forty-five minutes, but I was done after twenty. Math—a cinch, no stress to me at all. Not so with this Inca business. How was it that a reasonably intelligent person who was averaging A's in all her classes, with a ninety-eight average in math, could not decipher between the Incas, Mayas, and Aztecs? I had read through the pages detailing the diverse civilizations many times. All I needed was someone to explain it in fourth-grade terms. I thought about Gabe. He was good at history and could easily help me, and it even seemed like he wanted to.

But I didn't want to go to that next level of friendship with him. Passing acquaintances, occasional lunch partners, classmates, track teammates—those were all acceptable forms. But friendship beyond that with Gabe, the banana boat guy, was not something I wanted. I wondered if it was because of Sarah, and her disapproving look from lunch, or her derision of Gabe and how she seemed to hate him because of Bradley. Did her opinion still drive me? I was making a conscious effort to not be influenced by her in what she wanted me to wear, but maybe deep down inside I would always still care what she thought.

I carried that thought with me throughout the day, and it caused me to impulsively run up to Gabe after school. I knew I could google the Incas, find some *Incas for Dummies*–type explanation, or even ask my dad to dumb it down for me, but I chose a different option.

Gabe had pulled his hoodie over his head and was bounding down the outside steps toward the street. He was playing air drums with his fingers. I thought maybe he was wearing his iPod. I could see his yellow Volvo parked on the street across the lot. I picked up my pace and was next to him as he headed toward his car.

"Hey, Gabe."

He didn't hear me, so I reached out to touch his arm, stopping his air drums in the process. He pulled out his earphones and stopped walking.

"Ellie, hi." He looked down at where I'd grabbed his arm, and I quickly let go, dropping my hand to my side.

"So, I guess I could use some help with this Inca stuff. Do you really know everything there is to know?"

"Yeah, actually. I really do."

"Could you help me on my presentation?"

"Okay. How about tomorrow after school?"

"Yeah, okay. Thanks. That will be a big help." I managed a weak wave and then took a few steps backwards. "I'll see you tomorrow." I turned around and walked toward my car. Not something I generally did—approach a guy like that. I guess he had suggested it earlier that day, but I didn't want him to get the wrong idea, that I was interested in him or anything.

•••••

Our mailbox was at the end of our driveway, and I checked it before walking up to the door. The bare limbs of the aging oak tree in our yard swayed with the heavy breeze, and the tips of the limbs grazed our mailbox, scratching its aluminum exterior. Dad and I had spent a few weekends ago raking and bagging leaves from the oak tree. There was little left of the leaves. Instead, the remnants of snow still covered most of the ground.

I reached into the mailbox and pulled out a handful of letters. There were a few bills for my dad, a Stop & Shop circular, and some junk mail. And the usual Rick Thorton letter. We'd been getting random letters addressed to Rick Thorton for a while. I guess he lived in our house before us—just one of those wrong letters that always gets stuck in your mail. Dad used to write "not at this address" on the envelope and stick it back in the mailbox. I brought in the whole stack and set it on the kitchen table. I'd let Dad take care of it later.

FOUR

GABE PULLED HIS VOLVO INTO THE driveway, and I parked on the street in front of his house. I'd driven by the house many times, and people always told me it was haunted—whatever that meant. Gabe's family had always been considered eccentric; I don't think I'd ever seen his mom. Some people even called her a witch, but the word *haunted* seemed extreme.

I hesitated before walking toward the house. It was painted a dull gray and peeling in many places. The lawn had been mowed recently, but the bushes were overgrown, and the flower beds were crowded with weeds. A flimsy screen door squeaked with each blow of the wind. Gabe stopped and waited, so I grabbed my backpack from the car and followed him up the path to the front door. I didn't know why I'd come. I could have studied on my own. But I suppose I was in need of a little companionship, bored of going home after school each day with no one to hang out with. Couple that with a growing curiosity about who exactly Gabe was, and here I was, in front of Gabe the Weirdo's haunted house, about to venture inside.

I looked both ways before entering, hoping someone would see me go in, in case I was walking into my death. There was an old lady next door unloading groceries from her car. She looked up for a moment before closing her car door. At least there was a witness. I wasn't scared, really, but going to a strange boy's house was not the safest or most sound decision. And it certainly was not one my father would be pleased with.

Gabe stopped at the front door to pick up a UPS box from the stoop before going inside. I walked through the door, and Gabe shut it behind me. I smelled the faint aroma of cinnamon and noticed a candle's weak flame glowing on the coffee table. The beige carpet looked like it had recently been vacuumed, and the half dozen pillows on the beige couch were all straightened and ordered in a pattern. I wondered if it was the couch Bradley had been ordered to buy him as restitution.

He put the UPS box down on the coffee table. "Let me just go say hi to my mom. I'll be right back." He walked down the hall and knocked on a door. When he opened the door, I could only hear faint whisperings before he shut the door and was back.

"My mom said she just made apple pie, if you want some. Come on, let's go in the kitchen."

I followed him into the kitchen. It was small, but the white linoleum floor was immaculate and shiny. The countertops were clean and bare except for a line of storage jars that were labeled with words like *flour* and *sugar*. There was a pie platter on the center of the table, and Gabe put his backpack down next to it.

"My mom makes the best apple pie." He walked over

to the cupboard and took out two plates. From a drawer, he pulled out forks and a serving utensil. He dug into the pie and placed a piece on a plate. A small stream of steam escaped from the sides. "It's still hot," he said.

I sat down on a chair and took the plate he offered. "So, your mom is here?"

He licked some apple off his finger and slid into a chair next to me. "Yeah, she's in her room. She's not feeling well today."

"Oh. Well, that was nice of her to make apple pie even though she's not feeling well."

"I think she started feeling sick after she made it. Just like a migraine or something like that."

"Well, I can go if she's not feeling well."

He reached over and put his hand on my wrist. "No. She's in her room sleeping, so we won't bother her." He pulled his hand off mine and picked up his fork. Where he'd touched me felt cool and tingly. I concentrated on my arm for a moment, urging the feeling to dispel. As he sliced into the pie, my eyes were drawn to the series of small cuts along the inside of his arm. I couldn't take my eyes off his arm and wondered, for only a second, if all the stories about him being a cutter or a drug user were true. My imagination seemed to be running wild, and I quickly looked away.

I swallowed a bite of pie. The apples warmed my insides. "Mmm. Delicious."

"Yeah, she's great at baking, and she pretty much spends her day cleaning the house. It's almost obsessive."

"You have a very clean house," I said, looking around the kitchen.

"She does other stuff too. She's a great artist. That's what she spends most of her time in her room doing." He turned to point across the room to a small painting above the sink. "That's hers," he said.

As he pointed, my eyes were again drawn to the inside of his arm and the tiny cuts that ran down its length. I was relieved to realize that he was oblivious to my uneasy staring. I quickly averted my eyes toward the painting. It was a still life, a darkened table with a bowl of fruit and an overly ripe banana lying on the table outside of the bowl. It was rich in texture and so realistic you could almost reach out to grab a piece of fruit.

"She did that? That's amazing. She's very talented."

"She is. I'll have to show you some of her other stuff another day."

"Do you paint also?"

"No, I didn't inherit that at all." He shook his head and then smiled. "I'm getting to understand art a little though. She tells me about her paintings, and I go to the art store to pick up her supplies. I definitely know the difference between burnt umber and burnt sienna now."

I laughed and took another bite. "She sounds great."

"Yeah, she is." He nodded. "So, this oral presentation is twenty-five percent of our grade."

"I know—it's huge. I'm worried. History's not really my thing."

"I can help you. I've been researching Inca myths for a while. I'm sort of obsessed with them right now."

"Inca myths? I guess I don't know anything about them."

"Like I said in class, my dad was from Peru. His grandfather was a full-blooded Inca."

"That's pretty cool. I guess that's where you get your nice skin tone?" I hadn't meant to admit that I liked or had even noticed his skin color—a yearlong tan without even trying. He sort of smiled and then looked down at the table. I didn't have much of a way with boys—doing that whole thing of not letting them know what you think of them or how you feel. Sarah was an expert at that, and she was the one who usually reminded me when I said too much or should have kept my mouth shut. I could have used her advice right then. "So, tell me more about the Incas."

"My great-grandfather grew up in an Incan tribe in the Andes. Ever heard of Machu Picchu?"

"Yeah, I read something about that." I leaned down to grab a notebook from my backpack to take notes.

He played with the fork in his hand, pushing it against his empty plate. "It's the holy city of the Incas. Anyway, my dad used to tell me my great-grandfather's story. He left when he was young. He wanted to see the world but only got as far as Lima. That's where he met my great-grandmother, and they started a family."

"Have you ever been there?"

"No. I've wanted to, but my dad never wanted to go there. My grandfather left Peru when he was young. He had the same kind of wandering spirit as his father. He and my grandmother came to New York right after they were married."

"That's a really cool story."

"I haven't always thought that, but I do now. My dad really stressed the importance of family, of our past. That's why I'm so interested in the Incas."

"You said you were researching their myths. What are their myths?"

"Well, Inti was the sun god—their supreme god. To some, it's just mythology, beliefs that have no reality, but to others, like the Incan people, it's truth. That's what I like to focus on—the truth found in myths."

"Truth found in myths? Doesn't the word *myth* sorta mean it's not true?"

"To some people, it's myths; to others, it's real. It's their reality. Some don't want to see it and refuse to think it's possible, but for those who have seen it, it's the absolute truth and part of their daily lives."

"So do the people there—the Incas today—do they still believe in this stuff, these gods?"

Gabe looked at me and held my eyes for a second before nodding. "The same way you believe in your God."

"I'm not sure what I believe in."

"Do you ever think about where your mom might be?"

I looked down at the table, saw his hand outstretched in front of me. His long, tanned fingers padded the table softly, rhythmically.

"My mom is dead."

He pulled his hand in and rubbed his upper arm, nodding. "I know. But do you wonder where she went after she died?"

The question brought back memories of the token words I'd read in card after card following her funeral. Well-meaning friends, family members, and neighbors had sent sympathy cards—what you're supposed to do when someone dies, I guess. They're more of a courtesy, but does anyone believe those trite words actually comfort or bring someone peace? "She's in a better place" or "she's in peace" or "she went back home"—they all made me want to tear the cards to pieces, shred them until my fingers bled. Those words only brought more pain. They stood as tangible reminders that she wasn't coming back to *me*. "She went in the ground after she died, Gabe. She isn't anywhere. That's the end." I didn't like the idea that she could be somewhere, anywhere, out there in heaven or whatever people believed in. I couldn't imagine her being somewhere where I wasn't, where I couldn't see her or be with her.

"You don't believe she could be somewhere?" he asked.

"No. How can anyone believe any of that? Nobody really knows."

"I want to show you something. It's in the basement."

I leaned back in my chair and rubbed my finger across my notebook. "What is it?"

"It's something my grandfather gave me. He said it's an Incan artifact, handed down to him by his father."

"Wow. A real artifact?"

He rose from the table and held out a hand for me. "Come see it."

I took his hand and stood up, thinking he'd let go of it, but he didn't. He walked across the kitchen, and I followed. Through a door by the refrigerator, I followed. We went down a set of creaking steps made of bare planks of wood. The basement was dank, with cement floors. When we reached the bottom step, Gabe reached up to pull a string that turned a single light bulb on. He let go of my hand.

I looked around the nearly empty room. There was an old desk against a wall with a metal chair next to it. A stack of cardboard boxes was lined up in a corner of the room.

"It's over here," he said, walking toward the desk.

I followed him to the desk. He placed his hand on a wooden box. It looked hand-carved of light wood that had been sanded to a smooth finish. It was bare of stain or paint. Gabe slid his hand across it. "My father gave this to me. It's been handed down from my Incan ancestors for hundreds of years."

"It's beautiful," I said. It had fine carvings on the lid, some kind of tribal design. There were three wooden knobs that seemed to open very thin drawers. "Is it a jewelry box?"

He stayed silent for a minute before looking up at me. "No. It's not a jewelry box. It's a *huaca*." He pronounced it "wa-ka."

"What?"

"It's a sacred object. That's what *huaca* means. The Incas believe in performing worshipping ceremonies. They give sacrifices to the gods through a huaca."

"That's amazing. And you have one? Did your dad believe in all that stuff?"

"Yeah. It's not a belief, though. It's what we know—who we are." He bent down and picked up a cardboard box from the ground. He placed it on the desk next to the wooden box. "The Incas care deeply for their dead. They believe they could see them."

"Like a ghost?" I asked, remembering the rumors that the house was haunted.

"No, not like a ghost. The righteous ones who've passed on stay in Hanan Pacha. That's the upper world."

"Like heaven or something?"

He nodded. "Something like that. It's the sacrifice through the huaca that helps you see them."

"Wow, you could bring this to class. Zetlin would give you a ton of extra credit." I took a step back, hoping he was done showing me the thing. I was starting to get creeped out.

"I would never bring it to school. I want to show you something." He opened the UPS box and pulled out a long rubber band. He wrapped it around his bicep and put one end in his mouth as he tied and pulled it tight.

"What are you doing?" I asked, taking another step back.

"Please wait, Ellie." He inched closer to me. "Trust me,

okay." He waited for me to answer, but I didn't respond. I wanted to trust him, but I wasn't sure I could. He reached back into the box and pulled out some kind of needle and tube.

"Is this some kind of weird drug? I don't do drugs, Gabe." I turned around and started toward the steps.

"Ellie."

I had my foot on the first step when I turned around. Gabe held a small tube against the inside of his arm. He was drawing blood into the small tube. The rubber band was back in his mouth, and he untied it with the swift turn of his neck. I stared for a second at the determined look on his face. His eyes were focused. He did it so expertly, I wondered how many times he'd done it before. I turned and rushed for the next step, but he grabbed my hand.

"Let go!" I screamed as I tried for the third step.

"Wait, Ellie!" He tightened his hold on me, squeezing my wrist. He was using the arm from which he was still drawing blood. I swung my hand, trying to get it away from his grip. The movement made his hand slip and blood began to spurt. He pulled the tube away from his arm and looked at it closely, still not letting go of my hand. "Please, Ellie! Just wait."

"No!"

He tightened his hold and tried to pull me back down the steps. I stumbled down a step, and he steadied me so I wouldn't fall. As each second elapsed, all those fears and doubts about Gabe that I had pushed away the past weeks came back. Instinct had told me to stay away, that he was unstable, dangerous. But I hadn't wanted to believe it. I thought they were stupid rumors. Here I was, facing his wild eyes, watching him do disturbing things, and beginning to wonder what he was going to do to me.

FIVE

"ELLIE, PLEASE." HE SLID THE TUBE INTO his pocket and held me with both arms as I struggled against him. He pulled me over to the desk and squeezed his hands around my wrists. "Let me show you something."

"No," I said, trying to unclench his fingers from my wrists.

He pulled open the smallest of the three drawers from the wooden box. It wasn't a drawer like I had imagined—it was a small, glass tray. I stared at the tray, wondering what he was going to do with it, wishing I could trust him, but his strong hands on my wrist told me I couldn't. He released one hand as he took the tube and began to pour his blood onto the glass tray.

As he poured, I used my other hand to push against his chest and then tried to pry his fingers off my other wrist. His strength was overwhelming, and I couldn't make him budge.

"Ellie, just wait. Please." He spoke in a pleading voice. It wasn't harsh or scary.

I reached up to claw at his face with my stubby nails, and he swung my arm away. He released me, and I took the chance to run to the steps. He didn't come after me at first. I looked over my shoulder to see him push the drawer closed, and then he was right behind me.

I went up two steps, but then the whole room seemed to move, just faintly, like a small tremor. I held on to the railings and steadied my feet. I'd never been in an earthquake, but this felt like it could be one. I looked to Gabe to see if the sudden motion had disturbed him, `but he stood still, reverently looking toward a far corner of the room. There was a faint light that began to grow brighter with each second. Its brightness stunned my eyes, so I turned away. I started back up the stairs, but the tremor intensified, and I felt its vibrations through the railings I was strangling with my hands.

"Ellie," he said, reaching for my wrist. His voice was quiet, calm, unlike a few moments before. "Please come. I want to show you Hanan Pacha."

The upper world? What was he talking about? The corner of the room was now exceedingly bright, glowing and lighting a path before it. The brightness seemed to form an arch over an entrance, a sort of doorway that wasn't there before. Was it Hanan Pacha like Gabe had said?

My desire to flee had subsided, and a faint desire to trust Gabe set in. I took his extended hand and proceeded toward the beckoning light. The ground was now still because the tremors had stopped. I felt that I should follow him.

As I put my foot through the lit doorway, it seemed like an impossibility. A cement wall had been there, and now I was walking through it. I stepped into a lush patch of grass, and I knew it wasn't Gabe's yard. Our winter-worn lawns didn't look like this. This was shiny, green grass, the kind you want to run your toes through. We went around a tall hedge and into a large, grassy area. Just beyond that was an alcove of trees, rosebushes, patches of lilies, and tulips. When I turned around, I couldn't see Gabe's house. There was just an opening through a tall hedge.

Gabe was watching me, and he squeezed my hand and smiled. His smile cemented my trust in him, and the moments before when I feared him seemed so far away.

"This is Hanan Pacha," he said. He took a step forward and tugged gently on my hand. "Let's go find your mom."

I froze at the mention of my mother. "My mom?"

"Yes, that's why we're here. That's what I've been wanting to show you. Your mom."

I didn't even think of my mother when he'd mentioned Hanan Pacha. The idea of such a place seemed so foreign to anything I believed. It was Incan mythology he'd been sharing with me, not a real concept that could affect me or my dead mother. The sudden thought that I may be seeing her or some image of her both thrilled and terrified me. Of course I wanted to see her, but I had images of her long ago affirmed in my mind. What would seeing her now be like?

"I don't understand. How does this work? Will I really be seeing her?"

He nodded. "We don't have much time. We're sort of like intruders to Hanan Pacha. We belong in Kay Pacha—that's where we live. We're only allowed in here for about five minutes and then we're sent back home."

"Where is she?"

"Come on," he said, taking my hand.

I followed a half step behind him. Tendrils of dewy leaves fell from trees that towered into the sky past anything I could see. Leaves, vivid and green and larger than my palm, grazed past my shoulder through the tree-lined path. Just before us was a massive tree unlike any I'd ever seen before—nothing like the dogwoods and oaks back home. Its trunk was midnight black, and its leaves were tiny, perfect circles, like confetti, that hung from thin, low-lying limbs shadowing over a fifty-foot radius. As we passed quickly by it, I grabbed one of its emerald leaves and rubbed it between my fingers, feeling soft silk, before I let it fall to the ground.

Tiny pebbles, smooth and white, crunched beneath our feet. We followed the path for only a few seconds more before Gabe stopped and pointed ahead. "There," he said. He pointed to a pristine river. I saw her hair first—the long, brown hair I'd inherited. It was swaying with the gentle breeze. She was sitting down at the edge of the river, her ankles crossed. I recognized the bright red wraparound dress with white polka dots she was wearing—it was one of her favorites. She would often find reasons to wear it. "Let's go to a play or an art opening," she would say, so she could wear that dress.

I hurried to reach her. "Mom!" I yelled as I started to sprint.

Gabe quickly held me back. "Wait, Ellie. She can't hear you. She can't see or hear you. You can see her, but there's no way to communicate."

The thought sobered me, and I stopped midstep. I looked back toward her and continued on. It didn't matter. I could still see *her*.

When I reached the water's edge, she didn't turn. She couldn't even sense our presence there. Her eyes remained on the gentle lapping of the topaz-colored water before us. I knelt down beside her and watched her. She looked exactly the same as the last time I saw her. Her thin lips pursed in the slight smile she always wore. The small wrinkles curved around her eyes as she squinted against the bright sky. It was my mother. I wanted to reach out to her, to hug her and have her comfort me in the way only she could, but as I reached for her, I touched only air. I couldn't feel her.

"I'm sorry," Gabe said, sensing my disappointment.

I knelt beside her, watching her, taking in each detail that I missed daily. Her arms were wrapped around her legs as she sat. I stared at the small freckles that dotted her arms—they had been a constant in my life. I remembered those arms and their freckles from when she held me as a toddler. I would often curl up against her arms and stare at the freckles until I fell asleep. That was a memory from long ago, one I'd never remembered until this moment, when such images, memories, suddenly seemed so vivid.

I loved her. I loved her so much. It hurt to know that I could only get a brief glimpse of her before I returned to my life without her—the life that would now have an even greater void knowing that she was here, where I couldn't be with her or see her every moment, every day, like I wanted to.

I felt Gabe's hand on my shoulder. "It's almost time."

I nodded as tears began to fall. I was crying in front of my mother, and she couldn't see to comfort me or make me feel better as she had hundreds of time throughout my life. That thought weighed heavily on me and made me cry more, sobbing as I watched her.

Gabe helped me stand up and put his arm around me. "I'm sorry."

I wiped my eyes and shook my head, willing the sadness to go away. I wanted to feel only happiness. The tears would have to wait for later when I was alone in my room. "So she's the only one here?" I asked, trying to take the focus off myself. I couldn't see anyone else anywhere around.

"No, but she's the only one you can see. I'm part Incan,

so I can see everyone here. We're surrounded by people. You just can't see them. *You* only see the ones you're a part of." He pointed off in the distance, toward a majestic waterfall. "My father is over there, but you can't see him."

I looked toward where he pointed. All I could see was clear water plunging from a tall cliff. "I wish I could see him."

"You have to say good-bye, Ellie. It's time to go."

"Already? But we just got here."

"I'm sorry. We're expelled from here after five minutes. You have to get ready. The way out isn't nearly as nice as the way in. We're going to be thrown out with some force."

As he said the words, I felt the trembling return. It intensified rapidly with each passing second until I felt my body shaking and everything turned dark. I couldn't see my mother anymore, and I reached for the space in front of me where I thought she was. I felt nothing, and I couldn't see anything. My body shook until it slammed against something and dropped to the floor. When I opened my eyes, I was back in Gabe's basement. The brightly lit doorway was gone, and Gabe was on the ground next to me. I rubbed my shoulder, which had struck something. It hurt and was tender.

"Are you okay?" Gabe asked, crawling over to me.

"Yeah, I'm okay." I sat up and looked around. The room was the same as before. Nothing had changed, but inside of me, everything had changed. My mother was within reach. I saw her, but now she wasn't here. I was alone. I felt empty. "Can we go back?" I asked Gabe, who was now sitting in front of me.

He looked away.

"Please."

"Yeah, but it's better to wait until the next day."

"Why?"

"If you go back a second time in the same day, you only get half the time—a little over two minutes. That's all, and then you're sent back, expelled with even more force. The third time, it's about a minute and you get thrown back even harder. I dislocated my shoulder once trying to do it." He paused and then turned away. "It's dangerous."

I tried to understand, to be patient, but the thought of my mother nearby compelled me to persist. "Just one more time?"

Gabe scooted over and looked at me. "I would do it a hundred times for you. I'm just worried about you getting hurt. You don't understand how strong the power is. When you get thrown out, it's so much more intense than the time before. I don't care about the blood. I have a whole body full of it. I'd do that part over and over again if I knew you wouldn't get hurt."

"I'm sorry. I didn't think about you having to give more blood. I can't ask you to do that."

Gabe shook his head. "I don't care about that part. I'd do it."

"I guess we can wait until tomorrow." The thought of seeing my mother again, of going through those feelings I'd just experienced—the sense of loss, the inability to touch her or talk to her—was frightening.

"I have to work tomorrow right after school. Is Saturday okay? We can do it in the morning after our track meet. I don't have to work until noon," he said.

I nodded, and then he reached over to touch my hand. He hesitated at first, his fingertips lingering over my arm, but then he followed through and held my hand. I looked at his arm and thought about the blood he'd taken from it. He'd done that for me, to show me my mom. I couldn't even think of words to thank him or to talk about it.

"My dad first showed it to me when I was ten and I'd asked about my grandparents. He took me there and showed them to me. I thought it was a dream at first, because I couldn't believe it. It seemed impossible."

"I still can't believe it," I said.

"We didn't go often. He said it was only to be used occasionally. We don't belong there, he told me. We'd go about twice a year. He showed me how to use it, but he always used his blood. I didn't know that I could use my own blood until after he'd died.

"I tried it one day, about a week after he died. I just had to see him. I go about once a month now to see him. Sometimes, my mom comes with me."

"This is what you've been wanting to show me? That day you changed my tire, you said you wanted to show me something that I dream about?"

"Yeah. I didn't know how to tell you, but I've wanted to bring you here ever since I found out about your mom. When I first heard the news, it was my first thought. I didn't know you then. I didn't know how to tell you about it, and I wasn't sure I could trust you. I've never wanted to show anyone before, but with you . . . The way your mom was taken, it was so wrong. I just wanted you to see her again."

"Thank you. Thank you so much, Gabe. You gave me my mom back, in a way." I squeezed his hand and looked up at him. I would be grateful forever. Suddenly a thought struck me. My dad. "I have to get my dad. I have to bring him here." I pulled myself up and stood.

"No, Ellie." Gabe stood up and held my arm back. "You can't. You can't bring him here. You can't tell anyone."

"But he'll want to see her again. He can't even talk about her. He can't even mourn. He's just numb, still in shock. This might help him."

"I'm sorry, you can't. Promise me you won't tell your dad. I can't risk anyone else knowing. I trusted you with my secret. A sacred secret. You can't tell anyone."

"But, my dad . . ."

"No. If too many people find out about it—if the wrong people find out—I could lose it. Someone might take it away."

"My dad wouldn't do that."

"I can't be sure. Maybe not your dad, but if others find out about it, I could lose it forever. And lose my dad forever. I can't let you do that."

I understood. Adults couldn't always be trusted with secrets. "Okay, I won't tell him."

"Promise?" He reached for both my wrists and tugged gently on them.

"Yes, I promise."

"I trust you, Ellie. I trust you and no one else. Only you, me, and my mom know about it. No one else can ever know."

"Okay."

He pulled me toward him and embraced me, putting both his arms around my shoulders. "Saturday, Ellie."

SIX

UP UNTIL THE MOMENT I HEARD SARah's knock on my door, I hadn't thought she was coming. She hadn't said a word to me at school, and all I had to go on was the vague suggestion she'd made on Monday that we get together. But she was here, and I supposed our friendship was on again. I stopped in front of the hall mirror to look at myself. I was wearing my favorite jeans—the baggy ones that I have to wear a belt with or they'll fall down. My brown hoodie was on the floor in my room, but I was wearing a shirt—my *Les Mis* T-shirt from our freshman field trip—I knew Sarah didn't like. "Nobody wears theater T-shirts anymore," she'd told me. "That's so middle school." Well, I loved my *Les Mis* T-shirt, and it still fit. My mom had helped chaperone that field trip, and it was one of my favorite memories.

I was also wearing my brown Chuck Taylors, which Sarah definitely hated, but I was determined not to let her rule what I wore. She had to accept me for my theater T-shirt and boy shoes (that was what she called them.) When I opened the door, she quickly surveyed my wardrobe and frowned but didn't say anything.

"Grab a coat. Let's make lasagna," she said, not moving from the doorstep.

"Lasagna?" I asked. We'd made so much lasagna throughout our friendship. "Right now?"

"Yeah, for old times' sake. Let's go to the grocery store." She tugged on the collar of her belted leather coat. "Bring a coat. Your charcoal peacoat."

I was tempted to argue and grab my brown hoodie off the floor of my room, but she wanted to make lasagna—a small sliver of the old Sarah—and I didn't want to turn her off. So I opened the hall closet and pulled out the peacoat she'd helped me pick out last winter.

"I'll drive," Sarah said as she walked down the path to her Honda Pilot.

"Are we going to come back here?" I asked her.

"Yeah. You know how your dad loves our lasagna."

"Okay."

Sarah turned and glanced at me before she pulled out into the street. "I want us to still be friends, but it's going to be tough after what you did to Bradley."

"I didn't do anything to him. He did it to himself."

"I know. I know, Ellie. You always want to do the right thing, but this time doing the right thing got Bradley into a lot of trouble."

"He made that trouble for himself."

"I know. He was stupid. He was just so mad at Gabe because of stuff on the track team, and now the coach wants to kick him off the team. And, boys! They just don't think sometimes, you know?"

"Sarah, what Bradley did was really mean. He broke

into Gabe's house and burned his couch. What if nobody ever reported it? Nobody would know what had happened. It's like with my mom. What if somebody out there knows what happened to her? Or knows who killed her? But they're afraid to say something, so they keep it to themselves, and we'll never know. That's why I couldn't keep it a secret."

Sarah nodded and reached over to squeeze my arm. "I'm sorry, El. I didn't think about it like that. I know you're right, Ellie. You always are. But I really like Bradley. Senior prom is coming up in a few months and I really want to go. If I can't get him to ask me, I have to wait until next year. And I really want to go this year."

"Why?"

"Why?" She looked over at me with a scrunched forehead. "Because it's senior prom!"

"You can go to senior prom when you're a senior next year."

"But I want to go to senior prom when I'm a junior. I know I'll go next year, but the big thing is getting asked to go when you're a junior."

"I'm not sure I even want to go when I *am* a senior," I said, looking out the side window.

"I don't get you, Ellie. That's what high school's all about."

"That's not what high school is all about," I mumbled into the window.

She let out an exaggerated sigh and then jerked to a stop at a red light. "Ellie, I'm trying here. Okay?"

"I know," I said, turning slightly to face her.

"I know you don't care about what's important to me anymore. I don't know how it happened, or when, but what am I supposed to do? Just stop being your friend because you act like this now?"

"I'm not acting like anything. You're the one pushing me away."

Sarah continued through the light and then pulled into the Stop & Shop parking lot. "I'm not pushing you away. Look, let's just make this lasagna, okay?"

We walked toward the store in silence. Gabe was working tonight, and I wondered if we would run into him. I pushed the grocery cart around and followed Sarah down the aisles. We started talking to each other again, but just about dinner.

"Which sauce did we use last time?" Sarah asked, picking up a jar of Ragu. "The garden style?"

"I think it was traditional."

"Oh, right," she said. She put the garden style back and placed a jar of traditional Ragu sauce in the cart.

We moved down the aisle, and she scanned the pasta shelf. "Remember that first time we tried the no-boil noodles?"

I laughed at the memory and went to stand by her. "Yes, it was gross."

"What did we do wrong? I can't remember."

"We forgot to add the extra water. It needs extra water to cook the noodles all the way. Yuck."

"So your dad ended up ordering pizza." Sarah and I both started laughing.

I held my side and doubled over, remembering the pasty, tough noodles and how heartbroken we were at our wasted efforts. Dad topped off the evening by taking us out for smoothies after the pizza. "Should we just boil the noodles?"

Sarah made a face. "Yeah, I don't want to go through that again." She put a box of regular noodles in the cart, and I followed her through the store as we gathered the rest of the ingredients.

I pushed the cart to a line, and Sarah picked up a *People* magazine. She leafed through the pages as I eased further up in line. A couple stood behind us.

Sarah put her magazine back and was about to start unloading our groceries on the conveyor belt when she stopped suddenly. "Ew!" She turned to me in a harsh whisper. "Gabe, the banana boat guy, is our checker. Let's move to a different line."

I looked up and saw Gabe. He was finishing up with the lady in front of us. "No. And don't call him that. He's my friend."

"He's your friend? Since when?" She grabbed the front of the cart and started to push it back.

"Since I haven't had anyone else to sit with at lunch," I whispered to her. I pulled the cart away from her and started putting the groceries on the conveyer belt. "He's my friend, so can you just be nice about it?"

"I can't believe we're having this conversation. He's your *friend*?" She looked around the front of the store, scanning the checkout stands. She slumped her shoulders and crossed her arms, as if to hide from any disapproving eyes.

"Yes, I just said that." I finished putting all the groceries on and pushed the cart to the end of the aisle.

"Hey, Ellie," Gabe said as he started scanning items.

"Hi, Gabe," I replied, but Sarah had picked up another magazine and was using it to hide her face.

Gabe bagged the noodles and sauce. "Making lasagna?"

"Yeah," I said. "It's one of our favorites."

Gabe looked at Sarah and raised both eyebrows at me as he scanned the ricotta cheese. I didn't like the implications of those eyebrows. It was as if he disapproved of me spending time with my best friend. Just because he and I were friends now didn't mean he could have input on my other friends.

So I started bagging the groceries to get it done faster. Sarah's behavior was embarrassing, and Gabe's attitude about Sarah was annoying. What happened to the customer always being right? At that moment, I didn't feel like he thought I was right about anything.

Sarah shoved the magazine back and then handed me a ten. I pulled out another ten and paid Gabe. He took his time counting the change and then pressed it into my hand.

"Thanks. Good night, Gabe," I said, shoving the money into my coat pocket.

"Have a good night. Enjoy your lasagna." Gabe said. I hurried to follow Sarah, who was already to the door. I turned around for just an instant to see that Gabe was still watching me as he scanned the next customer's groceries.

"I can't see how you can be friends with him. That guy is so creepy," Sarah said as we walked to her car.

"Like how?"

She shuddered. "I don't know. Just creepy."

She helped me load the groceries in the back, and then I put the cart away as she started the car.

"His house is run down, and he drives, like, a fifty-year-old car."

I couldn't help laughing at her remark. "So?"

"So, that's creepy."

I buckled my seat belt and shook my head. Really, Sarah never used to be so shallow and annoying. Our friendship was based on something—something real. I just couldn't remember any of it at that moment.

Sarah turned down the radio's volume as she merged into traffic. "There's some weird stuff that goes on in that house. Gabe's house. I've never seen his parents. Some people say they don't even exist—that he lives there by himself."

"What's weird about that?"

"He's a kid. A kid living by himself, for who knows how long. And his house is seriously weird."

"Like how?" I pressed. I knew exactly what was weird about his house, had seen it myself, but I wondered how much she'd heard, how much she knew.

"Like, they say his mom is a witch or something."

"So does he live by himself or does he live with his witch-mom? Which story is the right one?"

"I don't know. I'm pretty sure the witch one."

"A witch?" I asked. I stared at her, my nose scrunched up, as she stopped at a red light. "Who says?"

"I don't know. I've just heard it around."

"So, is it like a witch who wears a black hat and rides around on a broom or more of a modern-day witch? You know, the Wiccan ones?" I didn't know why I kept arguing with her. It was like Sarah always thought she was right about everything, even when she was completely wrong. True, I had not met Gabe's mother yet. And there were strange events that occurred in his house, but she didn't have the slightest idea about any of it. She relied on pure rumor to make her opinions.

"Who knows? Who cares?" she said.

I let the argument die, like I had so many times with Sarah. It's just what I did.

Sarah pulled into my driveway, and we unloaded the groceries without another word about Gabe.

SEVEN

WE SILENTLY WENT TO WORK. WE knew this dance and had done it many times. Sarah knew where everything in my kitchen was, and she'd never been shy about getting what she needed. She put water to boil in a big pot while I opened the package of ground beef. After she salted the water, she unpacked the rest of the ingredients.

"I'm glad we're doing this, El," she said, pulling off the plastic peel on the ricotta cheese. "I'm sorry I've been so weird lately. I don't know why I'm so nervous about school this year."

"I guess because it's junior year."

"Yeah. I can't believe we're graduating next year and gonna be adults. Remember how we used to talk about it, dream about it? And now it's really happening."

"I know."

Sarah poured the ricotta cheese and began stirring it. She pulled out the cheese grater from under the counter and went to work on the mozzarella. "I guess it's just that this year is so important because it lays the social foundation for next year. Who you are and what you do this year makes or breaks senior year. That's what Bradley says."

"Senior year is so much more than social stuff. I mean, it's about what college you're going to go to and what major you're going to choose."

Sarah put the noodles to boil and turned to me. "El, that's easy for you. I'm not as smart as you. You're going to have your pick of colleges. I'm gonna be stuck in some Jersey college, which could completely cut me out of the right social scene."

"Sarah, college is not about the social scene. It's about becoming something."

Sarah grated the cheese onto a large platter. "Ellie, you're going to be something. Something important, somebody important. There's no doubt about that. I can only hope to be somebody important's wife."

"No, Sarah. You can be something important too. You're smart. There's a lot you can do. You just sell yourself short." I put the wooden spoon down on the stove and walked over to her.

"You don't get it, El. I'm going to be just like my mom. She went to college to get a man, not a degree. And she got him, all right. She set out to get a doctor and she got her doctor. She didn't get it by acting all smart and picking a major. She knew exactly what she was doing, and she got exactly what she wanted. A twelve-room colonial, a house in the Hamptons, and an unlimited expense account."

"And that's what you want?"

"She's got a great life, El. Goes to the gym every day, shopping and lunch in the city once a week, a new car every year, and nonstop phone calls from every charity and non-profit within a forty-mile radius that want her as their head.

How did she get that? By picking a major? No. I'm not the kind who picks a major. You are. I'm the kind who gets picked by someone major if I do everything right."

The meat sizzled, and I turned away from Sarah to pick up the spoon and stir. "That makes me kind of sad, Sarah. You sound so cynical. You can have a better life than that."

"What is a better life than that? Didn't you hear me? She has it made. Why wouldn't I want that?"

"But why are you already thinking about marriage?"

"It's not that I want to get married right away. I just need to make sure I'm doing everything, taking all the right steps in the right direction." She stopped grating cheese and looked at me. I guess she was hoping that I followed her logic, but I think she was disappointed by the face I made, because she turned around and kept grating. "Look, Bradley is going to Cornell next year. That means I have to act right now. If I do become his girlfriend, just think what that would mean. Even if things don't work out with Bradley, at least I have that to tell future guys. My ex-boyfriend goes to Cornell." It was like she was looking for ways to pad her resume, to find experiences that would look good for future jobs.

"I don't know, Sarah." I turned off the stove and walked over to the sink to drain the fat into a can I'd pulled out of the recycling bin. "Everything was so much simpler when we were kids. We just understood each other more."

Sarah stopped grating again. "I know. I miss it. The simpler times when all we had to worry about was whose house we were going to do a sleepover at or how far we would ride our bikes."

"We don't have to make it so hard, you know."

"I know. There's just so much more to consider now. That makes it hard."

I poured the spaghetti sauce into the pan and then checked on the noodles, separating them with a fork. "Sarah, I want us to stay friends, but I don't want to keep doing what you want me to."

She sighed and let the cheese grater fall to the counter. "This isn't middle school anymore where you could get away with just anything. Style and status really matter now."

"My style is my style." I had to stay firm and stand my ground with Sarah.

"Your style is no style, Ellie. I'm just trying to help you." She went back to grating, this time more rapidly. She grated three times and then dropped the grater back on the counter. "Remember in sixth grade when you and Jenna wanted to get perms? Perms! And I tried to talk you two out of it. Straight hair never goes out of style, I told you. And you listened to me and did the right thing. Remember Jenna the next day? She was in tears. Tears. She couldn't stop crying about how awful she looked—and she did look awful. Remember how you thanked me. You told me you were glad I talked you out of it. You," she said, pointing the chunk of cheese at me, "would have looked awful. Awful. That is all I'm trying to do now. Save you the embarrassment that Jenna went through that day." She turned back to grating. She'd already grated more cheese than we needed, but I didn't feel like telling her that.

I did remember that day. Poor Jenna. I knew what Jenna had been trying to do that day. It's what I was trying to do now: make my own decisions, follow what I want, and not listen to what Sarah says. I think that was the last time Jenna did that. From that day on, she followed Sarah's way of thinking and her advice on everything, from brand of jeans to what colleges to look at. It's why Jenna drove a Honda Pilot.

"I know you're trying to help, Sarah, but we have to do our own thing now and make our own mistakes."

"Let's just not talk about it anymore." Sarah brought over the cheese, and together we layered the lasagna. I always did the meat and sauce, and she always did the cheese. She put it in the oven, and I set a timer on my phone. We cleaned up our mess and then headed upstairs.

Sarah led the way into my room. "I haven't been in here in a long time. I used to practically live here."

"Remember this?" I said, grabbing a small scrapbook off my shelf. We'd made it the summer after freshman year.

"Yes!" We both sat on my bed, and she took the scrapbook from my hands. "Oh! Remember this day?" She fingered the embossed paper that framed a picture of the two of us. It was the day we'd taken the train by ourselves to the city for the first time. We'd gone to the Metropolitan Museum of Art and had eaten lunch in their little café.

"That was such a fun day," I said, remembering how scared I'd been about taking the train alone. Sarah, unwavering in bravery, had talked me into it and through it. In the end, I'd been so proud of our little achievement. We felt so grown-up walking through the museum, thinking we knew what were talking about as we analyzed the art.

"I can't believe we ever thought those clothes were in style," she said, pointing to our leggings and oversized sweaters. She turned the page to a layout of our swim team. "Remember Tim?"

Tim had been our swim coach, and Sarah had been crazy about him. She had a huge crush on him—probably the first one that made her really cry. I didn't know what she'd been thinking anyway. She was a freshman in high school; he was in college. I wasn't sure how she'd even thought that was possible. It was the only time I could remember when things had not gone her way. Prior to that, and ever since then, every boy she'd ever set her sights on had been hers. I thought it was heading that way with Bradley too, but I didn't feel like asking her about it. That was too much in the present, and at the moment, I preferred living in the past.

"I would never have done swim team without your help. Remember when I wouldn't even go in the deep end?"

She nodded. "Yeah. You were a great swimmer but just lacked confidence. I was so proud of you when you finally jumped off the high dive. There was no stopping you after that."

I turned the page. "I don't think I would have ever done it without you."

"That's why we make such a good team."

Really, it was a symbiotic relationship. None of those accomplishments would have happened without her prompting, without her friendship, just as running through sprinklers and having tea parties would not have occurred for her without me. Just as the friendship filled a void for me, it did the same for her. Because whereas her mother threw money at her, my mother indulged us both of us in the pleasures of childhood.

There was the summer Sarah and I spent most afternoons running through the sprinklers in my front yard. My mom sat wearing a large brimmed hat under an old oak tree. She took breaks from reading her book to get us Popsicles or lemonade or to slather us with sunscreen. That's how we spent most of that summer. One weekend, Sarah asked her mother if we could run through the sprinklers at her house. The next week, there was a crew in their backyard, digging a hole for a pool. That was Mrs. Winter's way. Instead of indulging her daughter in the simplicity of sprinklers, she built her a pool.

So that's why Sarah had loved spending time with my mother and me. Mom would sit on the carpet with us in my room with an old miniature tea set. It was an antique her grandmother had given her. There were small white saucers, cups with pale pink roses in the center. Some of the pieces were chipped, but we didn't care. My mom would make lemon tea and pour it into the small, ceramic pitcher. It was never hot—just lukewarm. She would make chicken salad finger sandwiches. Sarah and I loved the crunch when we bit down on the small pieces of celery.

Again, Sarah asked her mother if we could do that one afternoon. Mrs. Winter booked a children's tea party at the Russian Tea Room and invited six girls. The next day, we were all driven into New York City, dressed in lacy dresses and black Mary Janes. The girls were shuffled into a children's room for tea and blinis while Mrs. Winter met some of her friends for brunch.

My mother worked as a financial consultant for several years before my birth. After I was born, she cut her hours and worked from home a lot. When I started school, she went back to her rigorous schedule, cutting back each summer to spend time at home with me. In the summer, she worked from home, but I don't remember seeing much work happening. She spent her days with me and her nights with work.

Sarah spent many summer afternoons at my house. My mother, a willing participant in whatever our imaginations conjured up, would spend the afternoons with us, cutting up the new refrigerator cardboard box into a playhouse, sewing Barbie dresses, or drawing hopscotch on the driveway.

Sarah's mother was a stay-at-home mother, but she was hardly ever home. If she wasn't at Barney's or Saks, she was cochairing a garden club event or on the board of directors of an art museum. My working mother spent more time with me than Sarah's homemaker mother spent with her. So it was that void that our friendship filled for Sarah. With me, she was able to live the childhood forbidden at home. She could roller-skate in the kitchen, make a tent in the living room, and have tea and sandwiches on the floor in my bedroom.

It was a friendship that had enhanced each of our lives in different but mutual ways. But those ways had exhausted themselves after a while, it seemed, and at times, it felt as if that friendship had run its course. At least, that's how it felt lately.

The timer went off on my phone. "It's done."

Sarah closed the scrapbook and pulled herself off my bed. "Thanks for showing me that. It brought back a lot of memories."

"Yeah, I know." As we headed downstairs, I hoped that seeing the scrapbook would help her remember why we were friends.

I took the lasagna out and let it cool on the stove while Sarah set the table.

"So, my mom's redoing the basement. Again."

"Really?"

"Yeah. She wants to do a whole game room theme. New pool table and a huge projection screen to watch movies. It should be done soon. She's trying to get it done in time for my birthday party. She thought it would be cool to have my party down there."

"That sounds like fun."

"Yeah. I'm trying to narrow down the time and everything, so I'll text you when I know."

"Can't wait," I said.

"Remember my princess party?"

"Yeah. That was so fun. The company your mom hired was insane. They had everything—wigs, dresses, and glass slippers."

"Everything was so easy back then. Life just gets complicated the older you get."

"I know."

"So, I think Bradley is coming to my birthday party."

"And you really want him to?"

"Of course."

I heard my dad at the front door, and Sarah put on the oven mitts and brought the lasagna to the table.

"Hey, girls. It smells great in here," Dad said, coming into the kitchen. He put down his laptop case and came over to us. "It's been a while since you two made lasagna. What's the special occasion?"

"Just having fun reminiscing about old times," Sarah said, cutting into the lasagna. "Hope you're hungry, Mr. Cummings."

"Very." Dad walked over to the sink and washed his hands.

It seemed like old times, as cliché as that sounded. It was hard to recall how many lasagnas we'd shared at that table. Anytime we'd made lasagna, it was at my house. Sarah had mentioned the idea to her mother once, and she had suggested we could have a caterer bring us an Italian meal. It didn't have the same effect. Mrs. Winter just couldn't understand our penchant for making lasagna. I wondered if Sarah would become like her mother one day. I hoped she wouldn't. I hoped Sarah would indulge her future daughter by playing in the sprinklers, having tea parties on the floor, and making lasagna. Surely she would remember being that age and the importance of simplicity in childhood.

We ate the lasagna and talked about the mundane things

of our lives. Dad was good at keeping a conversation going, asking Sarah about her family and about school. He made the evening more comfortable. Sarah and I had quickly run out of things to say to each other, and it was good to have a buffer to keep the conversation light.

There was still one thing missing—my mother. She'd been present at all our previous lasagna dinners. With her absence and the discomfort so evident between Sarah and me, that day's lasagna just didn't taste as good.

EIGHT

I FOLLOWED GABE HOME AFTER THE meet, my hands trembling on the steering wheel. Being in my mother's presence was just minutes away, and I wanted to move past the formalities of parking the car, going inside Gabe's house, and watching him drain blood from his arm. The fact that we hadn't actually talked about my oral presentation hadn't escaped me. I knew he was willing to spend time talking about the Incas so that I could finish my project, but that was the furthest thought from my mind. As I pulled in behind his Volvo, Gabe, his hoodie covering part of his profile and his backpack slung over his arm, was waiting for me.

He threw his backpack down on the kitchen table and walked to the refrigerator. "Want a soda or something?" he asked.

"No, thanks." There was only one thing I wanted at the moment.

He took out a Coke and opened it. I put my backpack

next to his on the table and grabbed the back of a chair as I watched him drink.

"Is your mom here?" I asked, wondering if she knew that he'd shown me the huaca and taken me to see my mom. Did she care?

He nodded, putting down his Coke on the counter. "She's in her room. She's not feeling well today."

In my mind, I questioned how often she was sick. It seemed strange that I had yet to meet her; the two times I'd been here, she'd been tucked away in her room. I wondered if someone could be sick that often. The thought nagged at me, but for the moment, I let it slip out of my mind as I focused on the purpose for my visit. As I watched Gabe slouch against the counter, slowly sipping his Coke, I wondered if he remembered the first few times he'd gone to see his father through the huaca. Could he recall the anxiety, the overwhelming desire to leave here, to go to him, see him, feel his presence even for a brief moment? His casual stance and slow consumption of a twelve-ounce soda gave me the idea that he'd forgotten the desperation he once felt, the desperation I was currently feeling.

"Sure you don't want anything?" he asked when he caught me staring at him.

"Not to drink," I said, turning my gaze toward the floor.

He put the can down on the counter and wiped his chin. "You ready?"

I nodded and followed him to the basement door. I let guilt wash over me as I thought about what I was asking him to do for me, what he was willing to do for me. I turned away from him. He wasn't just Gabe, the freak kid from history, taking his own blood. He was now my friend—probably my closest friend at this point—and he was jabbing himself, freely giving of something vital so that I could see my mother. I couldn't watch anymore because even though he said it didn't really hurt, I knew it did. He was hurting himself for me, and there wasn't anything I could really give him in return. But he didn't care.

As my patience began to waver even more, I suddenly felt the trembling of the room and knew I'd soon see her. The quivering of the room that had once seemed so ominous was now comforting, like the soothing rocking of a baby—movements that would lead to a peaceful feeling. I felt Gabe grabbing for me, and I quickly took his hand. Together, we ran past the hedge toward where my mother sat at the water's edge.

After we were thrown out, I sat back against a wooden beam, trying to catch my breath as I recovered from being slammed to the ground.

"Are you okay?" Gabe asked me. He scooted over to me and sat cross-legged, facing me.

"Yeah, I'm fine. I'll get used to it."

"I'm sorry it has to be that way."

"I don't mind," I said, rubbing my knee, which had smashed right into the beam. "It's worth it." I smiled at him and then looked past him at the wooden box that lay on the desk. I stared at the box in awe of all the power held within it. It seemed impossible that a hand-carved wooden box had such great ability to bridge my world to my mother's. It was beyond my understanding and still seemed like a dream.

The three small drawers of the box were crudely carved out, uneven. Such an imperfect item—cut and carved by hand—could take me to see my mother. "What are the other two drawers for?" I asked Gabe, amazed that it was the first time I'd thought to ask.

Gabe looked at the huaca and then turned away from it. "Did I tell you my dad killed himself?"

"No," I said, quickly turning to him. "I'm sorry." I don't know why I said I was sorry, but the thought struck me that his pain must be much worse than mine.

"He suffered from depression his whole life. He'd been on meds, off meds, in treatment, out of treatment. I think, one day, he'd just finally had enough."

"I'm so sorry. How old were you?"

"Twelve."

The sudden change in conversation to his father's suicide didn't make me forget that he hadn't answered my question. I thought he was avoiding it, but I didn't want to call him on it. He needed that moment, and I wanted to respond appropriately to it. "That must have been very hard."

"It was. For a long time. I'm okay now."

"It's not your fault."

He looked briefly at the huaca and then turned to me. He kept my gaze and didn't say anything for a minute. "I know that now."

"Good."

"I didn't understand, though. For a long time I felt like I wasn't good enough. Like, if I had been a better son or a better person, he would have wanted to stick around. But I know now that he loved me and that I was the reason he held on for so long. Finally, he just couldn't take it anymore."

"How did you come to realize all that? Did your mom tell you?"

Gabe turned his eyes suddenly from me and looked back at the huaca, like it held all the answers. "Come here," he said. He pulled himself off the floor and offered a hand to me.

I grabbed his hand, and he pulled me to my feet. He held my hand as we walked to the desk, which held the huaca. He pulled out the second drawer and showed me that it was the same as the first, but with a wider glass tray.

"This one takes more," he said, reaching for his cardboard box of supplies. He took out another needle and tube and let go of my hand to pull up his sleeve.

"What are you doing?" I asked him.

"I want to take you back, but this time it's going to be different." He tied the rubber band around his bicep.

"Are you sure?"

He pulled it tight and then picked up the needle. "I didn't want to tell you about this one until you were ready. It will only last for a minute, but you'll be able to feel her. She'll feel you."

"What do you mean?" I grabbed his arm and turned him toward me. "How will I feel her?"

He unclenched his arm and placed it on my shoulder. "I didn't know about it at first. One day, I wanted to try the second drawer to see if it was different. When I got there, I saw my dad like always, but it didn't feel the same. I reached for him and I felt him. I could touch him. He turned to me and could see me. I couldn't believe it at first. We could communicate. Not, like, talk to each other. He couldn't hear me, but I could feel what he was feeling. It was only for a minute. It's hard to explain, but you'll see. I want you to see."

"She'll see me?"

Gabe nodded. "Sort of. That's how I knew about my dad and why he killed himself. I could see these images in my mind. What he was thinking. And I could see that he loved me, that I was the reason he didn't kill himself for so long—the reason he tried for so long. But then he just couldn't do it anymore. But I know he loved me."

"I want that. I want her to see me. I want to feel her."

He clenched his arm again and looked for a vein.

"Can I help you?" I asked, slowly reaching my hand out toward him.

He held his arm against his chest for a moment before nodding and extending it out to me. He handed me the tube and untied the elastic band. I noticed he was using a larger tube, and I watched as it began to fill with his blood.

"I'm sorry you have to do this. I wish that you didn't."

"I'm used to it. I don't mind." He opened the second drawer and held out his hand for the tube. I gave it to him, nodding that I was ready, and he began to pour the blood. He stopped midway. "Be ready. It goes so fast. You'll only be there a minute, and then we're going to get thrown out even harder."

I nodded, not caring about the consequences. I watched Gabe's hand as he slowly slid the drawer closed. Instantly, I felt how it was different. It didn't start out as a tremor like before. This time, I felt the room moving as if someone had picked up the house and was shaking it like a baby's rattle. I reached for the wall to steady myself but couldn't hold on, and I fell to the floor. I could feel Gabe scrambling behind me. The shaking lasted for half a minute and then we were behind the hedge again.

I hurried around it and spotted my mother sitting at the water's edge. Gabe followed, and I turned around to face him. I wanted to feel my mother, to get a bit closer than before, but fear needled its way through my legs, and I couldn't move. What if my expectations were so much greater than what I would actually feel?

Gabe sensed my apprehension, and he reached for my hand, squeezing it before tugging me forward to where she sat. Mere feet from her, I slowed down, still facing her back. Part of me thought she would sense my presence and run to me. But I was within arm's reach and she didn't even know I was there. I wanted to call out to her, but Gabe had said she still wouldn't hear me. If she didn't answer, I'd be crushed.

I reached her and tried to summon the nerve to step forward. So much of my minute had elapsed, and I would only have a few seconds with her. Gabe pulled me around, and I stood facing her. Her smile tugged at the corners of her eyes—a smile she would give me every day after school. She didn't seem surprised to see me. She rose to her feet, reached for my hands, and pulled me into an embrace.

It was as though a surge of electricity entered my body and coursed through it. Instantly, images flashed through my mind, so quick I could barely take them in. It was like I was seeing a slide show at superspeed. There were mental pictures of me as a baby, at birthdays, Christmas. All of the pictures were of me by myself or with her. Some of the memories, I remembered. Others were so long ago. As the images passed, her smile increased, and she squeezed her eyes together and pressed my hands tightly. The images didn't stop, and many of them I couldn't focus on. One image grabbed me, and I held onto it as long as I could. My mother was standing next to me, her hand was on one of my cheeks, and she kissed the other side of my face. I felt her love through that image she shared with me and through the strength of her hands on mine. I knew the time was almost up, and I started shaking with fear, scared I would never feel so loved again.

The images in my mind continued quickly, and I started sobbing as the intensity of the moment increased with each second that passed. Our joined hands started trembling and then were ripped apart. I reached for her, but a great force pulled me back.

"Mom!" I screamed.

She clasped her hands together, kissed them, and then waved them toward me.

I screamed her name again, but as I was pulled back, I couldn't see her anymore. Darkness enveloped me. The images were gone, frozen at the one of my mother kissing my cheek. I held onto it to carry me through the dark moment. The force pulling me intensified, and I felt a squeezing in my stomach, as though a rope were tied at my waist and being pulled tightly. I wrapped my hands around my waist to ease the pain. Then the force whipped me around and propelled me forward, throwing me out of my mother's world. I didn't belong with her, and I was reminded of that as I barreled into Gabe's basement.

I was thrown farther than any of the previous times, and I landed by the stairs in one pounding thrust. My head hit the bottom step, and I bounced like a rag doll. I eased myself up to a sitting position and reached for the back of my head. It throbbed under my hand, and I squeezed my eyes shut, feeling a sharp pain in my back.

"Are you okay?" Gabe was beside me in an instant. His hands were on my shoulder and then feeling down my arms. "You all right?"

I nodded, ignoring the pain, worried that he would use an injury as a reason to not go again. "I'm fine. It was okay." I withdrew my hand from its clutch on my head and patted his hand on my shoulder.

He slid down to sit beside me, rubbing his knee. His hand moved in slow circles as his fingers dug into his corduroys.

"Are you okay?" I asked him.

"Yeah, it wasn't bad." He pulled his hand away from his knee and planted it firmly on the cold cement beneath us.

A few minutes of silence elapsed as we each settled into our bruises. I stared at the concrete floor, rubbing my fingernail across the scratches and fissures that ran across the room. "I need to go again."

He nodded and kept his gaze down. "I know. I know how you feel. It's how I felt. I wanted to keep going, to stay there and not come back. But we can't. We belong here."

"I know. I know that. But it went so fast. Too fast. I need to see her again."

"We will. We'll go again, but not today."

I hated to ask him, to ask for his sacrifice. I nodded and turned to face him, but he was still looking down. He must have felt my eyes on him, because he looked up at me. His dark brown eyes softened as he looked at me, and he reached over to touch my cheek. "I know how you're feeling right now. It's the one thing you've dared to hope for over and over as you lay in bed each night. It's how I felt."

I gulped down the emotion his candid declaration elicited. It was the one thing I had hoped for against everything that I knew to be true. I never believed it could happen, but I hoped despite the disbelief. It was as if he'd pulled the curtains of my room apart on any given night and glimpsed inside to see me sobbing into my pillow. "Please."

"Yes, Ellie. Of course. But not today. If we go back now, you can only stay for half the time—thirty seconds. Thirty seconds will only make it worse, make you miss her more. I know. I've done it. It's only fifteen seconds the third time; seven the fourth. Then you almost don't even see her and you're thrust out just as you get there. Tomorrow, we can go again. You have to get your full minute."

I understood, but fifteen seconds of having her arms around me—feeling the love I never thought I would experience again—would be enough. One second more is all I needed if that was all that was allowed. "I just miss her so much."

"Tomorrow. You'll get your minute, I promise." He reached up and gently ran his hand over my head, stopping suddenly when he touched the lump that was starting to form. He sighed. "I don't want you to get hurt. The power intensifies with each time. If we go again, it would be so strong. You could really get hurt or break your arm or something. Please. Let's wait until tomorrow."

The physical pain he described was no match for the emotional ache that ran through me, but I didn't want to push it. He'd already given me so much. "Okay. Tomorrow."

He kept his hand on my head and smoothed down my hair. I leaned over and put my head on his shoulder, and we sat on the cold cement floor in his darkened basement. I didn't want to go anywhere. This was the closest place to my mother, and I just wanted to sit and think about her a little longer.

"I have to go to work in a few minutes," Gabe said, turning his wrist to look at his watch.

I knew it was close to dinnertime, and my dad would be home soon, but I didn't want to go there, to the emptiness that my mother left behind. I wanted to stay in Gabe's basement.

"I guess I should go home." I pulled myself off the floor, and Gabe stood up beside me. "Thank you. Today was amazing. I can't wait to see her again."

He slid his arms around my waist and pulled me into an embrace. I felt his breath on my ear as he rubbed his cheek along the side of my face. "I'll miss you tonight. The last place I want to be is at work."

"I know."

He pulled away, and we walked up the stairs to the kitchen. My eyes adjusted to the brighter light as I walked toward the door. "What time do you have to work tomorrow?" I asked him.

"Six."

I opened the door and leaned back on the doorjamb. "Okay. I'll see you at school."

"You going to be okay?" he asked.

I nodded, not sure if I was. How would I be okay knowing that my mother was just a few minutes away but I couldn't be with her or see those loving images in my mind?

He kissed my forehead and rubbed the back of my head. "Put an ice pack on your head when you get home."

"Okay." I smiled. "You put one on your knee, okay?"

He smiled back and nodded. "All right."

I'd been holding it in for Gabe's sake, but once I was alone, out of his sight, I broke down. The silent sobbing in my room that I usually indulged in was not enough today. I erupted in hacking cries, my shoulders trembling, and I could barely keep a grip on the steering wheel. Tears streamed down my face, blocking my view of traffic, and I knew I should pull over, but I wanted to be home. I wanted to run to my room and wrap myself in her quilt. I wanted to lie in bed and try to revive each image that had filtered through my mind earlier that day.

A stoplight in front of me suddenly turned red, and I jerked down on the brake. I whipped back in my seat and gripped the steering wheel in a choke hold. My breaths were coming in short, quick spurts, and I pried my hands off the steering wheel. I wiped my face with the sleeve of my sweatshirt as I tried to refocus my eyes on the road.

The light changed, and I made an effort to concentrate on the drive home. It was only a few blocks more. As I pulled into the driveway, I saw that my dad's car was already there. I grabbed the rearview mirror in the car and dabbed at my face. My eyelids were pink and my mascara was smudged with little black rivulets running down my face. I dug into my backpack, pulled out an old tissue, dabbed it on my tongue to wet it, and used it to clean off the black smears. It did little to remove the evidence of my crying. I threw it to the floor of the car and opened the door.

I was hoping to make it past my dad unnoticed, so I opened the door quietly. I could hear him in the kitchen, whistling as he made dinner. He'd mentioned last night that he wanted to make cream of celery soup. I hurried past the entrance to the kitchen and padded onto the first step, forgetting it was the one that always creaked.

"El?"

I stopped on the second step. "Hi, Dad. I'm just going to run upstairs for a sec. I'll be right back."

"What's up?" he asked. I turned around, surprised that he was already right behind me.

"Nothing. I just—"

"What's the matter?" He walked up the first step and looked at me. "You look like you've been crying."

The determination to hide my emotions from my dad deteriorated quickly as I looked at him, his forehead creasing as his eyes searched my face. I bit my lip to hold back the sobbing that threatened, dismayed that there were still sobs left to erupt. I thought I'd already released each sob, each tear, left inside me.

He put his arms around me and cradled my head as I buried my face into his chest. "I just really miss her," I managed to say between sobs.

"I know, El. I know."

"I wish I could have her back." I wanted to tell him everything about seeing her—the memories and being able to see inside her head. I wanted him to experience it all with me, so he could have that great sense of love I felt today. There was no way to explain why I was so emotional without telling him what had happened. But I'd promised Gabe, and, really, I didn't think my dad would even believe me.

He slowly released me and looked at me, reaching up to wipe my eyes with his thumbs. "I'm sorry, El. That's why I think it's best that we don't think about her too much. She's not coming back. We just have to move on."

The words hit me more heavily than any other time he'd said them because I felt that I could never move on. She might not be coming back here, but I could go to her, and there was no way I could stop thinking about her. "No. No, Dad. I can't do that."

"I know it's hard, but it will be easier in the long run. If you keep her too close to your heart and think about her a lot, you won't be able to focus on your life now. You can't live in the past, El."

His words stung. Living in the past was for washed-up high school football players who tried to relive their glory years, not for daughters whose mothers were murdered and who still had a connection to them. Living in the past didn't apply to me, and hearing him say those words made me want to get as far from him as possible. "You can't just put her out of your mind. That's not how it works. She's still in here," I said, pointing to my heart. I pointed to my head. "She's in here too. She's everywhere in here. Everywhere."

He dug his hands into his pockets and looked down on the ground. "I'm sorry. That's not really how I meant it. I just hate to see you so sad, so hopeless."

"I'm not hopeless. I'm filled with hope. But, yes, I'm sad. I miss her and I'm sad, and that's okay."

He nodded, keeping his gaze on the ground. "I'd better go finish up dinner. You go ahead upstairs and get cleaned up."

I watched as he walked away, and a moment later, I

heard him resume chopping. Up in my bathroom, I wiped the remnants of my eye makeup with a cotton ball and then washed my face. I kept my hair in a ponytail and slathered moisturizer on my face. My eyes hurt, and I closed them for a few minutes as I relaxed my shoulders and tried to calm my nerves. Raw emotion still lingered. I felt like my mom had been taken from me all over again. I'd had her within my grasp, actually touching and feeling her and knowing her thoughts. For a minute she had been alive again—alive to me. But now she was gone.

I stripped down and left my jeans and sweater on the floor in the bathroom. Then I went back into my room to put on a pair of red flannel pajamas that had belonged to my mom. I sat in the recliner and draped my mom's unfinished quilt over me, rocking back and forth for a few minutes until I heard my dad call me down for dinner.

He pulled out a loaf of bread from the bread machine and set it on the table next to the pot of soup. I walked into the kitchen and sat across from him. He frowned as he looked at my pajamas but didn't say anything. After ladling soup into two bowls, he began slicing the bread. I picked up my spoon and turned it over in my hand. Hunger was far from my mind. I wondered if I would ever think about eating the same way—or think about anything the same way ever again. The amazing experience with my mom was all I could think about.

"I'm sorry about before, El. I hope I didn't upset you."

I shook my head and slid the spoon into the bowl of soup in front of me. "I'll be okay." I stirred the soup but made no effort to taste it.

"Why don't you and Sarah go shopping this weekend? I'll give you my credit card."

Shopping and Sarah. Two things I hardly cared about

anymore. Shopping went along with Sarah, and she'd moved on, left me behind in her aspiration to get asked to prom. "I don't know if Sarah really wants to go shopping with me."

"Things still not getting any better with Sarah?"

I let go of the spoon that had yet to come out of the bowl and put both hands in my lap. I rubbed them on the warm flannel of my mom's pajamas. "No. She's too busy trying to get Bradley to ask her to prom."

"Don't you want to go to prom?"

I shrugged and then brought my legs up to the chair and rested my chin on my knees. "Not really. I don't think I care about prom, especially not this year. Next year? Who knows?"

Dad spooned out the last of his soup and then refilled his bowl. "So have you made any new friends? Who are you hanging out with these days if it's not Sarah?"

I hesitated to answer him because the answer would be Gabe. And how would I talk about Gabe without talking about the huaca? "A friend from track."

"Who is it?"

I brought my feet down to the ground and leaned in to take a spoonful of soup. It was a new recipe and the first time he'd made it. It was okay, but it couldn't beat Mom's ham and potato soup. At least he was trying. "His name is Gabe. We get together to do history sometimes."

"So, is he a boyfriend or a boy who's a friend?"

I laughed at his lack of subtlety. "I don't know. Just a friend for now." I knew he was more than a friend, but I couldn't explain the deep connection we'd forged in so little time. He cared for me. A lot. I knew that because of the gift he'd given me and because of how freely he gave it, drawing blood for me so I could see my mom. It wasn't the typical gift a guy gives a girl he likes—it was more, much more than

I could ever put into words, much less explain to my dad.

He watched me as I took another taste of soup, putting his spoon down so he could study my face. "Well, I guess I'm going to have to meet this Gabe. Just a friend for now? Maybe more later?"

I didn't know how to answer that, because he was already more than that. But not quite a boyfriend because we hadn't even kissed yet. "Yeah, maybe sometime."

NINE

A LOT OF THOUGHT WENT INTO what I was going to wear on Monday. Making lasagna with Sarah on Friday had brought back brief glimpses of our decade-long friendship. I wanted to bridge off that and see if it would get better. But then I didn't. I didn't want to know that she could control me and make our friendship contingent on my wardrobe and behavior. And hanging out with Gabe and seeing my mother again made me feel like I wasn't that same Ellie who'd been best friends with Sarah.

After I showered, I sat on the end of my bed in my towel trying to decide. Would I let her win? Would I continue carrying my Louis Vuitton handbag, flat-ironing my hair, and squeezing into skinny jeans? Or would I make her choose and see if she'd accept me for me, as she once had?

I towel-dried my hair and ran my fingers through the long, tangled tresses. I picked up the skinny jeans I had pulled out the night before. I thought about it for only a minute before throwing them back into the closet and pulling out my old Levis with the frayed hems. The Louis Vuitton handbag that we'd bought together freshman year was a must-have for high school, she had persuaded me. She'd gone through at least two others, varied only by size. I still had the same one. Nothing could convince me to drop another four hundred dollars on an identical-looking purse. I dumped its contents onto my bed and tossed the overpriced purse into my closet.

Somewhere in the process of towel-drying my hair and thinking of the thirty minutes it took to straighten, I resolved against bowing to Sarah's demands. Keeping up with her wishes didn't guarantee a friendship—not a true friendship, like we'd once shared. It only meant Sarah letting me hang around to witness her foray into senior popularity. I wasn't sure that was where I wanted to be. I threw the stuff I had dumped on my bed into a cloth shoulder bag my mom had given me years before.

•••••

On Thursday, we had winter track practice. Gabe and I stopped to get smoothies after and talked about my upcoming oral presentation. He gave me some notes he'd written down about the Inca civilization. I finally felt ready for my presentation at the end of the week.

I'd wanted to ask him if I could go over to his place to see my mom, but it was getting close to dinnertime and we both had a lot of homework. So we said our good-byes at the smoothie place, and I didn't even bring up the idea.

I pulled into the driveway and sat for a minute, trying to garner the energy needed to drag my backpack and myself into the house. Winter track was really kicking my butt. I went to push open my car door, but then I froze. As a man emerged from my backyard, I quickly locked it. He appeared between a pair of trees that were on the side of the house. He saw me and then ran across the front lawn toward a car parked a few houses down. I strained to see the license plate, but he was gone before I could read it clearly. I thought about driving away from the house, scared to venture inside, but I was frozen. I kept looking behind me to make sure he was gone, that he wasn't coming back.

I reached for my phone in my backpack on the floor of the car. When I sat back up, I let out a scream. There was a car pulling up directly behind me. My instinct to search for the number nine on my phone was quelled when I realized it was my dad's Lexus, but I hesitated to unlock the door until I could be certain it was my dad. He stepped out of his car and waved at me.

I pushed open the door and ran to him.

"What's the matter, El?"

"There was a man here in our backyard, and he came out and then drove off. It scared the crap out of me. You need to go after him. He left just a minute ago."

My dad looked down the street both ways. "Which way did he go?"

I pointed. "That way. You have to go! We have to call the police!"

"Now, hold on. I don't think I can catch up to him."

"Well, let's call the police." I ran back to my car, where I'd left my phone on the seat.

"We will in a minute. Let's get you inside. Let me find out what you saw."

"But they might still have a chance to catch him. He couldn't have gone very far."

He looked around the street and then pulled me toward the door. "Come on, El. Let's go inside."

I followed him inside. I marveled at his composure. I

was shaking, the image of the man emerging from the trees branded in my mind. I thought of the last time a stranger had lurked in our home, had broken in, had killed my mother . . .

I was scared of what we'd find inside, if the man had broken in. But the locks were intact, and my dad unlocked the door. He was gone, I kept telling myself. I was safe. We were safe. I followed Dad into the living room and sat down at his insistence.

"What did he look like?" he asked.

Despite the mental image that wouldn't go away, I could hardly answer the question. "I don't know. Middle-aged, middle-sized. White guy, brown hair, big blue coat."

"What about the car?"

"A white one, Ford maybe. I'm not sure. It happened so fast."

"Okay. It's okay, El." He squeezed my shoulder and stroked my arm. "He's gone, El. It's going to be okay. He didn't take anything, and he didn't do anything."

I shook my head, tightened my jaw, and tried to keep from crying.

"Did he say anything to you?" Dad asked.

"No, he saw me and then ran."

"Okay. I'm glad you're okay. It sounds like he was just looking around for stuff outside he could steal. Mrs. Jenkins from two streets down told me that the bench from her front porch was stolen last week. There's been a bit of that going on around Westfield. Not breaking into homes—just stealing things of value that are left out. He was probably just looking for something like that in the backyard."

"Aren't you going to call the police?"

"Yeah, of course. I will. I'll probably just go down tomorrow morning and file a report."

"You should call them now! Have them come over so they can look around, see if he's still prowling the neighborhood."

"I'm sure he isn't. He's probably getting as far from here as he can."

"But, Dad, you should call them now."

"Ellie, I'll just go down to file the report tomorrow. It's best to do it in person."

"Shouldn't I go with you? So I can describe him, maybe see some mug shots."

He laughed. "Ellie, you watch too much TV. Really, it's best this way."

I wanted to protest, to make him call the police.

"Come on, Ellie. Let's go out and get some Chinese food."

"I don't really want to . . ."

He stood up and pulled me to my feet. "Come on, El. You just need to get out for a little while."

I was tired from track and exhausted from my scare, and the last thing on my mind was food. But we went out for Chinese. My dad just had this thing about getting his way. My protests were no good; he just laughed them off or argued them away.

♦♦♦♦♦

I had track practice the next day, but when I got home, I was eager to ask Dad about the police station.

I came into the kitchen and grabbed a water bottle from the fridge. "Hey, Dad."

He was reviewing a stack of mail at the counter. "Hey, El. How'd it go?"

"Fine. So did you go to the police station?"

"Yeah, I did the incident report. They said they'd had some similar reports yesterday from a few other folks in the neighborhood. Someone had given them a pretty good description and even a plate number. So they have some good leads to go on. They're pretty confident they'll pick him up by the weekend. I asked them if you should come in to give them a description, but they said it shouldn't be necessary."

"Are you sure?"

"Yeah, they have a description of the guy and can ID the car."

"Well, good."

"Yeah, hon. I know you're spooked, but it's going to be okay. They'll get this guy. And he hasn't hurt anyone. He was just looking for stuff to steal."

He was trying hard to make me feel better, but it only slightly worked. I knew I would be looking over my shoulder constantly for the foreseeable future. He kissed me on the forehead, and then I headed upstairs to take a shower.

•••••

It was the Wednesday before Thanksgiving. Dad had the day off, and we needed to go grocery shopping. It had been our tradition, for some time, to go the day before. It had started out that way because we were always so busy and things didn't slow down until Wednesday. Even on slower years, we just kept the tradition—grocery shopping on Wednesday afternoons. Maybe it was something about the hurried crowds, the displays of boxed stuffing and canned cranberries, or the rushed feeling that helped set the tone for the holiday.

Thanksgiving was a small affair at our house. Dad didn't have any family. His parents had passed away before my mom met him. He had some distant aunts who lived in Oregon, but I'd never met them. My Aunt Melissa, my mom's sister, lived in a town about twenty minutes away. She was coming tomorrow with her two kids. Even though it was only a twenty-minute drive, it seemed like we just didn't see her that often, not since my mom died. This would be our first Thanksgiving without my mother. Neither of us had really said anything about it out loud, but I knew we were both wondering how we would get through it.

Dad was at the kitchen table making a list when I walked in. He was already on the second page. He was a list-maker. It used to drive my mom crazy sometimes. I guess you do need a list sometimes, at least for Thanksgiving dinner.

"Did you put cranberry juice on there?" I asked. It was my mom's favorite for Thanksgiving dinner.

"Almost forgot," he said. "I'll jot it down."

I peered over his shoulder, scanning the list. "Is Aunt Mel making the potatoes again?"

"Yes, and the stuffing."

"Oh, good. I love her potatoes."

Dad added to his list. "Think you can handle the pies?"

"As long as you don't mind canned pumpkin."

"I'm sure it will be great, El. Ready to go?"

I grabbed my coat, and we headed out to his car. Stop & Shop was our grocery store of choice. It's where we always went.

It was just as I had expected. Shopping carts were filled to the top, brimming over with stalks of celery and loaves of bread. Dad always started in the produce section, which didn't make sense to me because wouldn't you want all the heavy stuff on the bottom and the produce on top? Years of me explaining my theory did little to dissuade him from his routine. So we started with the produce and bagged onions, tomatoes, and apples. He grabbed the celery and some broccoli.

"I'll go take a look at the turkeys, El. You want to go grab the ingredients you need for pies?"

"Sure, Dad." I headed toward the canned food aisle.

I grabbed a can of pumpkin and read the recipe on the back. That was usually how I made pies. I had been in charge of pies for the past few years. Everyone just humored me about them. I knew they weren't gourmet or bakery-style by any means, but everyone was nice to eat them. It wasn't that hard; after all, how hard was it to read a recipe on the back of a can? It took me a few minutes to find condensed milk, and I remembered I still had pumpkin pie spice from the year before. I was sure it was still good. That stuff didn't have an expiration date.

As I turned the corner to head back to the produce section, I almost ran into Gabe speeding toward the back of the store.

"Hey, Ellie." He stopped in front of me and looked around. "Were you looking for me?" he asked.

"Pumpkin," I said, holding up my can. "I'm here with my dad, getting Thanksgiving stuff."

"Oh, right," he said. "Yeah, it's crazy busy. I'm taking a quick lunch break." He held up a white shopping bag, and I assumed it held his lunch. "Then I have to work until midnight. They don't think it's going to slow down at all."

A lady pushed by us with an overfilled shopping cart, and there was a line of shoppers coming toward us from the other direction. Gabe and I sidestepped into an aisle and out of the way a little. "You get tomorrow off though, right?"

"Yeah. So is your dad here?"

I pointed toward the meat department. "He's picking out the bird."

"He's not getting a frozen one, is he?"

"I have no idea."

"He should get a thawed out one. The frozen ones take a few days to thaw out."

"Okay," I said, smiling. "I guess I'll tell him."

"I bought mine frozen, but it's been thawing in the fridge for a few days now."

"Yours?" I asked. "It's your turkey?"

"Yeah, my mom does the baking—rolls, pies. But I'm in charge of the turkey."

"You know how to make a turkey?"

He smiled and looked away. "I've been making the turkey for a few years now. I've pretty much mastered it. Tender, juicy. Really, it's the best. Makes the best day-after turkey sandwiches. I'll bring you one on Monday."

"Okay. So you have to work all weekend?"

A lady with a crying baby in her cart and two pig-tailed girls holding on to each side of the cart squeezed past us.

"Yeah," Gabe said, taking a step toward me. "Here." He pulled something out of the white shopping bag he'd been carrying. "My mom made oatmeal raisin. Has walnuts too." He handed me a plastic bag of cookies.

"Are you sure?"

"Yeah, take them. There's a lot more at home, and she's already started baking for tomorrow. So they're yours."

"Thanks, Gabe. Tell her thanks for me. Her cookies are pretty awesome."

"I'll tell her. Bye, Ellie. Have a good Thanksgiving."

•••••

Dad usually woke up early on Thanksgiving to start the turkey. I was trying to sleep in, but I could hear him downstairs, moving pots around and rummaging through cabinets. I pulled a pillow over my head, trying to drown out the sounds, but there was no use. It was time to get up. I looked over at my clock: eight thirty. I had really hoped to sleep in past that, but it was Thanksgiving, and there was a lot to do.

I shuffled downstairs, yawning as I went. Dad was in the kitchen, mixing a marinade for the turkey. I dropped myself onto a barstool and lay my head on the counter to watch my dad with his whisk.

"What time is Aunt Mel coming?"

"Two o'clock."

"You need any help?"

Dad looked up from his cookbook. "I think I'm okay. If I can just get this big guy in the oven, the rest should be easy."

I sat there and watched him for another five minutes before mustering enough energy to peel myself off the barstool. After a shower, I was ready to start the pies. As I mixed the pumpkin with the other ingredients, thoughts of Gabe at Stop & Shop came fleeting through my mind. He was probably cooking his turkey by now. It still made me laugh that he called it his turkey.

I was looking forward to seeing Aunt Mel. She was a single mom, having been divorced for four years. Lucy and Jackson went to visit their dad in Pennsylvania every other holiday. They were coming today, but that meant that they wouldn't be here for Christmas. That was hard. We all loved having the kids around at Christmas. It's what made it Christmas, and having them gone was hard for everyone, especially Aunt Mel.

At two o'clock, I'd finished the pies and they were cooling on the counter. I had already set the table, and Dad was putting the finishing touches on the turkey. I heard Lucy and Jackson at the door before I even heard the doorbell.

I opened the door, and a blast of cold air came in with them.

"Lucy, your hair looks so cute," I said, running my fingers through her short pixie haircut.

"Thanks, Ellie. I just got it yesterday." Blonde Lucy was eleven and was just hitting the age when she was beginning to really care about her clothes and looks. I just hoped she would never hit Sarah-proportions of vanity.

Aunt Mel came in carrying a large pot. Jackson was behind her, carrying a brown shopping bag from Trader Joe's. I took Jackson's bag and closed the door behind him.

"Hey, Ellie," Aunt Mel said, holding the pot to the side to give me a kiss on the cheek.

"Hey, I missed you. I can't believe it's been so long since I've seen you guys." I hadn't even seen them at Halloween like I did some years. They had spent the day with their dad in Philly.

"I know, El. We need to get together more. This just seeing each other at holidays is not working out. I miss you."

"I know. I miss you too." I followed Aunt Mel into the kitchen and put her bag down on the counter. Dad came over and greeted everyone.

"Can I use your laptop, Ellie?" Lucy asked, coming into the kitchen.

"Sure. It's upstairs in my room."

Lucy shed her coat on the barstool and ran up the stairs. Nine-year-old Jackson sat at the kitchen table and pulled out his Nintendo DS.

Aunt Mel sighed. "I just can't keep these kids unplugged. They always want to be on the computer, watching TV, and playing the DS. Even on Thanksgiving." She gave Jackson a disapproving look. "Only a half hour, and then it gets turned off for the rest of the day. Thanksgiving is about spending time with family."

"Mom!"

"No, Jack. I'm not kidding. Thirty minutes." She sighed and turned back to her pot. "Daniel, can I warm up these potatoes? The stuffing's in that bag, Ellie. Can you get it?"

I brought the stuffing to her, and Dad helped her start warming them both up. I pulled down some serving dishes and brought them over to the stove.

As her dishes were warming, Dad started carving the turkey. We're simple at my house and bring the carved turkey to the table instead of making a whole big presentation of it. That was for TV, not for little, put-together families like ours. We weren't the traditional Thanksgiving family, anyway—just a small group of people who had no one else out there to go to, so we went to each other. And that was okay with me because I loved Aunt Mel.

Since her divorce, all she had was us. I had another aunt who lived in Colorado, but Mom and Mel's parents were both gone. Their father died when they were in college, and their mom, my grandma, died of cancer five years ago. I remember my grandma's funeral. She was my last grandparent. I felt I was too young to not have any grandparents left.

"El, here's a book I just finished. I think you'll love it." Aunt Mel handed me a worn hardcover book. When my mom was alive, the three of us had formed a mini book club. We'd pass books around, read them, and get together every few months for dinner to discuss them. We'd each take turns picking the restaurant, and we would talk about the books, what we liked and what we hated. We didn't do it as much anymore or in the same way, but once in a while Aunt Mel would tell me about a book she really enjoyed. I mostly didn't read them, just tucked them on a shelf somewhere. I really didn't want to do the whole book thing anymore now that my mom was gone, but I didn't want to tell Aunt Mel that.

"Thanks, Aunt Mel," I said, putting the book down on a nearby shelf.

We worked together to get everything on the table. There were several awkward moments as we began passing dishes. The clinking of forks on plates was the most audible sound as silence engulfed the mismatched members of the small family that gathered in our dining room. If a stranger had merely peeked into our frosted window that afternoon, all would have appeared ordinary—just a typical family consisting of a mother, father, and three kids. We were anything but ordinary—a widower, a divorced woman, two young kids whose father was alone in a small apartment in Philadelphia, and me.

There was an enormous void that no amount of turkey or pie could fill. It was felt by all, and it made me wish we had forgone the holiday altogether.

"So," my father said, clearing his throat. "Lucy, how's school going?"

She shrugged. "Okay." She moved around some mashed potatoes on her plate. "Mom, I don't really like turkey. Can I just finish the potatoes?"

"Sure, honey. And the corn too."

Aunt Mel turned to Jack and gave him an instruction about what he needed to finish on his plate. "So, is anyone up for Black Friday sales tomorrow? Ellie, how about you? You and Sarah waking up early to go?"

"No, I'm not that into shopping anymore."

"Yeah, it's way too early to get up just to save a few bucks on Christmas gifts." Aunt Mel turned to Jackson. "Besides, I'm thinking of not doing Christmas gifts this year."

"What?" Jackson said, sitting up on his knees to face his mom.

"Just kidding, Jack."

Thanksgiving dinner continued like that. Long stretches of silence followed by small snippets of conversation that seemed forced. Dad and Aunt Mel did their best, but there was no mistaking that this was not how any of us wanted to be spending our Thanksgiving.

•••••

Jackson was glued to his video game. So much for Aunt Mel's directive from before dinner. Lucy and I were watching a Disney movie in the family room. As fast as she was trying to grow up, eleven-year-old Lucy was still a little girl, allured by Disney princesses.

I could hear Dad and Aunt Mel cleaning up in the kitchen and wondered how awkward that felt without my mom's presence. I wanted—not really needed—a second piece of pumpkin pie, so I headed to the kitchen.

"But I don't understand why," I could hear Aunt Mel telling Dad. I didn't go in, but instead stayed just outside the kitchen where they couldn't see me.

"Because I already told you. It was private to her. I respect Olivia's privacy. *I* haven't even read them."

"But I just want to see what was bothering her."

"No, Melissa!"

I didn't want my presence known, but I wanted to know what they were talking about.

"She was my sister. I should have some say."

"Don't push me on this. I'm in no mood to be pushed by you," I heard my dad say. Then I heard the clatter of pots in the sink. He stormed past me and up the stairs. I didn't think he saw me, but I pushed myself against the wall anyway.

I took a deep breath and walked into the kitchen. Aunt Mel was wiping her nose with the back of her hand. "Hey, are you okay?" I asked, walking up to her.

She forced a smile. "Yeah, El. You know. Holidays without Olivia are hard."

I nodded. "I know." I paused and waited to see if she would say anything else. "So, what's going on with Dad? Why were you two arguing?"

She shook her head. "Oh, Ellie. Nothing. You know it's just a hard day for both of us."

"What won't he let you see? Aunt Mel, tell me."

"I just wanted to read some of her journals, see what was on her mind just before . . ."

"And Dad said no?"

She shrugged. "It's okay. I know it's hard for him."

"You said you wanted to know what was bothering her. Why do you think something was bothering her?"

"Ellie, you were eavesdropping."

"Sorry, but she's my mom. I want to know."

"It's just that she texted me that night, upset about something, but she wouldn't say what. I just want to know if there was something in her journals."

"Then we should look in them."

"Your dad's pretty adamant. He wants to protect her privacy. He doesn't want us to look."

"But—"

"No, Ellie. Let's just leave it. He was pretty upset. I don't want you to say anything."

"Well . . ."

"Ellie, it's not going to change anything. It's okay."

I nodded and walked away. I didn't feel like having that second piece of pie anymore.

TEN

SARAH TEXTED ME, GIVING ME ALL the details of her birthday party. "B ther n b cool," it said. I wondered if both directives went together. If I was going to be there, I had to be cool. If I wasn't cool, maybe I shouldn't attend. Funny how the intent of something said can be so evident in a text—a few words on your phone. I didn't think I could get as cool as she needed me to be in a week and a half, so maybe I should make other plans for that night.

I spent part of the afternoon in my room, blasting Bon Jovi while trying to decide if I wanted to go to Sarah's birthday party. Of course I wanted to go; it was something I did every year—just part of my early December plans. But my December this year might not include her birthday.

I thought about the year before when we'd gone to the Bon Jovi concert. The four of us had taken the train into the city by ourselves. I think that had been the beginning of the unraveling of our friendship. I hadn't really thought that at the time, but, in retrospect, I could see small seeds of dissension had formed that night.

It had been Trina. Starting that night and over the past year, she'd slowly been picking away at our friendship. On the train, she'd shoved me aside— albeit a small shove—to be next to Sarah. They sat next to each other, and several times during the ride, their conversations had become private, leaving Jenna and me to grasp for some semblance of conversation.

I don't think Jenna was very happy that night. She and Trina had been best friends for a long time. We hadn't met them until middle school. They'd gone to a different elementary than Sarah and me. As the elementary schools fed into the middle school, new alliances were formed. Sarah had decided to join forces with Trina and Jenna. It had been quite a methodical decision for her, one that she had researched and explained to me in quite some detail.

Trina had been desirable from the beginning. Her father was in the same plastic surgery practice as Sarah's father, Dr. Winter, and most important, Trina's mother was a correspondent for *Vogue* magazine. It didn't hurt that Trina had perfectly straight hair and perfectly straight teeth to match. Her sense of style rivaled Sarah's. Those facts had been indisputable when Sarah had made the case to bridge our friendship with theirs.

Jenna had been a package deal and only tolerable to Sarah. Her mousy hair had gone through an array of styles in order to reach its now perfect cut and color—soft, brown highlights achieved only through an overpriced stylist in the city. She was working hard to retain her status as Sarah and Trina's friend. I guess she deserved it, for all the hard work she put into it. Jenna's parents were divorced. Her father worked at one of the Big Four accounting firms but was only a lower-level accountant, nothing to impress Sarah. And her mother lived in the city and worked at one of the smaller art museums. Jenna spent a lot of weekends with her mom in a studio apartment overlooking the park. We'd had a few sleepovers there, giving Jenna a few points on Sarah's score sheet.

My stats, now that I thought about it, were not that impressive, either. It was no wonder Sarah was now considering kicking me out of her alliance. If it hadn't been for our years of friendship, there is no way she would ever have considered me in the first place.

The next day at school, I saw them walking ahead of me. They'd all come out of Sarah's car, and I wondered how long they'd been coming to school together. Jenna was a step behind Sarah and Trina, but they all had matching Louis Vuitton handbags. They'd probably all gone into the city to buy them. I don't think I would have gone with them even if they had invited me. I slowed down, watched them go into the school, and noticed how they all seemed to go together. I suddenly realized that I would definitely be the one you'd circle in a picture of what didn't belong.

But I didn't seem to care today. I was confident I didn't belong with them—not if they expected me to follow their ways and leave my own behind.

•••••

I started going over to Gabe's to do history homework a few times a week when we didn't have track practice and he didn't have work. He didn't always take me down to the basement, and I was okay with that. I didn't want him to think that was the only reason I was coming over, because it wasn't. I also didn't want my visits to my mom to become a mundane occurrence. Rather, I wanted the visits to be special, poignant moments in my life.

Our had been assigned to do history projects, and they were due in two weeks. I had decided to conduct my research on Ellis Island. Gabe was still writing on myths. I recalled our initial conversation at lunch when he had explained to me that he wanted to research the truth found in myths. I had become a believer in myths; I could see the truth found in them and had seen it for myself.

We sat on Gabe's couch, each with a laptop open on our knees. I was doing research. He was already halfway done with his research paper. I scrolled through a Google search looking for information on the groups of people that came through Ellis Island. I was particularly interested in the Scottish people that came through. My dad's side of the family was Scottish, but not many people of Scottish descent came through Ellis Island.

I copied a few links to read through later, did some research on my Scottish last name—Cummings—and read through a history of Ellis Island. I wasn't exactly sure what I was going to focus my research on, but I was trying to get some ideas. I envied Gabe's clear idea of his project, as well as his personal attachment to it. He was intent on his work, typing quickly and rarely stopping to think or edit a sentence. I turned to look at him, his face staring straight ahead at his laptop, so focused on his task. He caught me watching him and paused, his fingers hovering over the keys.

He turned to me. "How's it going?"

"Okay, I guess. I'm still in the baby stages. I have so much more to do. Have you started the PowerPoint yet?"

"I have a few pages done, but it's not complete yet. Don't worry. You'll get there. Getting started is the hardest part. Once you get going, it will come fast."

"I hope so." I turned back to my article and finished reading it.

Gabe leaned back against the couch and scrolled through his document, reading over what he'd written. He wiped his other hand against his jeans and then placed it on the couch next to me. I was very aware of his hand's proximity to me, and I wondered if he'd done it with some intention in mind.

It was distracting, and I kept reading the same paragraph over and over. I think I gained a pretty good understanding of how Ellis Island was founded. I felt him watching me but didn't turn to look at him, instead keeping my eyes fixed on my laptop screen. The next thing I felt were his knuckles brushing against mine. My fingers froze. I didn't move. Concentrating on my research was impossible. All I could think about was Gabe sitting next to me. I didn't want to pull my hand away. I wanted him to grab it. I wondered if he was actually reading or if he had given up just like I had. Somehow, I didn't feel that his attention was on Inca myths.

His fingers slowly pried through mine until he was holding my hand. I didn't hear any movement at his laptop; he'd probably given up on accomplishing any work. I ventured to turn my head to look at him. He was watching me, a shy smile spread across his face. He'd taken a chance, and I was glad he had.

I smiled back and then squeezed his hand.

After the initial formalities of that first handhold, we were able to turn back to our tasks. He continued scrolling through his document, using the down arrow key on his keypad while I read through my article. We sat like that for twenty minutes until my cell phone rang.

I let go of his hand and reached for my bag on the floor by my feet. "It's my dad," I said, answering. Gabe smiled and went back to typing with his free hand.

"Hey, El."

"Hey, Dad."

"Where are you?"

"I'm at a friend's house, studying. We're working on our history projects."

"Oh, good. Well, I just got home and was wondering where you were. I'm getting started on dinner. Try to be home in about forty-five minutes. It will be almost seven by then. I should be done with dinner."

"I didn't realize it was that late. Okay, no problem. I'll be home."

"Okay, El. So did you have a good day?"

"Yeah, it was really good." I couldn't help but smile as I talked to my dad. I was glad he couldn't see me. He would have asked me why I was smiling like that.

"Well, I'll see you in a little bit. How do you feel about chicken teriyaki stir-fry?"

"Sounds great. Bye, Dad."

"Bye."

I turned to look at Gabe, who pulled his eyes from his screen and smiled. A lot of smiling was going on today. "What was really good?" he asked.

"My day."

"Mine too."

"My dad wants me home for dinner."

"Okay. I have to work from noon to six Saturday, but maybe after work we can go somewhere."

"You mean, like an actual date, Gabe? You asking me out?"

He turned back to his laptop and ran his index finger across the base. "Yeah, I'm asking you out on a real date. I guess it would be our first, right?"

"Yeah, our first."

"But it won't be awkward—you know, that first date kind of feel—because we've been hanging out a lot."

"Yeah, and we already got past our first awkward hand-holding."

Gabe laughed. "I was awkward?"

"No, it was sweet. Really sweet."

"So, I guess I'll see you Saturday."

"'Kay." I got up and started packing up my laptop.

•••••

Sarah decided to go simple on her birthday party this year—just a party in her basement. Her parents had just finished having it redecorated—new hardwood floors, a projection movie screen with two rows of theater seating, a pool table, and a game room. I hadn't actually seen it. I knew it had been finished for a few weeks, but she hadn't invited me over. I only knew it was finished because I had heard Trina and Jenna talking about it in PE.

In a different time, a time when Sarah and I used to be best friends, she would have had me over almost every day to see the progress of her new basement. But it wasn't that time anymore. That time only seemed to exist in my memories now. I didn't think I'd see that time again.

So, her basement was done, and that's where her party was going to be. She had texted me the details about a week before. I'd read and reread the text many times, glad that I'd received it in the first place, but annoyed that the invitation came via text. Other years, I'd been with her every step of the way, helping to plan her party and knowing each detail well in advance. Now, I was a mere recipient of a mass text.

I was still going, though. I had thought about it over the past week since I'd received the text. I had decided not to go, then decided I should go. I vacillated between going for old times' sake and ditching in protest of the mass text and my demotion from best-friend status. But it was a Friday night, and Gabe was at work, so I decided to go.

The party was in two hours, but I had already started getting ready, figuring out what I was going to wear. I was torn between making a statement and pleasing Sarah. It was, after all, her birthday. I knew she would be glad she invited me if I showed up in skinny jeans and layered tops instead of my hoodie and Chuck Taylors. But then she would know she'd won and that I would keep complying with her wishes just to remain her friend.

I finally made a compromise with myself—I would wear the skinny jeans and layered tops with my Chuck Taylors and red hoodie, the newer hoodie without fraying sleeves. I'd keep the "gross" brown one at home. Surely she would see that I was at least trying.

I hoped she would be pleased with her birthday present—a gift certificate for her favorite manicure place. We used to go together on our birthdays and Valentine's Day. That was before manicures became obsessive for her and she had to go every other week. That was too much for me; I could only take a little primping and prodding. I didn't like having my cuticles pushed back more often than a few times a year. I went because she loved it—and it was time spent together. Once it became an obsession for her to upkeep her acrylic nails, I was done. I knew Trina and Jenna still went with her often, but it had been a long time since she'd invited me. I guess she got tired of my simple clear coats, when she was getting embellishments and blingy things put on hers.

I put the gift certificate in the birthday card I'd bought for her and sealed the envelope. I was hoping that the gift would remind her of our times spent in the past. Perhaps she'd invite me on her next manicure. Not that I wanted one, I thought, looking at my chewed up nails and overgrown cuticles, but I did still want the friendship. Despite all my misgivings over the past few weeks, it was something I wanted to cling to. I was not, however, willing to give up myself. This appearance at her birthday party was my way of showing her I still wanted to be her friend, but it was not going to be solely on her terms. If she couldn't accept that, then that was it. I was done. You both have to want it to make it work. If only one of you wants it, then what's the point? It's never going to work. *Just like a marriage*, I thought.

I tied my Chuck Taylors and went into the bathroom. Mascara was a must—my decision—but the lipstick was for her sake. She'd always encouraged me to try different shades, and I'd done so in the past to appease her. Tonight, it was a small token. But no eyeliner or eye shadow. I had to draw a line somewhere, and it wasn't going to be on my eyes.

I messed around in my room for a while, playing on my phone, listening to music, passing the time—just trying to muster up courage to face her. I didn't know why I needed the courage, but I knew this was not going to be like other birthdays.

I pulled onto her street and parked in front of her house. It was my usual spot, where I'd parked hundreds of times before. This was somewhere I'd been so many times, yet it was almost as if I were going in for the first time. The usual butterflies and nervousness associated with such an event overwhelmed me, and I thought about going home.

Instead, I took a deep breath and forced myself out of the car and up the walk. Sarah's mother, Mrs. Winter, answered the door. Her familiar face comforted me. This was a scene that I'd encountered many times before.

"Ellie, hi." Mrs. Winter stalled at the door, not letting

me in immediately. I wondered if Sarah had turned her against me.

"Hi, Mrs. Winter." I stood on the doorstep a second longer than I was used to.

"Come in, come in." She led me inside. "Um, so Sarah's not here. Didn't she tell you?"

Heat rose to my face, and right away, my eyes started to sting. "Tell me what?"

Mrs. Winter crossed an arm in front of her and rubbed the side of her face with her hand. "They moved the party. They left about an hour ago to go to a club in the city."

"Oh."

"I'm sure she texted you. Check your phone." She reached for my shoulder bag before I'd even had a chance.

I pulled out my phone to check. "It's okay," I said, mostly to allay her uneasiness. I'd known Mrs. Winter long enough to know she was about to go into disaster-relief mode. It was how she handled herself the summer that the catering truck broke down an hour away from the humane society benefit she was hosting. She rubbed her arms up and down, alternating between both arms and both cheeks.

I'd been on my phone for the last hour and wouldn't have missed a text. I shook my head and tried not to meet her eyes. "No."

"Well, let me call her. She had so much on her mind."

"No, no, don't, Mrs. Winter. It's okay." Sarah *had* sent me a message, not the text kind, but a very clear one. I was not wanted there, and I was not about to start groveling via her mother. My groveling ended with the lipstick; I refused to go past that.

"Yes, I know she wants you there. She just changed plans last minute, and she called about ten kids earlier this week, and I'm sure she just assumed she had called you. She must have forgotten or something. I mean, it doesn't make sense. You're her best friend." She tapped her kitten heels against the marble of the entryway and went into the kitchen to pull her cell phone out of her Louis Vuitton bag.

Her best friend—I hadn't been that for a long time now. I guess Sarah hadn't bothered to tell her mother.

"Mrs. Winter, no. It's really okay. I don't think I'm up for going into the city tonight."

Mrs. Winter ignored my pleas and dialed Sarah's number. She scrunched her forehead when it went to voice mail. Sarah always answered her mother's calls. "I don't know the name of the club. It's a new one—a teen club that just opened up. I was reading about it in the *Times*. Let me look up that article." She walked farther into the kitchen and popped open the small laptop she kept on her granite island.

"Mrs. Winter, it's okay. I'm not going to go to the city just to show up at some club where Sarah is having her party. I'm fine."

"But you're always at her birthday parties. She'll be devastated."

"No, she won't." I pulled Sarah's birthday card out of my shoulder bag and laid it on the smooth, granite surface. "Just give her this."

"I can drive you in. Really, it's no problem. And you can take the train back with them." She walked toward her bag and reached inside for her keys.

"I'm going to go home. Tell Sarah I said 'happy birthday.' Thanks, Mrs. Winter."

Mrs. Winter frowned and rubbed the side of her face. I even saw her French-manicured pinkie go between her teeth—something I hadn't seen since the flower arrangements she'd prepared for the garden club all died, over five years ago. "Ellie, I'm sorry. I don't know what is going on with Sarah lately, but I'm going to have a talk with her about it."

"Please, don't. Not on my account. We're just headed in different directions. I just think she realized it before I did. I'm not mad. This was going to happen eventually. It's okay."

"You're her best friend."

I shook my head. "Not anymore. I used to be, but not anymore. And I think I'm okay with that."

"You know I'll always love you, Ellie. Call me if you ever need anything."

I wanted to get out of there before she would need an emergency manicure. Most of the French was gone from her pinkie, and she was starting to work on her ring finger. "I know, and it means a lot. Bye, Mrs. Winter."

"Bye, Ellie." She walked me to the door, as she had many times before. But, unlike those times before, I knew I wasn't coming back again.

I felt relief—like I didn't need to try anymore. There was no reason for it. I could get rid of my various lipstick colors and cashmere sweaters. Skinny jeans and ballet flats were practically in the trash already as I drove back home.

My dad was in the family room watching cable news. I gave him a hurried greeting before rushing upstairs. I knew he would listen, give me sage advice and the hug that I needed, but I couldn't talk to him. His responses were always logical. He would give me a series of steps to follow in order to fix the problem.

I needed my mom. I wanted my mom. I wished that she were here and would just hold me and listen to me cry. She wouldn't say anything. I didn't really need it. I just wanted someone to hold me until it stopped hurting. It wouldn't be my dad. He didn't hold me like that. With him it was always just a quick hug.

Instead of breaking down and allowing myself the indulgence of a good cry, I got to work. I grabbed a cardboard box filled with school stuff from the top of my closet. Quickly, I emptied it onto the closet floor and left the remnants lying by my feet. I started tearing clothes off their hangers. Abercrombie. The Gap. Banana Republic. BCBG. Every piece of clothing that had been purchased by way of a Sarah suggestion was thrown into the box. I pulled skinny jeans off hangers, some still with tags, and dropped them in the box.

UGG boots and ballet flats were the next to be evicted from my closet. Louis Vuitton made it into the box too. All that was left were Chuck Taylors in a few colors and an assortment of flip-flops. I went to my makeup drawer and quickly emptied half its contents—things I only wore occasionally, when I knew Sarah would notice. I went to my bathroom to see what else there was. My flat iron for straightening my hair—that was perhaps the item that brought me the most pleasure to discard. I hated it. I hated straightening my hair and hated the feel of my hair afterward. It wasn't like I didn't have straight hair already. My hair was straight, no curl to it at all. But even naturally straight hair was not straight enough for Sarah. It had to be razor straight like the covers of *Vogue*.

I sat on my bed after filling the box. I didn't want any of that stuff in my room. I wanted it all gone, along with everything that Sarah had ever made me do. On my bedside was the little scrapbook that Sarah and I had looked at that evening we made lasagna. That seemed so long ago now. It *was* long ago—along with every event documented in the scrapbook. They had happened in another lifetime, perhaps even to another person. The usual sentimentality that accompanied my thoughts of Sarah was not overriding anymore. It had simply faded or been chased away by the unkindness of one who I'd once thought of as a best friend, a sister. That was not the case anymore, as was made obvious by where each of us was on that night.

She was celebrating her birthday, and I wasn't there. For the first time in almost ten years, I wouldn't be beside her as she blew the candles out. The fleeting thought reminded me of a Bon Jovi song we'd sang aloud on so many nights in this room. We had that entire album memorized from the first track to the last. We'd formed a bond over those songs that talked about being there for each other. All of it seemed meaningless to me now. It apparently didn't matter to her anyway. The Bon Jovi CD went in the box. The last item that I put deliberately on top was the scrapbook.

I grappled with that decision. Part of me wanted to keep it because it meant so much to me. It demonstrated a great friendship that I'd shared with Sarah. But those years were in the past. They weren't part of this moment, my present, where I was left feeling empty, lonely, and completely unsentimental.

The scrapbook was the bow on top of the present I was going to take to Sarah. I'd let her keep the manicure gift certificate. I wondered if she'd actually use it or if guilt would preclude her from even opening the card.

I picked up the box and carried it downstairs. As I came down the stairs, my dad turned off the television and walked over to me.

"Hey, I was wondering what you're doing home. Isn't Sarah's birthday party tonight?"

"Yeah, it was."

He looked down at the box I was holding. "What happened?"

I bit my lip, refusing to cry, not wanting to ruin the

moment of empowerment I'd just had upstairs. "She moved the party to a club in the city and didn't tell me."

"Oh, El. I'm sorry." He clenched his fist over the remote he'd been holding. "I can't believe she would do that."

I lifted the box I was holding. "This is a bunch of stuff I have that doesn't really belong to me. It's all Sarah's, always has been."

"What are you going to do with it?"

"I'm going to take it to her place and dump it on her front step so she sees it as soon as she comes home."

A wicked smile formed on his lips. "That's my girl. Don't let her win, El. I know she was your friend, but she deserves this for what she's done to you. You don't need her in your life. It's better to cut her off before she hurts you anymore."

I was glad he wasn't going to interfere with my payback strategy. He kissed my forehead and asked if I wanted a ride. I told him I'd be fine and then set the box down to put on my coat. I walked out to my car and placed the box on the passenger seat.

I can't say I wasn't surprised with my father's reaction. Aren't parents supposed to talk you out of vengeful and immature actions? Wasn't he supposed to say, "El, are you sure? Don't stoop down to her level"? He didn't say any of those things.

So I walked out into the cold. Sarah and her friends were out dancing, and I was on my way to her house, about to cut myself out of her life.

ELEVEN

IT HAD BEEN A WHILE SINCE I'D HAD A date. Maybe Sarah had been right after all about doing something with my hair and makeup.

I did blow-dry my hair, but my flat iron was still on Sarah's doorstep. I wouldn't want to use it anyway. It reminded me too much of my old self, the one who tried too hard for nothing in return. I did my basic mascara and a little blush, but that was it. I wore my favorite jeans—the ones with frayed hems—navy Chuck Taylors, and a red v-neck sweater. A "nightmare of a first-date outfit" is what I imagined Sarah calling it. I had to stop thinking of what Sarah would say or think. It was an old habit, one that was hard to break, and I hoped I could soon give it up.

I listened to Bon Jovi on my phone, and even that reminded me of Sarah. I had to start finding a new favorite band. Gabe was picking me up, and in a way, I was glad Dad wasn't home. He was in the city at a dinner for work—some end-of-the-year presentation.

I heard the doorbell and hurried downstairs, pulling my coat on as I went. He was wearing jeans I hadn't seen before. They were probably new. His hands were deep in the pockets of his wool coat, and he was wearing a navy stocking cap.

"Hey," I said, pulling the door closed behind me. I pulled my mittens on as we walked to his car.

"Hey. So, are you hungry?"

"Sure."

"Let's go to my house. I have pizza dough rising. It should be almost ready. I'm going to make you homemade pizza."

"Yum. Sounds good."

"What do you like on your pizza?"

"Mushrooms, pepperoni, black olives."

"Check, check, check."

When we walked into his house, I took my coat off and put it on the couch. I followed him into the kitchen. "So did you do all this?"

"Some of it. Remember, I was at work most of the day. My mom did the dough, got it ready for me. I did chop the mushrooms, however."

"Is your mom here?" I asked.

"Yeah, in her room. Working on a painting. She's almost done with it. I'll show you when she's done. She said I could have it."

"What are you going to do with it?" I asked, looking around the kitchen.

"I'm not sure. I think I'm going to hang it in my room. My walls are pretty bare."

Gabe took the dough out of a bowl and began rolling it out. "There's some sauce in the fridge. Could you get it?"

I opened the refrigerator and scanned its contents. I

spotted an unlabeled glass jar with sauce and pulled it out. "Want some help?"

"No. I'm supposed to be making dinner *for* you."

"We can do it together."

I watched his hands work the dough and spread it onto the pizza pan. His long fingers pressed down on the dough, the small veins in his hands bulging out in the process. I didn't do much in the way of helping. He knew exactly what he was doing, and I just let him do it. He reminded me of my dad. Dad had learned quickly over the last few months since my mom died, how to handle himself in the kitchen. He wasn't an expert by any means, but he did his best to make varied, healthy meals. He experimented with different recipes and techniques. They didn't always turn out, but sometimes he surprised the two of us and we knew the recipe was a keeper. That's how the Crock-Pot roast came to be, and we both decided right away we'd put it in the meal rotation.

Gabe put the pizza in the oven, and we sat at the table drinking Cokes.

"Can I ask you a question?" I asked.

"Anything."

"So, I've been wondering about the huaca. I don't understand how your people got such a powerful object."

"This is how my father explained it: The Inca really value their dead, worship the dead, and understand the importance of keeping that bond past the grave. They believe the world is composed of three aspects. There is Uku Pacha, which is the past, the interior world. Kay Pacha is the present, here," he said, pointing to the ground. "Hanan Pacha is the future, the supra world. These worlds are represented as concentric circles." He made a circular motion with his fingers. "Each of these worlds is inhabited by spiritual beings. They believe that human beings can access all three dimensions. Once future, present, and past are not conceived as a linear structure, but rather as concentric circles, then human beings can access the three dimensions. Once the belief is there, then access is granted. But true belief can only be obtained through sacrifice. If the sacrifice is not there, then the belief is not there."

"But how did they figure it out? How is it possible?"

"Legend explains that the Inca rulers have a deep connection with the gods. The Incas call their rulers Sapa, which means 'the only one.' So, the leader is Sapa Inca. Through the connection with the gods, the Sapa Inca makes the huaca. He is the only one that can make one. He alone must search for a ceiba tree, which is considered very sacred. It is a revered tree, and some say that the Mayans from southern Mexico even believed that man sprang from a giant tree. Ceiba trees can grow to be up to a hundred and fifty feet tall."

Gabe looked at me and paused, to see if I was following and keeping up with all the information he was throwing at me. Silently, I answered him and nodded for him to continue.

"After he blesses the tree with a special prayer, Sapa Inca cuts down enough wood to carve the wooden box. It is a pinkish-white wood and has to be finely sanded down to a smooth finish. Then Sapa Inca seals the wood with a sacred mixture of his tears, his blood, and oil made from the seeds of the ceiba tree. Finally he performs a sacred ordinance to ready the huaca for use to communicate with the dead."

"But if this Sapa Inca is the only one who can make it, how did you end up with it?"

"Well, Sapa Inca was like an emperor. *Inca* means emperor. And Sapa Inca was the ruler of the empire. Manco Capac was the first one, and it is believed that he was the son of the sun god, Inti. His son became the next Sapa Inca, and the title was handed down from father to son since the 1200s. Each Sapa Inca created the huacas and would present them to valiant men that provided important service to them. It was presented on a rare basis to only the bravest men. It was a privilege, and my father said that it was given to one of our ancestors and handed down from father to son until it came to me."

"That's really amazing. So your ancestor must have been a very brave man. And I can't believe that it was kept in the family and really handed down all this time. That's incredible."

"It's hard to believe because of our understanding of the world and our belief in myths. If we call these beliefs *myths*, then we're dismissing them as invented stories and as imaginary, unproven beliefs. An unbeliever doesn't accept these beliefs as truths, but as myths, just as an atheist does not accept God as a truth, but also as unproven."

"But why is it only for Incas?"

"Just as most people believe in an omnipotent God, the Incas believe in their gods. They're not myths; they're truths—*their* truths. Incas were forced to abandon their beliefs when Spain invaded and basically destroyed the Inca Empire. But some of them clung to their beliefs. They followed the traditions of their fathers, kept the religion, and kept the idea of sacrifices. For those few, the huacas still work. My dad had a theory—all groups of people possessed, at one time, some kind of access to their dead. Most groups either lost their belief or their desire to communicate with the dead. I don't know. He thinks there are others out there who might possess some kind of access. He doesn't know what kind or who. But, for Incas, caring for the dead was such an important aspect of their culture, they never abandoned it."

The timer on the oven went off. The pizzas were ready. Gabe rose from the table. "I hope that all makes sense."

"Sort of," I said, getting up to follow him to the oven. "It's just all very hard to believe, even though I've seen it."

He picked up two oven mitts and opened the oven. "It's no different than those who believe in God, in miracles."

"Well, thank you for sharing it with me. I don't think I can ever show you how grateful I am."

"And thank you for keeping my secret. I'm sure you see how important it is to keep it."

"Yes. You don't ever have to worry about me."

"Thanks, Ellie. So, you ready for pizza?" He walked over to the table and set down two round pans.

The pizza was good. I ate half of a small one. Gabe polished off the other half, and there was another small one left.

"That was great sauce. Is it homemade?"

"Yeah, I made it yesterday."

"You made it?" I asked.

"Yeah, it was one of my grandmother's recipes."

"Wow. Was she Italian?"

Gabe laughed. "No, just a good cook." He wiped his mouth with a napkin and then balled it up. "So are you sure about this movie tonight? Don't want to bore you on our first date."

We were going to watch a World War II drama. It was getting some Oscar buzz, so I knew it would be good. "Now I've got a full stomach, so I might just doze off during the movie."

"Well, we can do something else."

I started laughing. "I'm kidding. I want to see it. I've heard good things about it."

"You sure? I mean, I know history is not really your thing."

"I know, but it sounds good. So you really like all this history stuff?"

"Yeah, I do."

"What do you think you're going to do after graduation?"

"I'll probably go to school in-state. I need to stay close to my mom. I do want to major in history. Try for my PhD."

"Wow, that's impressive. I can't wait for college, but I just have to figure out exactly what I want to do."

"There's time. You don't have to decide everything right now. I'm sure you'll figure it out."

"Yeah, I'm sure I will, if I can just be done with high school."

"I'm ready to be done with high school too."

I wondered if Gabe knew what kids called him or what they said about him. It didn't seem to bother him; he didn't care. He was just living his life, making the best of it. He had so much he could complain about, but I couldn't remember ever hearing one complaint from him about anything.

He finished his Coke. "Ready to go? Or do you want some more pizza?"

"I'm stuffed. Thank you."

He got up and started putting everything away. "I'm glad you liked it. Maybe you can come over again, and I'll make you something else."

"I won't say no to food," I said, smiling. I got up, and we walked to the living room.

We put on our coats and walked out into the cold night. The heater in his Volvo took a few minutes to warm up, and I felt myself shivering.

"Sorry it's so cold," he said. He turned the heat vents toward me. Then, he grabbed my hand and put it into the pocket of his wool coat. Once inside his pocket, he rubbed my fingers with his hand. I then remembered that I had my mittens in my coat, but I didn't want to say anything. I didn't want to pull my hand out of his pocket to put them on.

The air blasting from the Volvo's heater finally started to get warm, and he adjusted the level, letting go of my hand. I reluctantly pulled my hand out of his pocket and put it in my lap. He looked over at me and smiled.

He drove downtown and found a parking spot on one of the side streets. We walked a few blocks to East Broad Street where the Rialto was located. On weekends, a lot of kids from the high school hung out downtown to get pizza, go to Starbucks, or watch a movie at the Rialto. There was also a lot of shopping that happened on weekends too—The Gap or Banana Republic. If you went to downtown Westfield on a weekend, you were sure to find someone you knew from school. Sometimes that was a good thing, but not always.

The Rialto was packed, with lines going outside. Most everyone was in line for the Tom Cruise thriller. Gabe and I were there to see the World War II epic. I think I was slowly getting into the whole history thing. I knew it was Gabe's thing, and so I was looking forward to it. At least it was better than anything Tom Cruise was in.

Gabe paid for our tickets, and I kind of felt bad letting him pay, knowing that money was tight at his house. But it was our first date, and I knew he wanted to do it. He took my hand as we squeezed through the Tom Cruise crowd to get to our theater. We walked down the aisle and Gabe stopped about midway.

"Is this okay?" he asked, pointing to a row.

"Looks good."

He started into the row and pulled me behind him. "Oh, I forgot to ask you. You want some popcorn or a Coke?"

"No, no. I'm good. I'm still full from dinner. Thanks."

Gabe was still holding my hand. "Are you nervous? You know, it being our first date and everything."

"No. You?"

"Maybe a little."

I tugged on his hand. "You don't seem the nervous type to me. What could you be nervous about?"

He looked away, staring down at the ground. "For a long time, I really wanted to talk to you, but you're just so out of my league."

"Whatever," I said, pushing his arm off the armrest. "I'm not out of anybody's league."

"You are. You just don't know it. That's what makes me like you even more. All those times I wanted to talk to you, I never had the courage." He finally looked up and turned to look at me. "And then I saw you, sitting by yourself in the cafeteria, and I finally had my chance. And then I kept saying all these stupid, stupid things every time I saw you."

"They weren't stupid things. Actually, they were kind of wise things."

"Wise? Ha."

"Well, I'm glad you kept trying."

"I like your hair like this," he said, reaching over to comb his fingers through a strand.

"What? Stringy?"

"It's not stringy. It's natural."

"I got rid of my flat iron, you know."

"Good," he said, letting go of my hair with one final touch.

The reason for the missing flat iron appeared at my side, almost on cue.

"Can I talk to you for a minute?" Sarah said, bending down and grabbing my arm. She didn't acknowledge Gabe's presence, didn't even look at him, but she knew he was there.

I turned to Gabe. "I'll be right back."

He nodded. I could tell he'd wanted me to tell her no, but he didn't say anything.

Sarah pulled me up the aisle to the back of the theater. We walked to a corner. "What are you doing here with banana boat guy?"

"He is not banana boat guy. His name is Gabe de la Cruz, and we are on a date."

"Why are you doing this? Are you trying to get back at me?"

"No, Sarah. Actually, I think I'm done with you. Or didn't my gift on your doorstep give you a clue? I don't want advice on clothes, makeup, or boys anymore. I mean, we're not really friends anymore, are we? What's left of our friendship? Whatever was left of it was in that box."

Sarah frowned at me as a group of people passed by. She hushed her tone to a loud whisper. "Ellie, I tried with you. I tried to hold on to our friendship, but you did everything you could to sabotage it. It's like when two people are drowning. You try to save the other one too, but sometimes all you can do is save yourself. If you keep trying to save the other person instead of saving yourself, then you end up dying too."

I burst out laughing.

Sarah closed her eyes and shook her head.

"That makes no sense," I said. "I didn't sabotage anything. I tried to go along with your idiotic style, cramming my feet into those stupid shoes, frying my hair so it would look good for you. I tried to do all your stuff, but it wasn't good enough for you. I'm done trying. I just want to be myself. If you can't accept me for that, then why are we still talking about it?"

Sarah shook her head. "If you hang out with this guy,

you're never going to be able to make it back. I don't think I could even do anything to help you."

"Don't you have to go watch Tom Cruise shoot something?"

"Whatever. I tried with you, Ellie. Have fun in social obscurity."

It was best to let her get the last word. Getting the last word never made me happy. What was the point? The last word was something you usually regretted saying anyway. All I wanted was to be happy. And my happiness no longer lay in an old friendship that both Sarah and I had outgrown. Gabe made me happy. I had Gabe, I had my dad, and, thanks to Gabe, I had my mom. Sarah's presence in my life had once made me happy, but not lately. Lately, it only brought me pain, sadness, and a longing for what once was. I turned away from the corner where we'd probably said our last words to each other. I saw the back of Gabe's head and wondered if he'd seen any of it.

Gabe looked at me as I approached our seats. "Everything okay?"

"Actually, yes. It's very good. I think Sarah and I are officially broken up, if you could call it that."

"Are you okay about it?"

"Yeah. I think everyone knew it just wasn't working anymore. I guess it took me the longest to figure it out. She had a birthday party last night, you know."

"Did you go?"

"In a way, I guess I did."

He took my hand, more easily this time, and laid his arm on the armrest between us. "What do you mean?"

"She told me last week it would be at her house, but when I got there, her mother told me Sarah had changed it to some club in the city. Sarah never told me about the change. She did it on purpose because she didn't want me to come."

"I'm sorry. You should have called me."

"I was okay. It's like I finally got her message, loud and clear. She'd been trying to tell me for months, subtly, I guess. I just didn't get it. It took last night for me to get it, to finally accept it."

"What did she say just now?"

"To have fun in social obscurity." I started laughing. "Kind of a good line, I think. Sounds like a good Facebook status. 'Ellie Cummings is having fun in social obscurity.' I might post that when I get home. I wonder if she's already unfriended me."

Gabe laughed too. "I think I'm in social obscurity as well. And, if you ask me, it's a lot of fun."

"You should have seen it yesterday. When I got home from her house, I started packing a box of all the lame stuff she's had me buy over the years. All the skinny jeans, my cashmere sweaters, the Louis Vuitton purse . . ." I started counting things off on my fingers. "Those stupid, stupid ballet flats, every single layered shirt I own, a bunch of lipsticks, anything with the name Abercrombie and Fitch—I packed it all up and just dropped it off on her doorstep."

"Really? Just dropped it off? You probably could have sold all that stuff on eBay. Made some money."

"I know. I thought about that. But I think the message I sent to Sarah is worth so much more than the money I could have made on eBay."

Gabe smiled and squeezed my hand. The lights dimmed, and the previews started. I wondered if he was going to hold my hand for the whole movie, and I realized that I wouldn't mind it.

I tried to concentrate on the movie, but thoughts of

Sarah lingered. Was it really over? Would I be able to lay aside the worry of what to wear every morning? Could I break the habit of looking for her spot at lunch? Maybe it was finally time to stand on my own and not rely on Sarah's grasp in the deep end. I could do the deep end all by myself now.

Gabe's squeeze of my hand brought me out of those few thoughts that remained. He was a tangible reminder that I didn't need Sarah to be happy. He was real, sitting next to me. He had opened up a world of possibilities, in which I could make choices based on what I wanted and not on what someone dictated for me.

After the movie, I was glad we didn't run into the Tom Cruise crowd. Gabe pulled on his stocking cap, and I put my mittens on as we walked out into the cold night. Gabe grabbed my hand and put it into his coat pocket again. He ignored the fact that I was wearing mittens. It didn't really matter.

"I hope it wasn't too boring," Gabe said as we crossed the street.

"No. It was good. I always have a hard time with holocaust scenes. I could never read Anne Frank's book."

"Yeah, it's not an easy thing to read."

We were to my house by the time the Volvo finally heated up. Gabe walked me to the door, and I braced myself for one of those awkward doorstep scenes.

"Thanks for the pizza and movie," I said. I pulled out my key and opened the door.

Gabe hesitated for a just a moment before he followed me inside. "A cliché first date. I hope you didn't mind that. I'll have to get creative for next time."

"I don't mind cliché. Creative sounds good too."

"So that means there will be a next time?"

I closed the door behind him, and he leaned against it. "Yes, but we're not done with this time yet."

He smiled and tugged at both my hands. "These mittens aren't doing a very good job. I can think of something better." He took off my mittens and let them slide to the floor. Pulling both of my hands, he slid them under his wool jacket and placed them on his chest. I could feel his heart beating just over his shirt, and I pressed my fingertips against it.

He placed his palms against each of my cheeks. I shivered at the icy touch, his hands still cold from the wintry night. His fingers pressed the back of my neck while his thumbs ran down my jawline. I looked up at him just as he closed his eyes and leaned in. His kiss was gentle, slow, but intensified with each passing second.

The cell phone in my handbag I'd discarded to the floor rang, and it was my dad's ringtone. Gabe paused and pulled slightly away, distracted by the ring.

"It's just my dad," I said.

"You'd better get it," he said. "You can't ignore your dad's call. I always answer when it's my mom." He slid his hands off my cheeks and quickly brushed his lips one more time against mine.

I smiled. I couldn't imagine Gabe ever ignoring his mom's call. I pulled my hands off his chest and bent down to pick up my phone. "Hi, Dad," I said.

"Hi, El. How was your date?"

I looked at Gabe and smiled. "Good."

"It *was* good or it *is* good?" he asked.

"Is," I said, not wanting to give away any more information.

"Where are you now?"

"We're at home. We're just saying good night."

"Saying good night?" he asked. "Let's finish up with the

saying of 'good night.' You know I don't like you home alone with a boy." He said it like it had happened before.

"Okay," I said.

"I'm on my way home and will be there soon. Text me in a few minutes, once he's left. I can trust you, right, El?"

"Yes, of course."

"All right. Love you, El."

"Okay. Bye, Dad."

I disconnected and turned to look at Gabe. A small, but growing smile spread across his face. "He wants me to go?"

"Yeah."

"He's a good dad," Gabe said. "I guess I'd better say good night one more time then." He leaned in, sliding his hand to my shoulder.

"Good night," I whispered. I wrapped my arms around his neck.

He kissed me again, the gentleness from before intensified, and I felt a bolt of electricity course through my arms and shoot down my legs.

"Good night," he said, pulling away slowly.

"Good night," I said again, kissing him one last time before I peeled my arms off his neck.

He grabbed the doorknob behind him and opened the door. He waved one last time before turning around toward the street. The exhilaration of a first date coursed through me. It was something I hadn't felt in quite some time. Right away, my eyes turned to the kitchen. It was an instinct to look there. That's where I'd often found my mom, where I'd run every time I had something important to share or confide in her. It wouldn't happen tonight. She wasn't here anymore. I couldn't tell her about Gabe, about our first date, or about how I was starting to fall for him.

TWELVE

IT HAD BEEN ALMOST A WEEK SINCE I'd seen my mother. That was okay. While I loved the feeling of being in her presence, I didn't want it every day. I wanted it to be special, something to look forward to. Plus, I didn't want to ask Gabe to make that sacrifice so often. Once a week seemed reasonable now that I was past the initial overwhelming amazement of the experience. Now, it just felt like a comfortable occurrence. Something to treasure.

I reached for her and, in an instant, I felt her thoughts, strong and emerging. They were reverent, tranquil at first. They were memories that I was too small to recall but that seemed to live within my mind: sitting in her lap on a grassy field, sharing an ice cream cone in my stroller. The warmth I'd longed for since it had escaped me after I first felt her came over me. I felt like I was flowing, gliding. As quickly as those images had evolved, they were ripped away, replaced by ones that felt foreign to me.

A man's hand clenched against my mother's neck. Her eyes widened with terror and pain. Her head pressed against her pillow. Her hands helplessly tried to pry his fingers off. There were screams I couldn't hear but could see, could almost feel. More than anything, I saw the shock, the immense shock in her eyes. And then they were gone. Those awful images vanished as quickly as they'd come. But nothing else came, just darkness. Darkness and silence engulfed me, and I wasn't sure if I was still with her or back in Gabe's basement.

The darkness then evaporated as one final image came into my mind. A knife quivering over her head as she let out a scream I couldn't hear. It was the last thing I saw before I felt the shaking begin.

"No!" I screamed as I felt my hand rip away from hers.

I didn't even recall seeing her face again before I was pushed out. The image of the knife about to strike her was burned into my memory, and it's what I took out with me. The tranquil, serene thoughts I had upon entering had been smashed to bits, replaced with a horrifying impression that was not likely to ever leave me.

Even the tremendous blow I encountered as I smashed against the cement wall couldn't rid my mind of it. I fell to the ground, out of breath and panting. Gabe was beside me in a second, also a little out of breath. My shoulder seemed to have taken the brunt of the hit.

"You okay?" he asked me.

I shook my head, wanting to scream out, but not finding any words to describe how I felt. I knew he hadn't seen the images, couldn't imagine what I'd seen. I didn't care about my shoulder; it didn't seem to even faze me. Again and again, I saw the same thing and the urge to shout wouldn't leave. Finally, I gave in.

"Uuhh!" I let out a shriek as I crumbled into a heap against Gabe.

He grabbed me and put his arms around me as I began to whimper into his shoulder.

"What is it?"

I still couldn't talk, couldn't answer, couldn't even describe what I'd seen or what I was feeling. It was as if I had witnessed her death, as if I had been there to see how it happened.

"I have to go back," I said quickly, sitting up. I wiped my eyes and nose with my sleeve and pushed myself away from Gabe. "I have to go back. I have to see." I'd seen it, almost as if I'd been a witness to the crime that took my mother. But one thing I didn't see. I didn't see his face. I saw his hand, saw her face, but not his. It was the one thing I needed—the one thing the police didn't know. I had to go back so I could help them find my mom's killer, so I could describe him and have them do a sketch—whatever witnesses do to help find murderers.

"We can't right now, Ellie. We have to wait."

"But I saw it. I saw what happened to her."

"What do you mean?" he asked, scooting up closer to me.

"At first, I saw good memories, of me and my mom." The recollection from only minutes ago filled me with a small fraction of the peace I'd felt earlier. "They were good. I felt so close to her. And then . . . And then . . ." Recalling those few minutes filled me with terror, wiping away the small amount of tranquility I'd managed to find. "And then, it was like I was in her room when she died. I saw her, the look in her eyes. And I saw the man's hand. I didn't see his face, but I saw her."

His arm around me tightened, and he pulled me closer.

"I'm sorry, Ellie. I'm so sorry. You shouldn't have to see that. I didn't know you would see that."

"But don't you see? I have to go back. I need to reach out to her again. Maybe she'll let me see more. Maybe she'll let me see images of him, of what he looks like so I can go to the police and give them a description."

Gabe shook his head as I spoke. "No. Ellie, how can you tell them that? What are you going to say? You can't tell them how you know, how you saw that."

"I have to."

"They wouldn't believe you. They would think you were crazy."

"But I have to. It's the only way. They're never going to find who killed my mother. They've already given up. It's the only way we'll ever know, ever find him."

He sighed. "We can't go back now. We'll think about it, see when we can go back, and what we can do."

"We have to go back."

"Tomorrow?"

I didn't want to wait until tomorrow, didn't think I could wait. I knew that I would carry the image around with me for the rest of the day and all through the night. The only way to rid my mind of it was to see what was next, to go back and have her show me what happened next. I needed to know who it was so I could tell the police and put an end to it.

"Tomorrow, Ellie. You'll have more time."

"I know. I just can't stand it. I have to know. I have to see."

"Are you afraid?"

Afraid wasn't the word to even begin describing how I was feeling. It was more anxiety. I was anxious to know more, find out more, and figure it all out. It was the only way

I'd be able to help my mother. "I just don't want to go home. I don't want to go to bed with this image in my mind. I want to see the rest and put an end to it."

"I don't know if it's that easy. You're not sure what you'll see. You don't control what you see or feel. She does. Going back doesn't guarantee you'll see who did it."

"I know, I know. But what am I supposed to do?"

"We'll go tomorrow. We'll see what she wants us to know."

"Okay. When?"

"I have to help open tomorrow. They like me to come in early on Saturdays, so I'll be gone by 6:00 a.m. How about when I get off?"

"Okay. Call me when you get home."

"I can come pick you up."

"Okay."

"Are you sure you'll be okay tonight?"

"Yeah, I will."

He put his arm around me and pulled me in toward him. "Call me if you need me."

We sat on the cold basement floor for a few more minutes. I tried to focus on the happy memories my mom had sent me, to think about those happy times I spent with her. But, involuntarily, the dark, scary images of the moments before her death crept in, dissolving any peace I could find.

As we climbed the steps back to the kitchen, I heard the water running. At the kitchen sink stood a blonde woman. She was washing strawberries and didn't see us right away.

"Hi, Mom. Feeling okay?" Gabe asked as he walked toward her. He touched her shoulder, and she turned around to smile.

"Hi, Gabey." Then she noticed me standing by the steps. "Oh, I didn't know anyone else was here." She turned off the water, put the strawberries down into a drainer in the sink, and wiped her hands on a dishcloth.

"Mom, this is Ellie. Ellie, my mom, Susannah de la Cruz."

Susannah looked at me for only an instant and then forced a smile as her eyes sunk to the ground. She took a few steps toward me, holding out her hand. "Hi, Ellie. It's nice to meet you. Gabey, I mean Gabe, has told me a lot about you."

I took her trembling hand and shook it. "It's nice to meet you too. Hope it's okay that I'm here. I know Gabe said you weren't feeling well."

"Fine. It's fine," she said, rubbing her hands together. She turned back toward the strawberries. "I was just starting on a strawberry shortcake. Maybe you would like to have some."

"Thank you. I'm sure it will be delicious. Gabe gave me some of your apple pie once. It was very good. And your cookies. Your cookies are amazing."

"I'm glad you liked them." She looked up at me for a quick smile and then began to cut the strawberries on a small wooden cutting board. I studied her profile and recognized Gabe's cheekbones. It was the only feature he seemed to have inherited from her. He did not have her blonde hair, her pale and delicate skin, or her slight nose. His skin tone and dark hair definitely came from his Peruvian father. If not for the cheekbones, I wouldn't have believed this petite, angelic-looking woman was his mother.

"You need some help, Mom?" Gabe asked her.

"No, hon. I'm almost done. I made the cake earlier. I just have to finish up the topping."

"You want me to do anything?"

She kept her focus on the strawberries as she shook her head. "No. I left you a grocery list on the table if you wouldn't mind picking those things up tomorrow before you leave work."

"Sure." He walked over to the table and picked up the list.

I looked over his shoulder at the rather long list—chicken breasts, celery, peaches, eggs, toilet paper, tampons. The list went on and on.

He folded the list in half and tucked it into his wallet. "Can you stay for cake?" he asked me.

"Yeah," I said, looking at my watch. "My dad won't be home for another hour. I know he wants me home for dinner, though."

"Okay," Gabe said. "Mom, do you mind if I take Ellie to your room? Show her what you're working on?"

She turned her head quickly to look at Gabe and then back at the strawberries. "Um, okay," she said as she began chopping erratically, her speed increasing with each strawberry, her blonde ponytail swaying with each movement.

I watched her for a minute and then turned to Gabe, shaking my head. "It's okay," I whispered. I didn't really want to go to her room. She didn't seem comfortable with the idea, and I didn't know why Gabe had brought it up.

He took my hand and pulled me down a narrow hallway. "Come on."

"No, it's okay."

"Just come, please?"

I hesitated and pulled my hand out of his hold. "Why?"

"I just want to show you."

I let him take my hand again, and he tugged gently. Turning to look in the kitchen once more, I saw his mom look away from me to place the chopped strawberries in a bowl. He pulled me again, and I followed.

There were four doors down the hall, all closed. He stopped in front of the first one. "This is her bedroom. It's where she paints. I just want you to see how talented she is, how amazing she is. Then maybe you'll understand her." He opened the door and closed it as we entered. "She's not the typical mom. This is why." With his hand, he gestured around the room.

If he hadn't called it her bedroom, I wouldn't have believed it to be one. With the exception of a thin mattress on the floor and a blanket folded neatly on top of it, this room held no resemblance to a bedroom. There was a large folding table against one wall, covered with art supplies, paints, brushes, and soiled rags. Hanging above the table was a framed print—it looked like Van Gogh. It was of a man sitting on a chair, his head turned downward. Around the room were large canvases stacked against each other. They seemed to be completed paintings but were covered by each other and facing the wall. There was an easel in the middle of the room, holding a large, unfinished canvas. A dark blue sky was painted across the top half. There was a lone pencil sketch hanging from a thumbtack on a nearly empty wall. It was Gabe and seemed to be from a few years ago. I recognized his smile. It was something he rarely exhibited, but I would know it anywhere.

"She's good," I said, walking toward it. "Very good." I paused in front of it and studied the quick pencil movements, the sharp angles that shaped his face. "Why doesn't she show the other ones?" I gestured around the room where stacks of paintings lay against the wall.

"She doesn't think they're very good, but they are." He walked over to one stack and picked up the first one. It was a forest, dark green paint against a murky, blue sky. It was nighttime, and the trees were obscured and gloomy.

"They *are* good," I said, studying the forest. "Just like the one in the kitchen."

"She gave me that one in the kitchen," Gabe said. "She doesn't want the other ones hanging in the house. But I had asked her for one for my birthday, and well, since it's mine I told her I should be able to hang it where I want. I love it in the kitchen. I wish she would let me hang up the others." He walked over to a different stack and turned the paintings, one at a time, searching. "Here's another one." He picked one up and brought it over to me. I recognized it as the Westfield train station. I would know that place anywhere. It was a realistic portrayal, almost photographic. It was nighttime, and the darkened sky hung over the railroad tracks.

"That's amazing. She's so talented." I looked around the room, wanting to see all of them. There were more than twenty stacks, with at least four or five paintings in each of them. "Are you sure she doesn't mind that I'm in here?"

He shrugged. "I want you to know her, and this is the best way. I think she understands that."

"I don't want to make her uncomfortable."

"She's always uncomfortable. It's how she lives." He walked over to the easel and ran his fingers down the edge of the canvas. "She has depression. Really bad."

"I'm sorry."

He nodded, looking down at the unfinished piece. "She's always had it, as long as I can remember anyway. Got worse after my dad died."

"It looks like you're a big help to her."

"She doesn't like to go out much."

"Has she gotten some help, like medication?"

He looked up at me, taking his eyes away from the canvas. "She's been off and on meds for a long time, in and out of treatment centers. She met my dad in a juvenile treatment center—they both suffered from mental illness. She says they fell in love—hard—and ran away. It always sounded a little too much like a made-for-TV movie where they live happily ever after. I guess they did for a while. And had me. And I guess I'm lucky I didn't get it. I don't think I'm crazy, anyway. Am I?" There was humor in his question, but the look in his eye said he wasn't sure. He wanted some reassurance that he wouldn't end up like them.

"You're not crazy," I said, walking toward him. "They're not crazy either—just ill. But you're not. If you're crazy, then I'm crazy, because I think you're the sanest, most has-a-grip-on-reality person I've ever met."

He laughed and looked away from me toward the Van Gogh. "I love my mom, and I'm trying to help her, but sometimes I wish she would just go get help again. She says it's never done any good."

I reached out to grab his arm and rubbed my hand up and down it. "You help her a lot. I don't know many guys that would go buy tampons for their mom."

He laughed really hard and grabbed his side. "Yeah, tampons. I know way too much about tampons for a teenage guy, way more than I want to know. But she's pretty particular."

"And I think you're pretty amazing to do all that for her." I put my arms around his waist and pulled myself toward him.

"She's not a bad mom; she's great. She just can't really help herself right now. I do the best I can. Working a little to help out; she's on permanent disability income through the state, but it's not enough. And art stuff is expensive, but it's the only thing that helps her. She paints all night long; she says it's her therapy. She doesn't care so much about the end result—the canvases. They don't really matter to her. It's the process of painting that helps her. And baking. She's not much of a cook, so I cook our dinner most nights, but she bakes dessert. It's also therapeutic, she says.

"I don't understand it all, how her mind works. I just do what I can to help her feel better. If painting and apple pie is what helps her get through it, then fine. It's better than when she's really bad. When she's really bad, it's . . . Okay, let me just shut up now. I know you don't want to hear all this."

"I do. Please tell me, Gabe. I want to know about her . . . about you."

"When she's really bad, it's bad. She just lies in bed." He pointed to the thin mattress on the floor. "She lies in bed and cries, all day. All day. She holds her side, like it hurts, and cries. And there's nothing I can do. Nothing makes her better. It goes on like that for days, and then she stops. And she's back to painting and back to cleaning and back to baking, and I know she's better for a while." He was shaking as he talked, and I pulled him even closer. "I don't know what I'm supposed to do for her, so I just buy what she needs . . . what she needs to feel better. Art stuff and groceries."

"You're a great son, Gabe. You're doing what you can to help her. She's very lucky to have you."

He shrugged. "I guess."

"Are you sure it's okay that we're in here?"

"Yeah. She knows you make me happy. She knows all about you. I wanted to explain her to you, so you know her, and I thought this was the best way."

"Thank you," I said. I had wondered about his mother—had wanted to know—and felt glad he had confided in me. I hoped there was a way I could help him, and her, but other than being understanding to the situation, I didn't really know how.

"I guess we can go now."

I followed him out of the room, and he closed the door behind him. We went back into the kitchen, but his mother wasn't there anymore. There were two large pieces of strawberry shortcake with whipped cream on the table. I glanced into the living room, but she wasn't there either.

Gabe looked at me, sensing my question. "She probably went into the garage. There's a sculpture she's working on in there."

I felt that perhaps it was more than the sculpture that had sent her to the garage, but I didn't want to say it.

"Let's dig in," Gabe said, handing me a fork.

"It looks really good. Is your mom going to have some?"

"Probably later." Gabe sat down and shoved his fork into the whipped cream. "She doesn't do that well with people. She did good with you, though. Thanks for meeting her and for staying after I told you everything."

"I'm glad I finally got to meet her. Thanks for telling me."

He started a tentative smile and then stopped. "This won't keep you away now, will it?"

"Not if your mom keeps making strawberry shortcake like this."

He relaxed into a smile, and then that smile lengthened, reaching his eyes, creating the look his mother had captured in her sketch. It was the image I hoped I would take with me after this emotionally exhausting day. I didn't want to think about those other images—not until tomorrow when I would have to reach for them to find the truth I needed.

THIRTEEN

ON SATURDAY MORNING, I WOKE UP wishing the day would hurry so that I could go back to Gabe's basement. Dad was making blueberry pancakes when I shuffled into the kitchen.

"Good morning, El. What do you have planned for this morning?"

I yawned as I reached over to fork a couple of pancakes off the platter he had placed in the center of the table. "Not much. I was wanting to go to Gabe's house this afternoon."

"Gabe's house, huh? Weren't you just there yesterday?"

"Yeah. His mom made us strawberry shortcake." I was hoping the mention of his mom would cool him off the subject. If his mom was there, we couldn't be doing anything bad, right?

"So, tell me about this Gabe. When do I get to meet him?"

"Whenever you want, Dad. I'm not trying to hide him."

Dad turned over a pancake. "Is he a boyfriend or is it headed there?"

"I don't know," I said, looking down at the pancake cooling on my plate. I think the warmth of the pancake had transferred onto my face. I couldn't look up at my dad, who was looking directly at me.

"Why don't you invite him over to dinner tonight? Then I can meet him, and you still get to hang out with him."

I didn't mind Gabe coming over, but what I really needed was to go to *his* house—his basement to be exact. "Okay. He's at work right now, but I can text him."

"Yeah, tell him to come over. What time does he get done with work?"

"I'm not sure. He was going to pick me up after work."

Dad poured more batter onto the sizzling pan. "Instead of picking you up to go to his house, you two can stay here, have dinner, hang out, and I can get to know this guy my daughter's been spending a lot of time with."

"Can I go over to his house for a little while first?"

Dad put his spatula down and turned around to face me. "Why do you want to go there first?"

I chided myself for asking him that. He was probably thinking that I wanted to go over to his house to make out or something. Maybe he thought that's what all teenagers think about. "He wanted to show me something."

"Show you something?"

Probably not my smartest answer. "His mom is working on a painting, and I think she was almost finished. She's a very talented artist." I was lying, which I didn't usually do to my dad. But I didn't want him to see through my lies and make up his own reasons for me lying to him. "No big deal. He can show me another day. I'll text him and have him come over for dinner." Maybe if dinner went well, I could ask Dad later after dinner if I could go over to Gabe's. By then, perhaps he would have forgotten all about that something Gabe wanted to show me.

I finished the pancakes and went up to my room to text Gabe. He said he would be done by four but that he had to drop off the groceries to his mom afterward. He would come over right after.

Dad gave me a short list of chores to do around the house while he went grocery shopping. I wondered if he'd run into Gabe at Stop & Shop but didn't mention it to him. Better for them to meet tonight.

After I showered, I got dressed. I put on my comfortable Levis jeans and a touristy "I heart NY" T-shirt. I felt so much better about myself and comfortable in my own choice of clothes, rather than Sarah's dictates.

I first vacuumed and dusted the living room. Then, Dad wanted me to clean the linens on our beds. I pulled mine off my bed and dumped them in the hallway while I walked into his bedroom. I didn't go in his room often; I guess it just seemed different now that it was only *his* room and not *their* room.

As I pulled the fitted sheet off his bed, a thread came loose from the stitching and continued to unravel as I tried to cut it off. I scanned the room to look for a pair of scissors but didn't see any. I walked across the room, toward his dresser, to look for a grooming kit. The top drawer held no clothes, just toiletries and a nail-trimming kit.

As I picked it up to get a pair of scissors, I noticed a tall stack of letters, some opened and some unopened. They were all addressed to Rick Thorton. I picked up the stack that was rubberbanded together and was surprised to see that some letters dated back several months. I always thought Dad sent them back to the post office. Why would he keep some, and why were some opened? And why had he put them in his dresser?

Those questions, although inconsequential, swam around in my mind as I cut off the loose thread and returned the scissors to their place. I suppose he got tired of always sending them back and having more come, so he just stopped doing it. I thought about it for a little while more as I started the load of laundry, but as I was in the midst of cleaning my bathroom, I let the trivial matter float away.

I thought about it again when I checked the mail. There was just the power bill and Dad's *Runner's World* magazine, and I put them on the counter.

Later that afternoon, I made a salad of spinach greens while Dad grilled chicken in the backyard. As I was setting the table, I heard the doorbell and was surprised at how my pulse quickened at the idea of Gabe at my house. It would be his first time meeting my dad. He wasn't technically my boyfriend, but it sort of felt like the proverbial meeting-your-dad kind of event.

I opened the door, smiling at the presence of Gabe on my doorstep. He was wearing scruffy jeans and a black hoodie. Just like Gabe to choose being himself over some lame attempt at impressing my dad with the right kind of clothes—whatever that was. I wasn't sure anymore.

"Hey, thanks for coming," I said, pulling him inside. "My dad wanted to meet you, since I've been going over to your place a lot. Just being fatherly, I suppose."

"Only seems fair. You met my mom."

"How's she doing?"

Gabe closed the door behind him and took off his hood, causing his hair to stand up a little in the back. "She's baking banana bread, so good, I guess."

"Maybe she can come over one day too?"

"I don't know."

I was tempted to brush his hair down in the back but figured Dad just had to accept Gabe as himself. I was done with trying to look the right way and trying to get everything to fit in.

I heard the sliding glass door in back and then saw Dad walking across the living room. He came up to the front door and extended his hand. "You must be Gabe. I'm Daniel Cummings. Nice to meet you."

"Good to meet you, sir. I'm Gabe de la Cruz."

"De la Cruz? So, where's your family from?"

"My dad's from Peru, and my mom's from Westfield."

"Well, welcome to our home. Come on in. Dinner's almost ready. Let's go into the kitchen."

I followed them in and finished setting the table.

"Have a seat, Gabe," my dad said. "I'm so glad you came. I just needed to meet this guy Ellie's been hanging out with. Make sure he's okay."

"Dad!" I said, nudging him in the arm.

"Come on, Ellie. I'm sure Gabe understands." Dad excused himself to go get the chicken off the grill while Gabe helped me bring the salad and baked potatoes to the table.

We served our plates, and I speared a piece of Dad's lemon-pepper grilled chicken.

"So, Gabe. Tell me about yourself. What do you like to do?"

Gabe cleared his throat and took a drink. "Well, I like history and running and rock climbing."

"Running? My kind of guy then. And rock climbing, huh? Ellie and I went once when we were visiting Olivia's sister in Colorado. We haven't been since. We should go again, huh, El?"

"Yeah, it was fun," I said, recalling the event from a

couple of years ago. I didn't even know that about Gabe. Good thing my dad was getting inquisitive. Maybe I would find out a little more about Gabe as well.

"So where do you go around here?" my dad asked Gabe.

"I go up to Allamuchy State Park. It's not too far, and they have a couple good sites."

"And who do you go with? You have brothers, cousins, in the area?"

"No. There's a group that meets at the outdoors store on East Broad every couple of months."

"Well, let's plan a trip, then. You, me, and El. When the weather gets nice, we'll go."

"That would be great, sir." Gabe took a bite of chicken and chewed slowly. "The chicken is very good, sir."

"Thank you, Gabe. I'm glad you like it." Dad took a few minutes' break from grilling Gabe to eat.

As we ate, the thought of Rick Thorton came to mind, and I was about to ask, but I thought it would be best to ask Dad after Gabe left. It was too weird a question to ask in front of company.

"So, Ellie tells me your mom is an artist."

Gabe turned to look at me. "Yes."

Dad put his fork down. "Is that what she does for a living?"

Gabe shrugged. "Sort of. I mean, she spends most of her time doing it, but she doesn't really make any money from it."

"Well, Ellie says she's really good. She probably should try to market herself."

"I guess I never thought about that."

"I have a friend who runs a gallery in the city. Maybe we can have her take a look at some of you mom's work and see if she'll display it. She can help sell it, if there's an interest.

That's if your mom can stand to part with it. I know artists have a hard time with that sometimes."

"I can ask her," Gabe said.

Dinner continued like that. My dad kept asking Gabe questions about himself, and Gabe answered them to Dad's satisfaction.

After dinner, Gabe and I cleared the table and took the dishes over to the sink. I was waiting for the right moment to ask Dad if I could go over to Gabe's house. I hoped that loading the dishwasher would soften him.

As I turned around to ask Dad, I stopped myself and watched him for a minute. He was standing by the counter, browsing through the mail. Dad grabbed a letter and then his cell phone rang, and he disappeared upstairs. Gabe continued clearing the table while I finished loading the dishes. He took the sponge out of the sink and wrung it out, wiping the table and counters.

"Thanks for helping me," I said, taking the sponge from his hand.

"No problem. I'd be doing the same thing at home." He leaned back against the counter and crossed his arms over his chest.

My dad came back into the kitchen, pulling his wool coat on. "Sorry, guys. I'm going to take care of something."

"At work?" I asked. It was a little late in the day to be heading into the city.

"No. Just something that came up." He stopped in front of Gabe. "So are you two going to hang out here?"

"I was going to go to Gabe's," I said, turning to him. "Your mom's home, right?"

"Yeah," he said, pulling himself away from the counter.

"Sorry I have to run," Dad said, buttoning his coat. "Thanks for cleaning up. El, I can turn the dishwasher on when I come back. I have to put a few dishes in there after I clean out the fridge." He turned to Gabe, extending his hand. "I'm glad I finally got to meet you. Hope to see you around some more."

"Thank you, sir."

Dad hurried out the door.

"I guess he likes you," I said. I walked over to him and put my hand on his. "Thanks for coming over."

He nodded, covering my hand with his. He interlocked our fingers. "You ready to go?" he asked gently. His question was soft, worried, and unsure.

I curled into him and leaned my head on his chest. My eyes closed, and I listened to the steady beat of his heart. It was the only thing I was sure of. Everything else seemed unsure, impossible. "I think I'm ready now. I'm glad I had a little time to not think about it, to try to forget what I saw yesterday. Thanks for coming over. It seemed to distract me from what I don't want to think about."

He held me close. I wished I could stay there and not return to the frightening moment I would face when I saw my mother, felt her thoughts, and saw her memories. I looked up at Gabe, and he leaned down to kiss me—soft, quiet.

I responded instinctively and wanted to suspend the moment, to stay in it. He ran his fingers along my forehead and down my face. They came to rest softly on my shoulder. We pulled away at the same time, sensing we should leave the moment for a time when it could be enjoyed without the ominous future looming before us.

"I'll be there. No matter what," he said, taking my face in both his hands. "Are you sure you want to do this?"

I nodded. "I have to."

FOURTEEN

AS GABE DROVE TO HIS HOUSE, THE usual anticipation of seeing my mother through the huaca was replaced with trepidation and fear of what she would show me. I hated the feeling of dread, of not wanting to see her. The usual excitement to see her on previous days was almost as glorious as actually seeing her. Today, I felt cheated out of those feelings.

Gabe reached over and squeezed my arm. Even the kiss had been tainted, robbed of the customary exhilaration associated with it. When Gabe pulled into his driveway, my movements were slow in getting out of the car.

He immediately reached for my hand, and we walked into the quiet house. As he prepared to draw his blood, I realized I could stop him. I could tell him I didn't want to go, that I didn't want to see the horror that I knew was awaiting me. But I didn't stop him. I had to go. I had to see.

I walked toward my mother's usual spot. She turned

around and took a step toward me. I walked slowly toward her and took her outstretched hand.

Instantly, my mind filled with images: she and I together in the city at a show, walking in Times Square, taking the subway. These were some of my favorite memories—watching Broadway shows together after going into the city early to find cheap tickets.

These images didn't last long. They were pushed away by quick, successive ones: Her thoughtful face. Her worried face. Her frightened face. A left hand clutched at her neck. There was a scream I couldn't hear. And then my mother was gasping for air. She grabbed at the hand. Pulled fingers away. The hand persisted. A familiar hand. A familiar ring on his finger. A knife above her head. The knife in her chest. A small trickle of blood. Her limp hand. Her devastated eyes. His kneeling body on top of her. The repeated thrust of the knife. Three, four, five times. The hand I knew. The arm I knew. The face I knew. The face that kissed my cheek every night, that whispered, "Good night, El" to me.

My father's face.

His hand pulled the knife out one last time.

"No!" I screamed. I tried to focus on my mother's face, to see her reaction as I processed what she revealed to me, but it disappeared when the images did. I felt my stomach being pinched and pulled back. "Mom!" I called out. I waved my arms aimlessly, hoping to hold on, to get some answers, but all the questions flooding my mind were answered with a slam against the basement floor.

My fists pounded on the cold floor, and I screamed. "No, Mom!"

Gabe scooted over to me. He placed his hand on my shoulder.

"What did you do?" I screamed, ripping his hand off

me. It couldn't be true—none of it. It had to be a hallucination, thoughts brought on by some force that worked its way into my mind. "What did you do to me? Your crazy box put these thoughts in my head."

"What happened?" Gabe asked. He reached for me, and I slapped his hand away. "What did you see?"

I pulled myself off the ground, ignoring the physical pain coursing through me. "It's wrong. How did you make me see those things? It's lying!"

"Ellie, please. Tell me what you saw."

"No!" I pushed him away and bolted for the steps, taking them two at a time.

"Wait! Ellie!" He was behind me in a flash and held the door so I couldn't open it.

"No, Gabe! I don't know how you did it, but you're messing with my mind."

"Ellie, just tell me what you saw. I didn't do anything."

"It's all lies!" I pushed him away, and he stumbled back a few steps.

He was right behind me as I pushed through the door.

"Ellie, come back," he said as I reached the front door.

"No, that box is crazy! You're crazy, and your whole family is messed up!" I jabbed my finger in the air at him with each statement.

I stopped in the street in front of his house, panting and shivering. He'd driven me. It was at least at four-mile walk to my house, but I wasn't sure I even wanted to go there.

I felt Gabe's hands behind me as he draped my coat over my shoulders. I didn't push him away, didn't run away. In the seconds it took for me to be standing there, I'd come to the realization that Gabe might be the only person I had left in the world.

I held my coat against me and sagged my shoulders. I

started crying quietly. The angry rush I'd experienced earlier was gone, leaving me beaten and hurting.

"I'm sorry, Gabe."

"Don't be. Tell me what happened. Want to go back inside?"

I shook my head and then turned around, collapsing into him. He put his arms around me and held me solidly against him as I began to cry—cry in earnest, cry as I hadn't since my mom died.

Somehow, Gabe managed to get me inside. I found myself seated on the couch.

"Ellie, please tell me."

I nodded, knowing I would have to eventually. "It has to be wrong, Gabe. Are the images ever wrong? Do they lie?"

He shook his head sadly. "No. You see into her mind, Ellie. You see what she's thinking, what's in her heart, and what she knows to be true. She can't make you see something that's not true."

"But what if she's wrong?"

"About what?"

"About my dad." I couldn't say anymore, couldn't formulate the words. The tears came back again. At this point, I wasn't sure if they'd even left, or ever would.

"Your dad?"

"That's what I saw, Gabe. Images of my dad. He was holding her down, and his hand was on her throat, squeezing."

"He killed her?"

I nodded, shaking away the tears. "No. I don't know. How could he?"

"But that's what you saw?"

"Stabbing her. I saw him stabbing her. But it can't be true. Why would she show me that?"

"Because she wants you to know. To protect you."

I shook my head, willing his words to go away. My dad couldn't have done it. He had loved her. He still loved her. He had taken it so hard. He hardly talked about her.

"You can't go there tonight," Gabe said. "You can't go home."

"But it's home."

"What if it's true? What if he did it?"

"But he's my dad."

"Could he have done it?"

"No!"

"Just stay here tonight until we can think this through. Text him. Tell him you're staying at Sarah's."

I didn't want to go home. Didn't think I could after what I saw. "Yeah," I said. "Can you do it for me? Text him." I reached into my pocket and handed him my phone. I watched as Gabe figured out my phone and punched in each letter, telling my dad I was going to Sarah's. "Ask him if he's home." I waited a few minutes, staring at the phone screen. The ringer announced his response. I suddenly felt his ominous presence in the room, like he was watching me, knew what I was thinking.

I looked away from the phone, not wanting to read his words. "He says he'll be home in a couple of hours. He said no problem about staying at Sarah's, but are you two talking again?"

"Tell him we're trying to patch things up—whatever. I don't know." Gabe typed back a response. I heard the ringer again but couldn't look at the words. "What did he say?"

"Said okay." I knew Gabe was lying, so I reached for my phone. *Good night, El. I love you*, read the text. His words, usually warm and endearing, were repulsive today.

FIFTEEN

SUSANNAH BROUGHT OVER A TRAY and set it on the coffee table. There were two steaming mugs of cocoa and two plates with Bundt cake. "Here you go, Ellie," she said, handing me a mug.

"Thank you," I said. "Thanks for letting me stay here tonight. I hope it's okay."

"Sure, Ellie. I hope things work out okay with your father."

Her hope seemed like an impossibility at this point, and all I could do was nod.

She turned to Gabe. "Make sure to put clean sheets on your bed before Ellie goes to sleep, and put a sheet on the couch before you go to bed.

"Okay, Mom," Gabe said, picking up one of the mugs. "Best cocoa," he said to me. "It has a secret ingredient."

"What is it?" I asked, blowing on it.

"You'll have to see," Gabe said.

"I'll be in the garage," Susannah said as she turned around.

"She'll probably work out there all night long and come in to sleep right when we're waking up." Gabe grabbed the remote control from the coffee table and turned the TV on, just as the late news was coming on.

I took small sips of the cocoa. There was a spicy taste. The secret ingredient, I guessed, but I couldn't place it.

The news detailed the death of a man whose body was found in Plainfield, a town about fifteen minutes away. It was a senseless death, like any death. The man was found in his home by a sister who said she'd run out to do some errands and had left him only hours earlier. She was sobbing, and another woman's arm was around her. The camera preyed on the woman's vulnerability; her recent loss was now fodder for the ratings race of the evening news.

"He was just fine when I left him. He was installing a new water heater. Who would do this?" The camera went back to the anchor, who said there were no leads. "Police are looking into a phone call that Joe Collins received around dinnertime. His sister states that the phone call agitated him, but Collins hadn't divulged the topic of the call or the identity of the caller. Investigators are going through phone records to determine who Collins was talking to at 5:30 p.m. that night."

The news story captivated me, preventing me from thinking about anything other than Collins. He had received a phone call around 5:30 and had been visited by his killer shortly thereafter. The timeline is what froze me in place as I thought about what I was doing at 5:30. I was doing dishes with Gabe, and my dad was upstairs on the phone. The fact that he left shortly after did not escape me. It was all I could think about. I didn't want to say anything out loud or share my suspicions with Gabe. I was still determined to believe that my father couldn't have done any of this. I couldn't bring myself to believe otherwise, or to compound the horrific idea with further scandal.

Gabe looked over at me and frowned. He reached over to touch me but hesitated and pulled his hand back. I wondered if his current line of thinking was similar to mine. Did he think my dad had anything to do with Joe Collins's death? He didn't voice his thoughts, and I wasn't going to ask him. I thought about his hesitation at touching me. I knew it was because I had already pushed him away twice. I had rejected his touch and had hurt him with my words.

"I'm sorry about what I said, Gabe. I didn't mean it."

"It's okay."

"No, it's not okay. I shouldn't have said those things. Of course I don't think you're crazy. I just couldn't believe what I had seen and I—"

"Ellie," Gabe said, reaching over to take my arm. "What you saw was horrible, more horrible than what you were expecting. You were ready to see a stranger's face, one you could identify and describe to the police. I know you didn't mean it."

I scooted over to him and pulled his arm around my shoulders. "You're not crazy. You're the least crazy—the only thing in this crazy world that is not crazy."

Gabe ran his fingers along my face and kissed me again. I wished we were in my kitchen again, doing dishes and kissing while my father was upstairs making an innocent phone call. I wished my heart could have the same love for my father and everything he'd ever done for me. Instead, I was here, running away from my dad and slowly beginning to realize that every word he'd ever said to me was a lie.

"I don't know what I'm supposed to think anymore," I said.

"We just have to work through all this in our heads.

Think about it logically and try to take the emotion out of it if we can. I don't know if it's possible."

His words made me want to cry. Emotion was all I could feel right now. Logic seemed impossible. Everything I knew was illogical at the moment.

"Let's think for a minute. Is it possible? Could he have done it? Not would he have, but could he have?"

I tried to take away the emotional stranglehold it all had on me, but I couldn't. Every possible way to think about it was laced with emotion. "I don't know," I said, shaking my head and wiping my tears.

"The police questioned him, right? He had an alibi?"

"Yes, he was at work all night. A coworker was his alibi—Simon Mercer. They were working together on an account and stayed in a hotel in the city. They were working on a proposal and had a presentation the next morning."

"So, there's really no way he could have come all the way back without Mercer noticing he was gone. Unless Mercer is lying for some reason? Unless he is in on it too?"

I shrugged. At this point, I wasn't sure of anything. I couldn't judge anyone's guilt or innocence. "I don't know."

"Is he a good friend of your dad's?"

"Not really. They just worked together. It wasn't anyone he hung out with. I don't even think he works there anymore."

"Let's find out." Gabe walked across the room and picked up his laptop. He typed as he walked back and was already doing a Google search on Simon Mercer when he sat down. He clicked on a link on the search page. "If this is the same guy, looks like he's with a consulting company—Warren, Engle. Is this him?"

I leaned over to look at his profile picture. "Yeah, that's him. He's Senior Vice President now?"

Gabe scrolled through his profile. "So he's the one that's going to help us get to the bottom of it."

"I can't just call him up and ask him."

Gabe clicked on his picture, enlarging it. "He's the key, though. We have to talk to him."

"How do we get a hold of him? Tomorrow is Sunday."

"Let's see if he's on Facebook." Gabe clicked away, and I sat back watching over his shoulder, feeling a small segment of peace knowing I was not in this alone. "Do you want to log in?" he asked me, handing over the laptop.

I logged in and handed it back to him.

"I think this is him. Current City: New York City. Employer: Warren, Engle. Let's send him a message."

"What would we say?"

"Hmm." Gabe clicked on the message button, and his fingers hovered over the keys as he thought.

"Here let me," I said, holding my hands out for the laptop. He handed it over, and I thought for a moment before I started typing. *Mr. Mercer, hello. My name is Ellie Cummings. I hope you remember me. My father is Daniel Cummings, and he used to work with you. I really need to talk to you urgently. Can you please call me back right away? Please.* I typed my cell phone number and then clicked the send button before I could rethink my words or change my mind. "I hope he's the type to get his messages sent directly to his phone. He might call back tonight or in the morning."

Gabe took the laptop from me and put it on the floor. He wrapped his arms around me and kissed the top of my head. "We'll figure this out, Ellie. If we don't hear from Mr. Mercer by tomorrow, we can go back and see your mom. Maybe she has more to tell you."

"No!" The thought of going back to see her, of seeing the

images she would project to me, was overwhelming. I didn't want to see her suffer like that again.

"Just think about it," he said. "Maybe we should get you to bed." He rose from the couch and held a hand out to me.

We walked into his room and I lay on his bed, my head on the fresh pillowcase, which had a sweet, flowery smell. Gabe sat on the floor next to me.

He ran his fingers through my hair once and kissed my forehead. He looked around his room and then started talking. "This was my grandmother's house. Grandmiller, I used to call her. My mom grew up here."

"Really?"

"Yeah, we moved in when I was in seventh grade."

"I think I remember when you moved in and started coming to school."

Gabe laughed. "Yeah. Goofy, overgrown hair and long skinny legs. You can't forget that."

His statement made me smile for an instant. "So, is that when you moved in here? With your grandmother?"

"Yeah. We were living in Atlantic City before that. Both my parents were working there at different casinos. My dad was a blackjack dealer, and my mom cleaned the hotel rooms. It was a good situation for her, because she didn't have to deal with people. She just cleaned up after they left. She's always been a neat freak, and cleaning creates order for her, which helps her, I think. It's why this place is always so clean."

"So, you lived there with them? Went to school there?"

"Yeah, we had a shabby little place there. Grandmiller would come visit a lot. Looking back now, I think she was really worried about them. I think my mom had pretty much stopped taking all her meds by then. She would tell Grandmiller that she was fine, that all she needed was my dad and me."

"Sounds like your grandmother loved you all so much."

"Yeah, Grandmiller was such a great woman, a force to be reckoned with. She stood five feet ten inches tall, and she took care of my mom for a long time. I think, Grandmiller said once, that she knew something was wrong with mom when she was little. She just wasn't your average happy girl. She was a real loner, hated play dates, and didn't want to spend time with friends."

"I'm sorry. That's so sad."

He nodded and then laid his head on the pillow beside me. "Grandmiller tried everything—diet, exercise, changing schools, different doctors, medications. Nothing seemed to work, she told me once. Mom was in and out of behavioral hospitals, given every diagnosis you could think of: OCD, depression, bipolar, schizophrenia, anxiety disorder, post traumatic stress. She met my dad in one of those hospitals. She'd been to so many—the private, expensive ones, the state ones. It was a state one where they met."

"I remember you told me that once. So, was your grandmother okay with their relationship?"

"Yeah, at first. I think because it was the only thing that had ever made my mom happy. Grandmiller told me that she'd never seen Mom smile like when she was around my dad.

"Once mom got out of the hospital, she and my dad would get together. Grandmiller or my granddad would drive her. But they were so young when they got married. I think that worried my grandparents. And then I was born, and things got pretty bad for my mom. She had to be hospitalized again, and I got bounced back and forth between my parents and my grandparents. When my parents moved to Atlantic City, that was hard because they were so far away. They worked at a few different casinos, and they had a hard time keeping a job, but they did their best, I guess. My grandparents were there a lot. They had a usual room they stayed in every time they visited. I would come stay here with my grandparents a lot too. And when my granddad died, Grandmiller would still come. She would take the bus sometimes or drive down the whole way. Nothing kept her away. Never gambled either. She was just there to take care of us. Busses filled with old ladies ready for slots, but never her."

"That must have been hard."

He shrugged. "I got used to it. It's all I knew. I think it helped me grow up fast, but I just always knew I had to help take care of my parents. They needed me. And it was okay for a while. I just stayed at home when they were at work—did my homework, did chores, watched TV. We were doing pretty well. And then, the summer before seventh grade, everything just got screwed up."

"What happened?"

He lifted his head off the pillow and looked down at his hands in his lap. "That's when my dad killed himself. Jumped off the top of the parking garage of one of the big casinos."

"I'm sorry, Gabe." I sat up from my position and dropped down to sit on the floor next to him.

"My mom . . ." he said, shaking his head. "I've never seen her like that. When she found out, they had to restrain her. Another ambulance came to take her away and made her check into the psych ward of the hospital. I had to go to child services until Grandmiller came. She stayed with me for a few months until they released Mom. That's when we moved here. The two of us took care of Mom. She was on some pretty heavy meds. Grandmiller helped us get settled here and helped Mom get on permanent disability. She just couldn't work anymore. Her social anxiety had gotten worse. She couldn't go anywhere."

"Did she start to get better?"

"A little. She started painting, and that helped. We did okay for a few years until Grandmiller died last year."

"Do you go see her sometimes? In the huaca?"

"Yeah, I do. Sometimes."

I reached over to grab his hand. "What did you do after she died?"

"It was hard. Mom didn't want to take her meds, and Grandmiller wasn't around to make her anymore. She left us some money after she died, so we were okay in that sense, but I was left alone to take care of Mom. It took us a while to get to where we are. We're doing okay," he said nodding his head. "We're doing okay right now."

I squeezed his hand. "You do so much."

"I can handle it now, but last year . . ." He shook his head. "I had to teach myself to drive. I started driving Grandmiller's old yellow Volvo around. No license. No insurance. But I had to drive. I had to get groceries. I rode my bike sometimes, but I couldn't always."

"And you never got caught?"

"No. I was lucky. I have my license now and insurance too, but it was a tough road after she died. Tough. I did my best."

"I think you did great. Your mom's doing okay now, right?"

"She never leaves the house. I don't know if I would call that okay, but I guess she could be worse. She could be back in a hospital. I don't think I could handle that."

"She's very lucky to have you, Gabe. You're lucky to have each other."

"You're going to be okay, Ellie. I know it's not easy.

Whatever you find out, whatever you're going to face tomorrow, the day after, I know you'll be okay."

"I don't know if I can handle it."

"You can handle way more than you think you can. You'll find that out." He kissed me one more time. "I'll let you get some rest now."

"Thanks. Thanks for talking to me—for everything."

He nodded and then was out the door.

•••••

It was eight thirty in the morning, and I didn't think that I'd had more than thirty minutes of consecutive sleep all night. I kept checking my cell phone to see if Mr. Mercer had called. Checking calls and checking the time—that's what I did all night long. I rolled over in Gabe's bed, his clean sheets wrapped all round my legs. I looked around at the room, wondering if I should get up or just stay in bed and hope to fall asleep for thirty more minutes.

He was probably awake, sitting up in the couch he'd slept on, doing something productive, thinking of possibilities, or searching for answers. He'd suggested going back to see my mom, to ask her for the answers I needed. I knew that was what I should do, but I was scared. I really didn't think I could face the answers I needed or face the emotions that would get me to those answers.

I sat up and pulled Gabe's sheets off me, letting them fall to the floor. They fell on top of my phone, which suddenly started ringing. I hurried for it before remembering that it could be my dad. Maybe he was calling me to see how my sleepover went. I slowly reached for it and looked at the number that was calling. It was a New York City number, one I didn't recognize.

"Hello?" I said in a raspy voice.

"Is this Ellie Cummings?"

"Yes, it is. Who's this?"

"It's Simon Mercer. You sent me a message last night."

"Yes, thank you for calling me back. It's such a relief to hear from you." I stood up, my anxiety forcing me from the comfort of Gabe's bed.

"Is everything okay? Is Daniel okay?"

"Yes, yes. Sorry if I made it sound like something was the matter. I just need to ask you an important question, if that's okay."

"Of course. It's been a long time since I've seen the two of you. How's your dad?"

"He's fine. Thanks."

"Good. Please give him my regards. So what can I answer for you?"

It had seemed so simple yesterday when I'd sent him the message, but now that I had him on the phone, I didn't know what to ask or what to say. "Well, I've just been thinking a lot about the day my mom died."

"I'm sorry, Ellie. I know that was a very hard time for you and your dad."

"Well, I was just wondering a few things about that night. I know you were working with my dad."

"Right. I remember that night. We were working on the Hunter-Avery account. It was a big one. Both our careers depended on it."

"So Dad was with you all night, right?"

"Yes. We were hunkered down at the Waldorf and had a long night."

"And he didn't go anywhere?"

"No. We worked through the night. I remember we both dozed off a few minutes here and there, but we worked through the night and finished the presentation. We were in the middle of presenting to Hunter-Avery when your father got the call the next morning." He paused for a minute. I didn't want to say anything or stop his thought flow. "So why all the questions now? Why are you wondering?"

I wasn't sure how to answer that, how to put into words my current suspicions—that I believed my father had killed my mother. "Just a lot of questions coming up, you know. Trying to get some questions answered for myself—I don't know, just to make sense of it all, I guess."

"There's no way to make sense of it, but I guess I understand. So they never found the person responsible?"

"No. The police are still working on it, I guess, but there are no leads."

"Yeah, I think the police were pretty thorough with what they had to work with. They questioned me thoroughly regarding your father's whereabouts. I can't believe that they could suspect him for a minute, but I suppose they had to rule out all possibilities."

"Yeah. What else did you tell them?"

"Just what I told you. We met that evening for dinner. Had room service in the hotel room while we worked through the proposal. We drank plenty of coffee and Cokes, hoping to pull the all-nighter."

"Right. Well, when you say you dozed off here and there, do you remember what time or how long?"

Mr. Mercer let out a long intake of breath. "No, Ellie. I can't remember those details. I know we never turned in for the night. I recall after dinner he said he needed a few minutes for a power nap and then he'd be good for the night. He slept on the couch for about twenty minutes or so while I finished a Coke. After he woke up, I took a little power nap myself. Then, we finished up the proposal and got ready for our meeting."

"And you're sure he never went anywhere? Anywhere at all?"

"No. Other than to take a shower in the morning, no. We worked together all night."

"Okay. Well, thank you. Thank you for calling me." I was grateful for his time even though I didn't feel he'd answered any of my questions. He had given me only more to think about.

"No problem, Ellie. I hope I was some sort of help. I want you to know I thought a lot of your mother from the few times I met her. She was really something, Ellie. Quite a loss to you and your father. I'm so sorry about that."

"Thank you," I said, the emotion catching in my throat.

"Please tell your father I hope he's doing well. I really enjoyed working with him and miss it, but I like my new company. It's going well for me."

"I will. Thank you."

"Good-bye, Ellie. You have my number now in case you think of anything else, right?"

"Yes, it's on my caller ID. And will you please call me if you remember anything else?"

"Certainly. Take care of yourself, Ellie."

"Thank you, Mr. Mercer."

My phone started buzzing from a text just as I heard a soft knock at the door.

"It's me," Gabe whispered through the door. "Are you awake?"

I walked toward the door, my phone still in my hand. I hadn't checked the text. I had guessed it was probably my dad, and I couldn't read words that he'd written, not now with all the uncertainty that loomed around me. All of Mr. Mercer's words confirmed my father had not done it, but why did I still have a sick feeling in my stomach?

"Morning," I said to Gabe as he shuffled in and closed the door behind him. His hair was standing up in the back, and his T-shirt was more wrinkled than usual. "Mr. Mercer called me."

Gabe sunk onto the bed. "What did he say?"

"He said that my dad was with him all night. They stayed up most of the night. Each of them took like a twenty-minute power nap, but that was it." I went to sit next to him. Both of us on his bed, side by side. "My dad texted me." I handed the phone to Gabe.

"Good morn, El. When are you coming home?" he read.

His question caused an inadvertent shiver to travel up my back. "Can you tell him I don't know?"

Gabe texted my reply.

"I don't know what to do, Gabe. If Mr. Mercer is telling the truth, which I think he is, then my father didn't do anything and I'm horrible to suspect him."

Gabe's hand went to my knee, and he squeezed. "You're not horrible. You know what you saw. You can't help but suspect."

"Maybe I was wrong. Maybe she was wrong."

"I don't know," Gabe said, giving me one more squeeze before he crossed his arms in front of him. "I think you should go see her again."

I shook my head. The thought of going to see her had once been the highlight of my day, what I wanted more than anything. But not anymore. It's what I most dreaded. "No. I think it will just confuse me more. Mr. Mercer said my dad didn't leave his sight for more than the few minutes it took him to shower."

"And while Mercer was sleeping."

"A power nap," I countered. "You can't drive an hour away, kill someone, and drive back all in the time someone is having a power nap."

"How can he be sure it was just a power nap? He can't know for sure he only slept twenty minutes. What if it was longer?"

I shook my head. "No. No, Gabe." Why was he trying to convince me? Why did it matter so much to him that I believed my father had killed her? Quickly, my mind flashed back to my initial thoughts after seeing the images. The huaca was lying. It was all a hallucination somehow engineered by Gabe. I didn't know what to think anymore, who to trust. Everything in my life seemed wrong and convoluted. Maybe what I needed was to see my dad again, to reconfirm his love for me. How could I eradicate a lifetime of love and care with a few images that lasted only seconds? "I should probably go home."

"I don't think you should," Gabe said, standing up. "How do you know it's safe? That he's safe?"

"He's my dad, Gabe."

"I know, but yesterday you were scared and so convinced."

"That's before I talked to Mr. Mercer. My dad's alibi is airtight. That's what the police concluded. He didn't do it." I walked around Gabe's room, collecting my socks, hoodie, and shoes. I took the phone from his hands and walked toward the door. "I think I should go home."

"What about last night? The news. I know what you were thinking, Ellie. I was thinking it too."

"That's a coincidence. He had nothing to do with that."

"I really don't want you to go back home yet. Not until we know for sure."

Each of Gabe's arguments was having the opposite effect he was hoping for. Each word he said solidified what I knew, what I should have known all along—my father was innocent. He was guilty only through a malfunctioning artifact or my misguided imagination or a teenage boy's machinations. I didn't know anymore. I just knew that I needed to be home, to see my dad, and be reassured by his hug and by the way he called me *El*.

"Let's go see her one more time."

"No, Gabe! No. I don't know why you're trying so hard to persuade me not to go home, but I'm going home. Do you want to take me or should I call my dad to pick me up?"

Gabe sunk his hands into his jean pockets. "You're acting like I'm the bad guy here. I'm trying to protect you."

"I don't need you to protect me. I need you to be my friend."

"Your friend? So, after all this, I'm back to friend status?"

"That's not what I mean." I should have walked over and held him. He was more than a friend. In the few weeks I'd spent with him, he'd become the best friend I'd ever had. He had quickly superseded the years' worth of friendship with Sarah. Gabe knew inside my heart; he knew me for my real self. I should have explained that to him, but at that point, I just wanted to go home, for the vindication of my father that I knew I would instantly feel the second I saw him. "Can you take me home, please?"

He nodded and led the way out the door. He grabbed his hoodie off the floor by the door and put it on, pulling his hood over his head. Silently, he walked out to the car and opened my door. I slid in, trying to think of the right words to tell him so he wouldn't be mad or feel sad, or whatever it was he was feeling.

"Thanks for letting me stay the night," I said as he backed out of the driveway. "I think it's what I needed to clear my head. I know my dad didn't do this and couldn't do this. Whatever I saw, it's not right."

His jaw was locked in place, and all he did was nod as he turned the corner.

Silence enveloped us the remaining three miles to my house. I knew I should show more gratitude toward Gabe and what he'd done for me last night, but I just wanted to get home.

A block before we reached my house, Gabe turned to me. "Can I at least come in with you and make sure everything is okay?"

I knew he was referring to my dad. He wanted to make sure he wouldn't hurt me. At first the thought angered me—Gabe still believed my dad was capable of hurting me and my mom. But I didn't want to argue with him, so I nodded.

Gabe pulled into the driveway, and we both walked silently up the path to my house. I opened the door, and Gabe followed me inside. I wondered if my dad was still upstairs, but I heard him moving around in the garage. We walked through the kitchen, and I noticed Dad had never turned on the dishwasher and probably hadn't cleaned out the fridge.

"Thanks for dropping me off," I said to Gabe, who was leaning against the counter, his hood still on.

"Can I stick around for a little while? Make sure your dad's home."

"I think he's in the garage." I walked through the kitchen, and Gabe followed me toward the garage. Dad was stacking boxes against a shelf. "Hey, Dad."

He jumped a bit when he heard me and dropped the box he'd been holding. "Sorry, El. I didn't hear you come in." He left the box on the floor and walked over to us. "Hi, Gabe. What are you two doing this morning?"

"Gabe picked me up from Sarah's. He was just dropping me off."

"That was nice. Thanks, Gabe."

Gabe nodded and then started looking around the garage, at nothing in particular.

"So are things better with Sarah now?" he asked.

I nodded, turning my gaze to the ground.

"You sure?" he asked, bending down to look at me.

"A little, you know. It'll take some time still."

"But you spent the night at her house. How did that come about?"

"We've just been talking at school more, texting a little," I lied.

"Don't let her hurt you, El. If she's just going to start doing the same stuff again."

"I'll be careful, Dad."

He nodded, frowning. "Are you two going to go out or anything?" my dad asked, his gaze turning away from us and toward the box he'd dropped on the floor.

"No," I said quickly, not turning to Gabe. "I want to shower and stuff. I didn't have time at Sarah's." As each moment passed, I gained small shreds of certainty. Here was my dad cleaning and doing what he did best—keeping order.

He was cleaning out the garage—what normal dads do, what my dad normally did. How could I have let yesterday's thoughts infiltrate my mind and dominate my night? He was no killer. He used knives to trim fat off of chicken before grilling it. The idea of a knife in his hand—the hand that I knew—to inflict pain on anyone was simply untrue, despicable even.

"Well, make sure to get some breakfast if you didn't eat anything." Always the purveyor of food, the one who knew what's for dinner that evening, and who knew exactly what I would be eating for lunch each day. That was my dad. How could I have believed anything else?

I looked at Gabe, his eyes on the ground of the garage. It was an ugly gray color my father picked out a few years ago, a color my mom had been opposed to. I never understood the argument. Who paints the garage floor anyway?

Those quick observations—all of which occurred within minutes of arriving home—helped me remember who my dad was. He wasn't the killer the images told me he was. He was my dad, who cleaned and cooked and fed me.

My dad walked back to the spot where I'd found him. "Well, if you want to go out later on, that's fine with me. I'll probably stay here and clean things out for a while. I've been meaning to."

"Okay, well. I'll see you later." I turned away from Dad and went back into the kitchen. Gabe followed me silently.

"You feel okay?" he asked me after I'd closed the garage door.

"Yeah, I do. I'm okay." I took a few steps into the kitchen, and I let the sight of the unfinished dishes slide. "I don't know what I saw yesterday. I can't be sure, but he didn't do it. He's my dad. My dad."

"I know, Ellie. I didn't see what you saw. I don't know. But if you even think what you saw could be right, we need to go again. We need to see her again."

"No," I said. "I can't. I already know what's true. Whatever images I saw—they're wrong. They can't be true. I can't go back there."

"It's the only way to know for sure, Ellie."

"No," I said. I pointed to my chest. "This is the only way I can know for sure. In here, I know he couldn't do it. He didn't do it. Yesterday, my mind was clouded. I don't know. Gabe, it's wrong. It just is. I know that now."

Gabe took a step toward me and reached for my elbow. "I just want you to be safe."

"I am safe. It's my dad. I've been safe with him since the day I was born."

He nodded, quiet for now, but I wasn't sure he was convinced. "Can I see you later, then?"

"I don't know. I feel like I need to stay here." Gabe's presence here or my presence in his house seemed unthinkable to me. Either one just served as a reminder of what I wanted to forget—those images. Those images that were both horrible and untrue. I wanted to stay as far from them as possible, and home seemed like the best place for me to stay. Away from Gabe and the images his huaca provoked.

"Can I call you later?"

"Yeah," I said.

He walked toward the door and opened it. "Are we okay?" he asked. "I don't think we're okay."

I nodded. "It's just been a long, hard day. Things will be better tomorrow at school."

"Ellie, I love you," he said, leaning against the doorjamb. "I love you, and I want you to be safe."

It was the first time he'd said it. I'm sure he wished it had been different—that's what I wished—but it wasn't. It was in my doorway, with me wanting him to leave, after a fitful night spent thinking my dad was a killer. It was the last place and time that I wanted to hear those words. And it certainly wasn't a time or place in which I could repeat them, even though I felt them. But when I did tell him those words, I wanted it to be the emotion I felt most at the moment. That wasn't how I felt—too many emotions were competing for priority.

"Thanks for everything, Gabe. You did so much for me last night, and I know that I haven't been very appreciative. But I have so much going through my mind. I know things will be better tomorrow after I've had a chance to sort through everything."

He swallowed hard and then nodded. I knew that my lack of acknowledgment and return of his sentiment had hurt him, but those words needed to come at a different time and in a different place. I leaned in and kissed him on the lips, hoping he could at least sense my feelings for him.

"I'll call you later," he said.

"Okay, bye."

SIXTEEN

I THOUGHT OF GABE MOST OF THE DAY. I thought of how he'd helped me last night when I thought my whole world was over, of how everything I thought about anymore was somehow correlated to him. The huaca, the images pounding through my mind most of the day, the doubts I ignored, which still lingered in my stomach—all of that came from Gabe. He was the central figure of my life at the moment. I didn't even think about Sarah anymore and didn't really care.

How was it that one boy had sequestered my every thought, had made me doubt my father? The man who made me turkey wraps for lunch and grated zucchini for bread just because it was my favorite—that was my dad. He did everything for me. Sometimes I felt like I was his whole life. Everything he did other than work revolved around me. And Gabe—in a matter of seconds, really, if you count the seconds the images flashed through my mind—was able to get me to doubt my father and wonder whether he had killed my mother. But my dad had loved her—loved her still—so much so he couldn't even talk about her.

Gabe's powers, if you could call them that, had possessed me and dominated my mind. How had he done that? Was he really what others said of him, haunted house and all? But that all seemed ridiculous to me, unbelievable. Even now.

I cleaned my room slowly throughout the morning, thoughts of Gabe never leaving my mind. He sent me a few texts, but I didn't reply. There were too many doubts clouding my mind to make way for any logical thought or idea. My trust for Gabe had been pure, untainted the night before. Now all I could think about was that he'd bewitched me, making me see images that weren't true and that told me my father had done something I knew he couldn't.

I dreaded Monday morning—school and having to see Gabe again. He would know something was wrong and would ask why I had ignored his calls and texts.

Dad was in the garage, organizing again. I wasn't sure I could face him, either. I felt he would read the guilt on my face and see how I'd betrayed him with my doubts, my thoughts.

"Hey, Dad," I said, poking my head in the garage.

"Oh, Ellie." He turned toward me, dropping a handful of objects to the floor by his feet. "Just trying to get everything organized. It's been needing it for a long time, and I figured it's finally time."

"Looks great, Dad." I glanced around the garage, noticing that not much had changed, but I didn't tell him that. "Want some help?"

"No, no. It won't take me much longer." He slid a lid on a large plastic tub and pressed down on it. "So what are you going to do with the rest of your day?"

"Don't know," I said, slipping onto an old bar stool that Dad kept saying he was going to throw out.

"Are you going to get together with Gabe?"

"Probably not. I don't know."

Dad wiped his hands up and down his jeans. "He seems like a good guy, El," he said, walking over to me. "I know we haven't really had a chance to talk since dinner last night, but I like him. He seems real, you know. And I know you've struggled with Sarah and her recent not-very-realness. Gabe's real—I can tell that. He's good."

Those aspects of Gabe—his being good and his being real had all been evident to me early on, and they were what drew me to him. But even that now seemed dimmed in light of the doubts that abounded with each thought of Gabe.

"Yeah, I know, Dad, but I'm just not sure about him."

He walked over to me, wiping a small bead of sweat from his brow. "What do you mean?"

I shrugged my shoulders and shook my head. "Don't know."

"Tell me what it is."

"Don't you think he's a little strange? Just a little?"

"Oh, El. That's so relative. So he doesn't dress like the guys around here. You don't care about stuff like that."

"It's not that. It's hard to explain."

"Well, you know better than I do. I trust your judgment." He brushed the back of his head and walked toward the door. "I think I'm going to go wash up. Feel free to invite Gabe over again any time. I approve."

I smiled as he walked away. I followed behind him into the kitchen. He had spent the better part of the night cleaning out the garage, and he was still wearing the same clothes from yesterday. Dedicated father—cleaning the garage, making dinner. I kept telling myself that to brush away the small but still-lingering doubts that remained even after Gabe had left.

I went to grab a bowl for cereal. Chex cereal for lunch on weekends. Mom and I would often have that when Dad had to work or was out of town. The bowls in the dishwasher were still dirty, and I remembered that Dad had said he was going to clean out the fridge and start the dishwasher yesterday. I guessed he got caught up with cleaning out the garage that he hadn't gotten to it. I opened the refrigerator door and started pulling out Tupperware containers of old leftovers. The soup from last week, the chicken no one was going to eat, the pasta I made that hadn't turned out very well—I dumped them all out in the garbage and finished loading the dishwasher. After I turned it on, I sat at the kitchen table to eat my cereal. Chex just wasn't the same without my mom, but I ate two bowls, remembering I hadn't had any breakfast.

Gabe called me but I didn't answer my phone. Things weren't quite sorted out in my head yet. I was just beginning to feel like myself again—like my dad was my dad and my life was my life. Haunting images of a killer, one whose face and hands I recognized, were just beginning to get vague, hazy, and I needed more time for them to completely dissipate. A few minutes later, Gabe texted me: *How are you doing? Call me.*

After cereal, I went upstairs to find something to do. I played around on my phone for a little while and then headed back downstairs. Dad had finished his shower and was doing some work on his laptop in his room. Part of me did want to be with Gabe, but back in the moment when we'd first kissed, when there was so much to look forward to in the world. Now, everything in my world seemed tainted, and I didn't want to be a part of anything.

I headed back into the kitchen and decided I should take

out the garbage bag I'd filled earlier. The combined smell of leftover chicken and pasta was permeating the room, and my Chex-filled stomach didn't much care for it. I left it on the front step and figured I'd walk it to the outside garbage can later.

I wondered if Gabe would text me again. I knew that I owed him an explanation, but my phone was upstairs and I didn't want to know if he'd called. I didn't really know what I would say yet. I dropped into a chair in the living room and closed my eyes. None of it made sense. Two men that I felt I knew with my heart and whom I trusted—both of them couldn't be right. One of them had to be deceiving me, but I didn't know which one. Time and blood had to win this contest—I had to trust my dad. He was, after all, my dad. Gabe was *just* Gabe, and I'd really only known him a few months. After that thought came and went, guilt washed over me. He wasn't just Gabe. He was more than just Gabe, and that was perhaps the hardest part of it all.

I squeezed my eyes tighter, thinking I would hear the familiar announcement of my phone upstairs, but I didn't. The sound of the doorbell seconds later quelled the thoughts of an impending text or phone call.

I knew it was Gabe before I opened the door. His curly brown hair was ruffled, his eyes were wide.

"Ellie, you're okay."

"Hi. Yeah, I'm okay. Why . . . ?" Realization started slowly to form. He thought something had happened to me. That my dad . . .

"When you didn't answer the phone or my texts," Gabe said, taking a step inside, and I stepped aside to let him, "I just . . . Why didn't you answer the phone?"

"I didn't know what to say, Gabe. I'm just so confused."

"I know, Ellie, but couldn't you have at least texted me

something? I've been scared. I almost called the police before I came over."

"The police!" I hushed my tone and turned around to see if my dad had come down yet. "What?" I turned back to Gabe, my heart racing. I took a second to calm down. "You were going to call the police on my dad?"

"I don't know, Ellie. What was I supposed to do when you didn't answer?"

I sighed, realizing that I shouldn't have ignored his calls or texts, not when just the night before we'd thought . . .

"I'm sorry, Gabe. I feel like I've been saying that a lot, but I am."

Gabe grabbed my arm and pulled me into an embrace. "I don't know, Ellie, but something just doesn't feel right. Something's wrong here. I know it. What you saw was real. Your mother is trying to tell you something."

His arms should have felt soothing, comforting—what I needed at that moment. But they didn't, not when his hug was accompanied by his words, words that accused my father.

"Gabe, please stop saying that. My dad is upstairs." I pulled him into the kitchen, away from the bottom of the stairs. I leaned in close and whispered, "Mr. Mercer said he was with my dad all night. There is no way he could have done this."

"But what if there was a way? A way we haven't thought about yet. What if you're in danger?"

"I'm not! He's my dad. I've been safe with him all my life. I'm safe with him now."

"Ellie, I know he's your dad, but—"

"No, Gabe. There are no buts. He's my dad, and that is all."

"Okay. Look, I just wanted to make sure you're okay. I'll

leave, but I don't think it's asking too much for you to text me back if I text you. At least that's what friends do."

"You're right. I'm sorry. I will."

"Bye, Ellie. See you tomorrow."

"Okay, bye."

I watched Gabe drive away, thinking that could have gone a lot better. I was sure I should have done more, but that was all I felt capable of at the moment.

SEVENTEEN

THE GARBAGE BAG I'D BROUGHT OUT earlier still sat by the front steps. I took it to the side of the house and lifted the lid of our large garbage can. It was almost full, and I noticed that Dad had stuffed a garbage bag in there, filled with paper and a few plastic bottles. He was always forgetting to recycle the bottles and papers. It wasn't the first time I'd fished out one of his bags. It drove him crazy. He said I was a little too obsessed with recycling.

I took the bag into the garage to sort out the items that could be recycled, tossing the bottles into a bin in the garage. There was a large stack of folded papers and envelopes, and I figured they could be thrown in with the newspapers and assorted paper. But before I threw them out, something about them caught my eye. I'd seen these envelopes before. They were all letters addressed to Rick Thorton.

Amid those envelopes, I saw a small, plastic baggie, smaller than a sandwich bag. Through the clear plastic, I could see three small, white pills. I pulled out the little baggie and stared at the small, white pills. They looked like aspirin, but their appearance in the little baggie piqued my interest and I spilled the three pills onto my hand. Each pill had the letters R-O-C-H-E carved on it with the number two. The other side had a scored line down the middle.

Quickly, I abandoned the garbage bag on the ground of the garage and raced upstairs to my room with the stack of letters and pills in hand. I opened my laptop and did a Google search for ROCHE. The search was not as quick as I had hoped. I had to scroll through two pages of possibilities. I revised the search to include a description of the pills—their color and markings. After scrolling through a few more pages, I clicked on a link that explained their color, the word ROCHE, and the number 2. It described the pills as Rohypnol—*ruffies.* I knew what ruffies were. Every teenage girl I knew had been warned about ruffies. We'd been told to watch our drinks and never leave them unattended. It's called the date rape drug because it makes people fall asleep and not remember once they wake up. I didn't know what my dad would be doing with them or why he was throwing them away. He had wanted someone asleep, I guess. Not to rape them, but why?

It was all too much for me to take in right away; I couldn't think straight. So I put the pills back in the little bag and stuffed it in my pocket. I wanted to look through the stack of envelopes and folded letters, but my dad was in his room down the hall. More than anything, I wanted to get out of the house—a place that had previously meant safety and comfort. Now, it just meant secrecy and confusion. I didn't know anything anymore. I grabbed my shoulder bag and quietly padded down the stairs. I would text my dad later.

I squealed my tires as I pulled away from the house. As

I drove to Gabe's house, I tried not to think too much. I didn't want to draw any conclusions until I'd had a chance to think about everything. I quickly texted my dad and told him I was going to Gabe's. Then, I turned off my phone. I didn't want to hear a response or hear anything from him at the moment.

Gabe answered the door quickly after I'd knocked. He seemed surprised to see me but happy about it too.

"Hey, can I talk to you?"

He pulled me inside. "Yeah. You okay?"

"I don't know, Gabe. I found some weird stuff at my house." I sat down on the couch, and he came over to sit beside me.

"What is it?"

"Some stuff my dad threw away. Yesterday, maybe." I pulled the baggie out of my pocket. "Ruffies."

"How do you know?" he asked, taking them out of my hand. He turned the bag over to examine it.

"I did a Google search."

"Are you sure? They could be anything."

"The description I read online described it exactly. They're ruffies."

"Do you think he's used them on someone?"

I shrugged. I didn't want to think about it or admit the thought that had come to my mind the instant I saw the word *ruffies* online. "Mercer. I think he used them on Mercer."

Gabe nodded, still staring at the baggie in his hand. I knew he'd been thinking about it too but didn't want to say it.

"I don't know what to think, Gabe. How can I think that about my dad? He's my dad." My voice started to crack, and I knew the tears I'd been holding back all day were coming. I'd been able to keep them at bay by using all my energy to keep denying the accusations in my mind and to keep finding details around my house that would support his innocence. I'd almost had myself convinced, via the tiny, mundane things he did for me every day. But there was no denying it anymore. Not with what my mom had shown me and the strange items he'd been trying to dispose of—all of it was evidence that he had something to hide, something to fear.

I quickly wiped my face with my sleeve and cleared my throat. I knew it was okay to cry. Of course it was when your whole life was falling apart, when everything you thought you knew was wrong. But I wanted to be strong for my mom. I wanted to find the truth for her because whatever I was going through was nothing compared to the fright she must have felt that night. To believe one thing and then, in a matter of minutes, have the person you thought you knew the most—loved the most—turn on you and hold your neck until you couldn't breathe anymore was terrifying.

Gabe put his arm around me and kissed the top of my head. "Let's go see her again. Maybe you can get some answers. We don't know anything for sure yet."

I knew he was right. I should have gone to her yesterday when he'd first suggested it, but at the time I'd just wanted to shut out those thoughts. Having those thoughts, allowing them entrance into my mind, had seemed a form of betrayal. But it wasn't. *I* hadn't betrayed anyone. I nodded and rose from the couch.

Silently, we walked through the kitchen to the basement. I knew the routine and had it down completely. Other times, the actions would have been accompanied by happier feelings, greater expectations. I didn't even know how to categorize the emotions that accompanied me then.

I watched Gabe do what he'd done many times for me before. He filled the tray with blood and closed the drawer. He did it with no hesitation, no demonstration of pain, and I knew he meant those words he had spoken to me earlier that day. He did love me. At that moment, I held on to that knowledge. I clung to it.

Quickly, we were in Hanan Pacha, and I could see my mother straight ahead. She sat at the water's edge, serenely, quietly. I wished I could just stay there and watch her instead of intensifying the moment by making her conjure up those images.

She turned around when I was a few feet away. Her smile was instant, and I wondered if she knew why I was there. We clasped hands, and I was wondering if she would start off with happy memories or if she would jump right in to what I needed to know. Immediately, the tears started streaming down my cheeks. They'd been summoned by the motley of emotion I was feeling—fear, love, sorrow. I missed my mom more at that moment than any other time. She was in front of me, holding my hands, but not really. And while I wanted the moment to be akin to a happy reunion, it wasn't. It was a preamble to a horror show I had no choice but to watch.

I saw her seated on the bed looking through a stack of letters, opening them frantically and pulling out letter after letter. Then she was on her laptop, doing a Google search, looking for something. Tears are what I saw next—tears from her beautiful brown eyes, now puffy and red. She was seated on our living room couch, alone, in the dark. In the next image, I saw her arguing and pleading with my dad. His face was hard, jaw set, eyes fastened on her—a way I'd never seen him look at her before. I almost didn't recognize him. In an instant, his countenance changed. His look softened, and he was the one pleading with her. She nodded at the words he gave her, a small semblance of explanation—whatever it was appeased her for a moment. He left with his workbag, and she was left alone to her tears and sadness.

The next image interrupted that sadness, and she was lying in bed, staring at the ceiling. The door opened, and my dad came in. Her face registered surprise at his arrival. She seemed relieved though and sat up in bed, looking at him expectantly. He approached her, but instead of soothing her agitation, he fed it. Her surprise turned to confusion, which was quickly replaced by fear, the same fear I'd seen in images before. I still saw it sometimes when I closed my eyes. That is when she began crying out for help. He then pulled out the knife, and that is when the images shut down, stopped entirely. I felt the familiar pull against my waist and the painful thrust to the basement floor that my body knew but was still unaccustomed to.

I pulled myself up to a kneeling position, ignoring the pain in my knees and shoulder. Gabe sat up next to me.

"You okay?" he asked.

"Yeah, you?"

"I'm fine. What did you see?"

"I don't know. It was so fast. I saw my mom and dad. They were arguing about something. She was looking through some bills, the mail, or something like that. She was mad at him, and he was explaining something, then he left. He came back later, and that's when he attacked her."

None of it made sense to me, but how could I make sense of such a senseless action as killing someone you loved?

"She confronted him about something, maybe," Gabe said.

"The letters!" I pulled myself to my feet and ran up the basement steps. Gabe was right behind me. I'd left the stack of letters and envelopes on the couch in Gabe's living room.

"What are those?" Gabe asked.

"I found them in the garbage with the pills. They're old letters for some guy that used to live in our house, I think. We get his mail all the time, and Dad sends it back to the post office. His name is Rick Thorton."

I unfolded one letter and studied it. "I don't know why Dad has held onto these for so long or why he never returned them."

"What do they say?" Gabe asked.

I closed my eyes for an instant and could see the stack in her hands; she had been reading them, searching them. It was the same stack of letters. I opened my eyes and looked back down at them. They were typed and were short letters, all addressed to Rick.

One of them said: "Hey, Rick. I'm an old friend from Clearwater. I was wondering how you're doing?" The next one said: "Hey, Rick. We really need to catch up soon. Let's get together for coffee. I'll be in touch."

I handed them over to Gabe so he could read them as I unfolded the next one. It read: "Hey, Rick. I see you've come a long way from Florida. Nice house."

"Who is Rick and why does my dad care about these letters?"

Gabe took the next one from my hand. "So, you said your dad told you these were from somebody who used to live in your house."

"Yeah, it's been a few months. He said that this Thorton guy maybe forgot to get all his mail forwarded. My dad said if any more letters came, to put them aside and he would take them to the post office and tell them nobody lived here by that name."

"Some of these are postmarked almost a year ago. So he just kept them all, instead of taking them to the post office?"

"I guess. I never thought anything of it. I mean, we get

mail for other people too, every once in a while. It's no big deal."

"Do you remember a lot of these letters?" Gabe asked.

"Not a lot. Every once in a while."

"There's no return address," Gabe said, turning the envelope over in his hands.

I opened the next one. It said: "So, Rick. Did you hear what happened to Loretta Maxwell?"

Gabe got up and walked into the kitchen. He came back with his laptop. He typed in "Rick Thorton" and "Clearwater, Florida." Several results came up, and I read over his shoulder after he clicked on one.

"Rick Thorton, age 17, is wanted for questioning in the death of his foster mother, Loretta Maxwell. Her body was found by a foster daughter after school. Maxwell had been stabbed several times. Rick Thorton was not named as a suspect, but police are wanting to question him. Witnesses say they saw Thorton in the downtown area of Clearwater, Florida, around five o'clock that afternoon, but police were unable to locate him.

"Thorton's biological mother, Jessica Thorton, is currently serving time for a drug charge, and Thorton has been in foster care for six months and has been living with Loretta Maxwell for five weeks."

Gabe clicked to go back and scrolled down for another story. This time, a small picture popped up of Rick Thorton. Right away, I knew it was him. I covered my mouth to keep back the gasp that I forced myself to swallow. The picture was over twenty-five years old, but I just knew. I recognized the dark brown eyes—my eyes. The picture showed his square jaw, the nose we shared, and the lips set in a straight line that he called his smile. Twenty-five years did nothing to disguise him—the man I'd lived with my whole life, the one whose face I looked into almost every day.

Gabe squeezed my hand. Even he could tell it was my father. He shut his laptop and slid it to the floor. He put both arms around me as I melted into him.

Everything I ever thought I knew about my family was a lie. I didn't know one solid truth about myself.

"Ellie, I'm sorry."

I cried, wetting his shirt, not holding back the sobs that I usually kept private. Even when my mother died, I didn't let myself cry like this in front of others. Except my dad. He was the only one who'd ever seen me cry like this.

Gabe's hold grew tighter with each of my sobs. I grabbed his shirt and squeezed my fists against his chest. I didn't want to think about anything. Any thoughts that came to my mind, I quickly converted to physical actions through the tightening of my fists, the biting of my lip, and the kicking of my legs.

I don't know how long we sat there. Gabe didn't say anything. Slowly, my tears tapered off, the trembling of my shoulders slowed, and my thoughts began to clear. I thought about what I'd just seen. The old image of my dad, of Rick Thorton. Was he my dad? Who was he?

It wasn't just a matter of could he have killed my mom. Who was he? Where did he come from? And what did he do before I ever met him? I knew that more answers were at my fingertips, but I couldn't look at the computer screen, much less search for more about my father. I knew enough. I now knew that he was never who I thought he was. I felt with great certainty that he had killed my mother and possibly one other woman. I didn't think I would ever know for sure the extent of his crimes.

"I'm so sorry," Gabe said into my hair.

I wiped my nose and pulled away. "It's hard to believe."

"Do you think your mom found out about this?"

I nodded. "I think she was looking at these letters in the images I saw."

"What about Mercer? He said he was with your dad all night."

"The ruffies."

"So he drugged Mercer and then drove back to your house?"

"I don't know what to do." I pulled myself off the couch and walked to the window. I looked at my watch. "He's probably wondering when I'll be home. I can't go back there. I can't see him."

"You have to stay here." Gabe rose and came to stand behind me. Gently, he put his hands on my shoulders. "You have to stay here, Ellie."

"Will you text him and tell him I'm staying at Sarah's?"

Gabe squeezed my shoulders and walked over to the couch where I'd left everything. He picked up my phone, and I could hear Gabe quietly pressing the buttons, giving life to the lie I was sending him. The lie I needed to give. I didn't know what I was going to do the next day.

Minutes later, I heard the familiar beep that let me know his response had come. It felt eerie, strange that I was still communicating with this man.

"He says, 'You have school tomorrow. Are you sure?' "

I didn't want to communicate with him, didn't want to tell him anything, but I had to buy myself time to figure out what I was going to do. "Can you tell him that we have a big project due tomorrow and that Sarah and I want to finish it up tonight?"

Gabe obliged and typed in the words. "He said okay. Do you want him to bring you anything?" Gabe talked as he sent the next text. "I just said you'd borrow some clothes from Sarah."

"Okay." I went over to him as he tucked my phone back into my bag. "What now?"

"We have to call the police. I don't know what we're going to tell them. But, Ellie, I'm scared. I'm scared for you. You're in danger, and I don't want anything to happen to you."

"We have to give them proof. Find as much proof as we can and take it to them. These letters." I picked up the stack of letters and moved them from one hand to the other as I spoke. "The pills. I don't know what else."

"Are they going to believe he drove all the way to the city, met with Mercer for a few hours and drove back to Westfield and then back to the city—all without Mercer waking up?"

"EZ Pass," I said just as soon as the thought came into my mind. "EZ Pass. His car has EZ Pass on it. We get monthly statements. He still has them all, I think. He keeps everything."

"You think he still has those statements?"

"Yeah, and they show the date and time the car passes through each location. It would probably have the time he went through the tunnel."

"We have to get them," Gabe said. "What time does he go to work?"

"He usually leaves the house by six thirty."

"We have to go tomorrow. As soon as he goes to work."

The idea of going back there started to sink in slowly; what I knew now gave my home a whole new meaning. It was no longer a place of safety from the outside world, a haven where I'd felt loved my entire life. It was now somewhere shrouded with lies, danger at every corner—a place wherein I could die. Nothing was safe there anymore, but I had to go. For her.

Lifelong love doesn't die easily even when you learn something awful. I tried to suppress whatever feelings I still carried for him and put them away for examination another day, another time. I tried to imagine that he was not my dad, Daniel Cummings, but rather Rick Thorton—a stranger, a man from Clearwater, Florida, with whom I had no connection. Gathering evidence to use against him would be easier that way.

Gabe came over to me and sat on the couch next to me. "Ellie, you're so strong. How are you dealing with all of this?"

"Thanks for being here for me. I don't know what I would do. I would feel so alone."

"You'll never be alone, Ellie. You'll always have me, for as long as you let me."

"I love you, Gabe. I've been wanting to say that to you. I was waiting for all this to end to tell you. But there's never the right time, the right place, to tell you I love you too."

Gabe put his arm around me and pulled me close. "It doesn't matter when you say it to me. It's always the right time, the right place. I will always love you, Ellie. I won't let anything happen to you."

♦♦♦♦♦

I told Gabe I wasn't hungry, but he went to the kitchen to make dinner. He suggested I lie down on the couch and take a nap, but I couldn't sleep. I wasn't much of a nap-taker to begin with, and all the thoughts going through my mind made it impossible.

I tried for a solid five minutes before going into the kitchen to help Gabe. He was browning ground beef in a pan. "What are you making?"

"Chili. Does that sound okay?"

"Yeah. Want me to help?"

"Sure. Will you work on this? I want to go talk to my mom and tell her you'll be staying here."

"Do you think she'll be okay with it?"

"Of course. I just think I need to tell her everything, you know. See what she thinks we should do."

I nodded and took the wooden spoon he held in his hand. I turned the beef over in the pan, something I'd done many times before. I didn't know why seeing the beef cooking made me start crying again. I knew it wasn't the chopped onions Gabe had thrown in with the beef.

It was the simple act of cooking beef—something I'd seen my dad do many times. I'd seen him shape meatballs, meatloaf, and hamburger patties with his hands. I'd seen him cook beef for tacos, lasagna, chili . . .

Maybe this would be something I'd experience with everything. Everything I would do for the rest of my life now seemed tainted. There would be memories of time spent with him in every corner, in every circumstance. All of those moments were fake. They were lies. My entire life was nothing more than a pretense.

Gabe came in a few minutes later with his mom behind him.

"Hi, Ellie," she said. "How are you holding up? Gabe told me about your dad. I'm so sorry." She came over to me and put her arm around me. "You know you can stay here for as long as you need. Gabe doesn't mind the couch."

"Thank you. I don't know what I'm going to do."

Gabe took the wooden spoon and finished up the beef.

His mom looked at me and smiled. "I think it's time to get the police involved. Gabe said you have some letters. Turn them over to the police and let them continue the investigation."

I nodded. "I know I need to, but I just want to wait until tomorrow. I need to get those EZ pass statements. I need to see them before I can really believe all this." Part of me was still in denial. It was probably the part that was keeping me sane up to this point. I just felt that I couldn't be absolutely certain he was a killer until I saw the EZ Pass statements. Those would prove he had driven back and forth. They were the absolute proof and, until I saw them, I couldn't call the police and accuse him.

"The police can search the house," his mom continued. "They'll find the statements, if they're there."

"But I need to see them. I have to see them before I can say that I think he did it."

She nodded and patted my shaking hand. "I understand. So you're going to get them tomorrow?"

"Yeah. I want to find them, and then I'll call the police and give them everything."

"And you're sure your dad is going to work in the morning?"

"Yeah. And I'll go home first thing, then call the police."

She nodded, and I sensed that the discussion was over. Gabe poured a can of beans in the meat and then put in some spices. He stirred the simmering chili while his mother took a pan of cornbread out of the oven. I didn't even know how it got there or when she'd put it in, but it was ready just as the chili was.

We sat in silence and ate. In different circumstances, at another time, I would have finished the chili, gone for seconds, and raved about its taste. It was very good, what little of it I ate. But today wasn't a day to dissect Gabe's recipe or find out the seasonings he'd used. I sensed that Gabe didn't take it personally that I didn't finish what he'd given me.

After dinner, Gabe walked me to his room. He put clean sheets on the bed, just as his mother had directed him to at dinner. Then he sank down to the floor at my feet.

"I wish I could sleep in here on the floor. You know, just to watch over you. I know that sounds dumb, but I can't help but be scared. I'm worried for you. My mom would never let me, though. She'll be checking the living room all night to make sure I'm on the couch."

I smiled. "She's a good mom, and you're a good son."

"Sleep well, Ellie. Tomorrow, we'll find what we need."

I bent down to kiss him. "Thank you. I love you."

"I love you too."

He rose from the floor and dragged himself out the door. I lay down and covered myself. I felt safe under Gabe's fresh sheets. I didn't want morning to come. I wasn't sure I was ready to face it all. Over the past two days, answers had come to me piecemeal—just enough for me to accept. Tomorrow, I would face the remaining pieces of this overwhelming revelation; I might finally know the truth about my mother's murder. It wasn't a journey I had been prepared to undertake or had even been aware of. It had found me through Gabe, the huaca, and my mother. And now it was up to me to face the truth that I still wanted to negate. But there was no refuting those statements. They would tell. The discomforting thought kept me up for longer than I had hoped, and I found myself wishing that Gabe was with me, sitting on the floor, holding my hand, and assuring me that I would survive facing the truth. *The truth will not destroy me*, I told myself over and over again.

EIGHTEEN

MY INTERNAL ALARM WOKE ME UP every morning at six thirty. Sensing that the importance of the day far outweighed anything as trivial as school, it didn't fail me Monday morning. I pulled myself out of bed and tried to pat down my hair.

I could hear Gabe out in the living room, and I hurried out to join him. He was on his laptop and didn't notice me at first. I wondered, for only a second, where I'd be if I hadn't gained such a close attachment to him. Would I have any cause to suspect my dad? Or would I continue to live in blissful obliviousness? I only wished it for an instant before forcing myself to the present, to Gabe, and to my impending search.

Gabe looked up at me, his hair poofy and standing up on one side. He ran his hand through it. "You okay, Ellie?"

I nodded and walked over to the couch. Behind him, in the window, I could see that there was a light snow accumulating. There were already tire tracks on the street in front, but the front lawn, walkway, and sidewalk were untouched. It made me think of what my mother had said once: the snow makes everything clean again.

Nothing seemed clean to me today, and I turned away from the unblemished blanket of white snow in front of me. From yesterday's clothes that I was still wearing to the task that lay before me, there was nothing around me that felt remotely clean. The snow did nothing to make anything clean, and I wondered how she had ever come up with such an inane thought.

"What are you looking at?" I asked Gabe.

"Just some more information about your dad. Trying to put some pieces together."

"Like what?"

"I'm trying to figure out who sent him these letters and why. Why were they trying to contact him? Who was it? Is there someone out there who knows the truth, who knows who your father really is?"

More questions. I thought we'd finally be getting answers. I didn't want to think about any more questions or face further implications about who he was and what else he had done. "Who do you think it was?"

Gabe shook his head. "I don't know. Maybe somebody was blackmailing him."

I didn't want to think about anything more than what was already on my agenda: EZ Pass statements. I had to see them. I had to see if he had made that twenty-six mile drive back to New Jersey that night.

"I think his train has probably left by now," I said, glancing at the time on my phone. "Let's drive by the station to see if his car is parked there."

"Okay," Gabe said, standing up. "Want something to eat first?"

I shook my head. "No, thanks."

"Well, let me go clean the snow off the car. It looks like it's really coming down out there." He put a stocking cap on his head and pulled on his heavy coat.

I stopped suddenly as a face in the newspaper on the couch caught my eye. "I've seen this guy before," I said, picking up the newspaper. "At my house. He was coming out from my backyard and took off running when I saw him. My dad said he would report it. This is Joe Collins, the guy who was murdered."

Gabe grabbed the newspaper from me. "We need to hurry, Ellie. We have to get that stuff and call the police."

I looked around for my coat and followed him out the door, pulling on my mittens as I went. His footsteps were the first disturbance of the snow covering the lawn. My own footsteps quickly followed, and together, we agitated the once-serene layers of newly fallen snow.

We drove past the train station and saw my dad's Lexus. It was parked close to the same spot it was every day, a thin layer of snow beginning to accumulate on its silver exterior. After a brief pause, Gabe continued toward my house.

Gabe pulled in to the snowy driveway. Fresh tracks had been left behind as my dad had pulled out of the garage earlier. The lawn and walkway were unblemished, new snow still accumulating. Our footsteps toward the front door were the first markers of the morning. Before going in, I stood on the front steps and looked out at the front yard. I thought about how the still white, almost-untouched lawn—now "clean" as my mom would say—would later be sullied, blackened by forthcoming footsteps.

I opened the door, and Gabe followed me inside. I'd only been gone a night, but everything seemed different to me now. Pieces of my life, scattered throughout the house, did not seem like they belonged to me anymore. This was still my home, but I didn't feel like I belonged anymore. Nothing seemed like it belonged anymore.

"All of his papers are upstairs. He keeps everything filed up there."

Gabe followed me up the stairs, and I went into my dad's room. His bed was neatly made, the maroon bedspread pulled tightly and evenly over the bed. Six throw pillows were arranged in the same familiar pattern.

I tried not to look around the room or notice the details that surrounded what once felt like a sanctuary to me. Now, it all felt cold.

We went inside the walk-in closet where his shelves held old shoeboxes filled with filed receipts and statements. Each shoebox was labeled—American Express, mortgage, phone, insurance.

I pulled the one that said EZ Pass, my hands shaking as I held it. Gabe took it from my hands, and we walked toward the bed, where we both sat down. I had thought about this moment all night—looking through the statements and finding the answer. Now that the moment was here, I couldn't proceed. I couldn't look for what I had to know.

"Want me to look through it?" Gabe asked.

I shook my head. "No. I have to do it."

Gabe handed me the box, and I took off the lid, letting it fall to the floor. It was in order, the most recent ones at the front. I leafed through the front ones, slowly making my way back to June. I found the statement that showed June and pulled it out, unfolding it as I lay the box on the bed next to me.

It had been June seventh. There weren't too many entries, because he rode the train most days. Once in a while, if there was an event or a meeting, he might drive. He had driven on June seventh and said he parked at the Waldorf, where he and Mr. Mercer had stayed and where they'd had their meeting the next day.

I scanned down the list of dates. June seventh. He had passed through the Holland Tunnel to NYC at 4:39 in the afternoon. I couldn't quite describe the feeling (it was possibly relief) to see that it was the only entry for June seventh.

That semblance of relief or whatever it was proved to be short-lived as I saw the next entry. It was for June eighth at 1:15 a.m. He had returned to New Jersey some time during the night and had passed through the Holland Tunnel toward New York City again at 1:15.

I could feel Gabe had reached the same conclusion as he let out a small gasp. I stared at the numbers as they blurred and came into focus again. My grip on the statement tightened as I shut my eyes. I felt Gabe's hand on my knee moments later. He was saying something, but I couldn't hear it.

All I could think about was how he had come back to New Jersey that night. He came back. All the way to Westfield? That could be the only answer.

"Ellie, I think we need to take this to the police. They have to see this. I don't know how they could have missed this when they questioned him."

I shook my head. "No. Not yet. We have to find more." I handed him the statement and then walked back to the closet. Bank statements. The last thing Gabe had said to me before we'd left his house came barreling back at me the second after I'd seen the EZ Pass entries.

Someone was blackmailing him.

Someone had sent Rick those letters and put him on guard. "I need to see his bank statements. See if there's anything unusual."

Gabe nodded. He seemed to sense what I was thinking.

I walked into the closet again. Taking a deep breath, I scanned the boxes, looking for the one with the bank statements. There was Allstate and AT&T . . . As I kept searching, his stupid, methodical way of organizing was blaring at me, and I couldn't stand it. Freaking alphabetical order. Control, order—it made me hate him, hate him for the way he boxed things up to make them look right. I grabbed the Allstate box and threw it on the floor. AT&T was next. I kept pulling boxes to the floor with swift, angry moves. I didn't realize I was shaking and sobbing until Gabe grabbed my shoulders and made me face him.

"Hey, Ellie. Hey," he said.

"I hate him! I hate him, Gabe! How could he do this?" I grabbed his shirt and let him draw me into his arms.

He stroked my back and whispered in my ear. I couldn't really focus on what he was saying. My mind kept thinking about the last six months, how I'd lived under the roof of this man, this monster. How he'd kissed my cheek and told me good night. How he'd cooked me dinner and made my lunches.

I wiped my nose with my sleeve and nodded at Gabe. I couldn't find the words to say anything, and he didn't pursue it. Instead, he walked over to the shelf of boxes and grabbed one near the bottom—the W's. It was Wells Fargo. He took my hand and walked me over to the bed.

I sat with my shaking hands in my lap as he searched through the statements. "March. There's a thousand dollar withdrawal on the nineteenth. Is that normal?" he asked.

I shrugged.

"April, the twentieth. Another thousand." He leafed through the next few. "It's the same for May and June. A thousand dollars."

I couldn't recall an occurrence when he would have that much cash on hand. It didn't make sense for him to be withdrawing a thousand dollars a month. There was only one answer—the answer Gabe had arrived at earlier that morning.

"I can't believe this."

Gabe nodded and then stood up. He boxed up the Wells Fargo box and then grabbed the EZ Pass statement I'd left on the bed. "Let's go."

I followed him downstairs wordlessly. I covered my eyes as we passed the hallway where framed pictures of my dad and me covered the walls. We were almost to the front door when I stopped suddenly and took a step back.

It had been gradual, the way he'd altered the pictures, little by little so I wouldn't notice. Until today. The wall had contained family pictures, at one point, of all three of us. Until today. I pulled my hand away from Gabe as I stopped in front of the wall and scanned each picture. Where was the picture of the three of us skiing in Vermont? Of us in Times Square? Of my mother dressed as Snow White for Halloween? They were gone. Seemingly unnoticeable until today.

Why hadn't I noticed? Had the previous arrangement of pictures been so indelible in my mind that I hadn't noticed the changes? He'd taken them down, boxed them up, and removed them from his life.

I locked the door behind me and hurried out to Gabe's car. We ran through the snowy lawn, and he quickly backed out, his tires spinning a few times on the way out.

"I think you should call the police. Tell them what we found," Gabe said.

I knew he was right, but I didn't know what I would tell them or where I would start. I stared at the evidence we'd gathered. It was on the seat between us. I reached for my phone, and it started ringing. I pulled my hand back as if I'd just touched fire and clutched it to my chest.

"What if it's my dad?" I asked.

"Check, Ellie. It's okay." He took his hand off the steering wheel to squeeze my knee.

I pulled my phone out of my pocket and had never been so relieved to see Sarah's number. I couldn't believe she was calling me after the last conversation we'd had. "Hello?" I answered.

"Where are you, Ellie?"

"Why?"

"Because your dad just freaking called me. He is like raving mad. He called me on my cell phone at school. Lucky I was on my way to the bathroom and answered it. He wants to know where you are. You're cutting school?"

"What did he say?"

"He said the school called him because you were absent. So he called me because you were sleeping over. I told him you weren't. Sorry, El. He caught me off guard. I didn't mean to tell him we hadn't hung out for weeks. You should have warned me. I would have covered for you, El. I would have."

"It's okay. What else did he say?"

"He thinks you're with that guy Gabe. I told him I didn't know. He thinks for sure you were with him last night. Were you, El? When did this happen?"

"Look, it's not like that. Okay? It's complicated."

"He tried to get me to tell him where Gabe lives. I told him I didn't know. I think I bought you some time, but he's pissed, El. I think he's trying to figure out where Gabe lives."

"Okay, Sarah. Thanks. It will take him some time."

Gabe passed by the train station, and I turned to look for the Lexus again. It was gone.

"That's what I'm trying to tell you! He missed his train because of the snow. He's still in Westfield. He's looking for you, and he's not happy."

"Oh, no!"

"Sorry, El. But you've got to come up with a story quick because I think you're in big trouble. Look, I'm sorry for everything."

"I have to go." I disconnected Sarah just as Gabe was pulling into the driveway. I scanned the street, hoping not to see the Lexus, hoping he hadn't figured out where Gabe lived.

"I saw that!" Gabe said, hopping out of the car. "Where is he? He's not parked at the station!"

"I know. Sarah said he thinks I'm with you. He's looking for us right now."

"My mom." Gabe ran toward his house, thrashing through the snow-covered ground. "Mom!" he yelled as he came into the house.

She came out of her bedroom, her eyes wide. "What is it, Gabe?"

"Are you okay?" he asked.

"Yes, what's the matter?"

"Ellie's dad is on his way here. We have to call the police." He grabbed his phone out of his pocket. "Let's get downstairs."

Susannah and I followed him downstairs. I was still clutching the papers to my chest. Gabe dialed as he descended the stairs. "I'm calling about the Olivia Cummings case. She was the woman killed here in Westfield back in June."

I was grateful that Gabe had taken over and made the phone call. I didn't think I had the courage to call and talk about my mother or turn my father in. It was all outside my realm of capability at the moment.

"We believe the killer is Daniel Cummings. He is also known as Rick Thorton. He is driving a silver Lexus, and I believe he is on his way over here." Gabe gave the operator his address and then turned to me, knocking me out of my stupor. "What's his license plate number?"

"Um, I, I, I'm not sure. I don't know." I tried to think, but nothing was coming to me at the moment.

Gabe turned back to the phone. "Because we just know. We have evidence that we'll show the police when they get here. They need to come now because he is on his way over here."

Just as Gabe disconnected, we heard a heavy knock on the front door upstairs. The knock intensified to pounding blows. Gabe tucked his phone in his back pocket.

"Gabe." His mother reached out for his arm and handed him the elastic band next to the huaca. "We need to leave here now."

He nodded and let her tie it around his bicep. I saw him draw blood as he had many times, but the desperation with which he did it was different than those other times. His hand was less steady. It was shaking, and he struggled a bit with the needle, so his mother took over.

As Gabe was pouring it into the drawer, we heard a crashing blow upstairs, followed by a booming voice. "Ellie!" My dad's voice increased to a shout. "Ellie!"

The slamming of several doors was followed by his feet storming down the steps. Gabe closed the drawer and the room began to tremble. It was an occurrence so familiar to me, but the feelings that surrounded me now were foreign, like nothing I'd ever felt. The fear that gripped me was so tangible, so immediate. I'd never feared anything like the way I feared my dad at that moment.

"Ellie!" he yelled one last time before grabbing my hair

and stumbling forward with the shaking of the room. As the light began to shine and summon us forward, we were pulled into Hanan Pacha.

"What the—?" My dad's voice seemed foreign to me now.

I didn't know what to do or how to feel. Gabe took my hand; he and his mom backed away from . . .

I was face-to-face with him now. The man I'd known my entire life. I had called him Dad for all of it until this moment when I didn't want to call him anything, didn't want to say anything.

"What is this?" he said as he looked around, taking in the environment that I'd already become accustomed to. His eyes darted from me to the lush, green grass, a world away from the snow-covered ground we'd left behind seconds before. He turned to face me.

"El, what is going on?"

"Don't call me El ever again."

"What is this place?" he asked, ignoring my angry statement.

"Take it all in," I said, taking a step forward. "Because it's probably the last time you'll ever see this place."

Gabe was beside me, but he didn't say anything. I thought it was perhaps because he was watching the time and counting the minutes as they elapsed before we'd all be thrust back to his basement, subject to our world's physical laws. Here, we were safe, if only for a time. He couldn't hurt us here. But once we were back in the basement, there was no telling what the man in front of us was capable of.

He turned his eyes away from his surroundings to look at me. But it was only for an instant. Almost immediately, his eyes looked beyond me, and I knew what held his attention before I'd even turned around. It was her. To me, it was not new. But to him . . .

I couldn't imagine what his feelings or thoughts were. He half walked, half stumbled, over to where she sat. She couldn't see him or feel him there. He called out to her as he increased his pace toward her. Unmoved by his calls, she stayed still, serene in her usual spot.

As he reached her, he grabbed for her, his hands outstretched, reaching for her neck, a place familiar to his angry, monstrous hands. But they touched nothing and went right through her. She remained unfazed by his presence, his disbelief, his anger, and by the harm his hands had hoped to inflict.

He turned his stunned face to Gabe, sensing that he was at the center of this mysterious place.

"You," he said, walking toward Gabe, who still stood in front of both me and his mother, shielding us. "What have you done to us? To her?" he asked, pointing at my mother.

"You don't belong here. This is a place of peace, where our dead have come to rest. You don't belong here."

"But how did I get here? How did we all get here?"

"You can't hurt us here. You can do nothing to us here."

He tried to reach for Gabe, to grab him by the shirt. Gabe let go of my hand and took a step forward, not backing down.

"Leave him alone!" I shouted, coming from behind Gabe. "Don't touch him!"

"Ellie," Gabe said, trying to shove me behind him.

"We know what you are and what you did. You're surprised to see her, aren't you?" I spat out.

The look of shock on his face prevented him from speaking, and he just stared at me.

"Aren't you?" I yelled.

"Ellie, look. We need to talk. There's something strange going on here, and somehow you're in the middle of it all. We have to get away from here." He took a step toward me.

"I'm not going anywhere with you. I know who you are, Rick."

My use of his name stopped him from advancing. "Ellie."

"No, Rick! You killed her. You killed my mom!" Saying the words aloud and in front of him caused me to start shaking. I was shaking so much that I didn't notice the sudden movement that overcame us and started dragging us back. We didn't belong here, especially not him. It was time to go back and face our world and the misery and consequences that awaited us there.

We all came tumbling back into the cold, hard basement floor. Three of us had experienced it before and were somewhat prepared, but Rick wasn't. He hit hard against the bottom step.

"Augh!" he shouted. He attempted to get up but fell down to his knees.

"Ellie, run!" Gabe yelled and pulled me to my feet. He shoved me and his mom toward the steps, and we all ran up.

It took Rick a moment to get oriented, but he was stomping up the steps right after us. He grabbed Gabe by the legs, causing him to stumble forward hard onto his hands. Rick pulled Gabe down the steps and grabbed him up by the collar.

"Gabe!" I yelled out and retraced my steps down to where they stood at the bottom.

"Go, Ellie!" Gabe yelled. "Go find the police!"

I hesitated. I didn't want to leave him alone in the presence of Rick Thorton because I knew all too well what he was capable of. I turned back toward Susannah, whose hand I'd instinctively grabbed as we had hurried up the steps. "Go see if the police are here," I said. "I'll help Gabe."

She nodded, turned quickly to look down at Gabe, and then hurried up the last of the steps.

Rick had Gabe by the collar and slammed him back against a beam.

"Stop!" I yelled, stumbling down the last of the steps.

Rick held a hand out toward me. "Don't move, Ellie." He punched Gabe in the stomach, who buckled forward from the impact.

Then, Gabe grabbed Rick around the waist and ran forward, barreling him against the opposite wall. Rick grunted as he hit the wall and kicked Gabe in the chest, sending him stumbling backward to the floor. I looked around helplessly for a baseball bat or something I could hit Rick with. The thought of hitting my dad stopped me for an instant, until I saw him pin Gabe against the wall and punch him in the jaw with strength I never knew he had. I ran behind the steps and grabbed a wooden board from a stack of mismatched scraps of wood. I looked up to see Rick's hands gnarled around Gabe's neck. Gabe was grasping at Rick's wrists, but he couldn't pull his strong, angry fingers off his neck.

The vision of those same hands around my mother's neck propelled me to move toward them with the board aimed high in the air. The board was in mid air about to come down on Rick's back when the piercing sound of a gunshot came splitting right in front of me. I jumped back and stumbled on the stack of wood scraps.

Rick screamed and grabbed at his shoulder. He stumbled a few feet back and rose quickly to his knees, attempting to get up, but the shock and pain of being shot kept him on the ground for the few moments it took for me to see Gabe run up the steps. Gabe stopped at the top of the steps, where Susannah was holding a gun with both outstretched arms, aimed right at Rick.

Rick roared another scream and forced himself to turn around. His eyes flashed around the basement and stopped on me.

"Ellie, come on!" Gabe yelled and reached a hand to wave me toward the steps. I ran up to him, and he pushed Susannah and me up the rest of the flight of steps. He closed the door behind him and pushed himself against it. "Go see if the cops are here!" he yelled.

Susannah collapsed into a chair. Gabe had taken the gun away from her and held it firmly in his hand, pointing it at the floor. I ran out of the kitchen to the front door. I could hear sirens in the distance. It only took a minute before I saw the first of the police cars hastily stop in front of Gabe's house.

I trudged through the snow to reach the two officers getting out of the cars.

"Is everything all right here?" one of them asked.

I pushed away the fear I'd carried with me for two days. "No. I think my father killed my mother. She was Olivia Cummings. He just tried to hurt us."

"Where is he?" the officer asked. The tag on his police uniform said Perkins.

"Downstairs. In the basement."

The other police officer pulled out his gun and continued into the house.

"Is anyone here hurt?" Officer Perkins asked.

"He is. He was shot." I turned and noticed that Susannah had come out of the house. She stood by the door, her hands clutched together at her stomach and her eyes fixed to the ground.

"Who shot him?"

"I did," she said, taking a step down, her eyes still on the ground.

"You shot him? Daniel Cummings?" Officer Perkins asked just as another patrol car pulled next to the curb.

He didn't wait for her to answer as he yelled over his shoulder to instruct the incoming officers. They hurried into the house, out of sight, but were back in an instant with Gabe behind him.

"He's gone, Ellie," Gabe said.

"The perpetrator broke a window in the basement," said one of the officers who'd come in the second car. "He crawled out of the basement window and appears to have fled on foot. There's a trail of blood in the snow. Mears and Pisano are on foot following the trail. I've directed Alvarez and Thompson to patrol the surrounding streets. They were on their way over on East Broad."

"There are other units on their way. If he just left, someone will catch up to him immediately. Take the patrol car and scour the area," Officer Perkins said.

"Got it." The other officer nodded and ran toward the street to the car.

Officer Perkins turned back to me. "So you're the daughter of Olivia Cummings?"

It was a relatively recent case, one that hadn't been closed. Everyone in town knew about it. "Yes, and Daniel Cummings is my father, I think."

"Why do you think he killed her?"

"He's been living under an alias. Rick Thorton is his real name, I think."

Gabe put his hand on my back and stepped forward.

"If you contact the Clearwater, Florida, authorities, you'll find that he's wanted down there for a possible murder."

"That still doesn't tell me why you think he killed Olivia Cummings."

"I have evidence," I said. "He lied about his alibi. He

drugged his coworker and drove back to Jersey from Manhattan that night. I have his EZ Pass records and also some letters addressed to Rick Thorton."

"Where is this evidence?"

"Inside," I said.

"I'll be right in," Gabe said. "I'm going to check on my mom."

I turned to look at Susannah and hoped today's events wouldn't set her back. "It's inside, Officer . . ." I said.

"Perkins. Officer Perkins," he said. He eased a gentle smile onto his lips. Perhaps he'd just realized that, although this was a job to him, to me this was my life—my falling-apart life.

The other officer caught up to us. "Daniel Cummings was apprehended right outside the train station. It looks like he was trying to get on board."

I froze at his words. They caught him that easily. He was trying to get away, go to Manhattan, where he would have been able to fade away among the millions that resided there and perhaps reinvent himself and create a new life. Who knew how many people he'd pretended to be already?

"And what is his condition?" Officer Perkins asked the other officer.

"Stable. GSW to the right shoulder. Paramedics are taking him in. Pisano and Mears are escorting to the hospital."

His condition? I knew he'd been shot. I'd been there when it happened, but suddenly it just hit me. My dad had been shot and was on the way to the hospital. Under ordinary circumstances, a daughter would be in the ambulance with her father, holding his hand, crying and praying that he would be okay. But I was here, at Gabe's house, standing in a foot of snow, trying to tell a police officer why I thought my dad had killed my mom.

"They're going to question him," Officer Perkins said, turning back to me. "But I need that evidence to show the investigator. He'll want to know what we have on him, if there are grounds for arrest."

Both officers followed me into Gabe's house. I couldn't remember where I had left everything, and it took me a moment to gather my thoughts. I had to keep reminding myself that I couldn't give them all the evidence, the ultimate proof of my father's guilt. That evidence was housed downstairs in the secret of Gabe's huaca.

I found the statements and the baggie with the ruffies. Officer Perkins placed them in evidence containers. "I don't know how much this will mean, but thank you. Perhaps it's a start. We'll see what the investigator says. I'm sure he'll want to talk to you."

Gabe had settled his mother in her room and then came to stand by us. "You okay?" he whispered to me.

I nodded, wondering if I would ever really be okay.

Officer Perkins watched me. "Do you have somewhere to stay? I'm sure there will be a warrant to search your house. Not sure if you'll want to be there."

"Yes. I can stay with my aunt."

"You can stay here," Gabe said, taking my hand.

I nodded, but I knew it wouldn't be a matter of a day or two, like I'd stayed at his house before. This was more, much more. I wasn't sure I would ever live at my house again. I would have to find somewhere to *stay*—indefinitely.

Officer Perkins stayed. He took our statements, walked around the house, searched the basement, and made detailed reports. I don't know why I was in such a hurry for him to leave. I had nowhere to go, nothing to do, but I couldn't wait for him to go.

♦♦♦♦♦

I went to meet with Detective Marshall, who'd investigated the case after my mom was killed. He had come to my house to gather evidence. It was the same detective who'd failed to find any tangible leads, who'd failed to find my mom's killer. Aunt Mel and Gabe went with me to meet with him.

It had only been two days since my dad had been arrested, but it seemed like a lifetime.

Detective Marshall sat at his desk, and the three of us sat on chairs he'd brought in just as we'd entered. I sat between Gabe and Aunt Mel. They'd both pulled me to the center, as if I needed crutches on both sides to hold me up or I would fall. But I had survived my mother's death; I hoped I would be able to handle this new blow without falling apart.

"Thanks for coming to meet with me," he said after introductions had been made and hands had been shaken. "I know this is really difficult for you, Ellie, but I want you to know everything we've discovered over the last two days."

"I already know about Rick Thorton."

Gabe scooted over to me and put his arm around the back of my chair. I turned to give him a quick smile to assure him I was ready to hear everything.

"Rick Thorton grew up in a series of foster homes. His mother—Jessica Thorton—spent time in jail for drug-related charges. We couldn't find any information on his biological father. We're working on obtaining a copy of his birth certificate."

"Gabe and I read about some of that online in a Clearwater newspaper."

"How did you know to look for him—for Rick Thorton?" Detective Marshall asked.

"He'd been receiving letters addressed to Rick Thorton. Dad . . . Rick told me it was a wrong address and he'd return them to the post office. But I found a bunch of letters. He never sent them back."

Aunt Mel broke in. "Why didn't you tell me any of this, Ellie?"

"It was just a few days ago, right before the police arrested him. I was trying to piece everything together."

"I wish you hadn't taken this on by yourself, Ellie. To think what could have happened." Aunt Mel reached over to squeeze my hand.

"Gabe was helping me."

Aunt Mel looked over to Gabe and then turned back to Detective Marshall.

On cue, Detective Marshall continued. "We examined the letters and found some fingerprints we were able to trace back to a Joseph Collins."

"Collins?" Gabe asked.

"Do you know him?" Detective Marshall put down a document he'd had in his hand and peered at Gabe.

"No. But Ellie and I saw a news report about him, about how he'd been murdered. The name just kind of stuck with me."

Detective Marshall nodded. "Yes, well Collins had been arrested a number of times for petty thefts, so we had his prints on file. We're investigating his murder and think Thorton may have had something to do with it. We're checking bank accounts, but I have reason to believe Collins was blackmailing your father, Ellie. It seems Collins has ties back to Clearwater and knew Thorton from there. Perhaps he threatened to expose him. There's still some investigation to do there. We don't know all of the details."

I nodded. I remembered the night we'd heard about Collins's murder; the feeling had quickly come to me that it had something to do with him. "What about the lady in Florida. Did he kill her too?"

Detective Marshall picked up his document and examined it for a moment before speaking. "Loretta Maxwell. That was Rick's foster mother. I read through statements from Maxwell's daughter. She believes Rick killed her mother and then went into hiding. Loretta Maxwell had found Rick was stealing from her. Apparently, Loretta confronted him, and it's still unclear exactly what happened. Clearwater authorities want to charge him on the case."

"So, three murders," I said quietly. "I guess I'm lucky to still be alive."

"El," Aunt Mel whispered into my hair as she leaned over to hug me.

"We think it could be four," Detective Marshall said.

"Four?" I said, sitting up and pulling myself away from Aunt Mel.

"Daniel Cummings. That name didn't come from nowhere. He has an authentic birth certificate and social security number. There was a Daniel Cummings born in Florida, but we have no record of his death. Your father stole his identity. Authorities in Florida are trying to find him—the real Daniel Cummings. They suspect that he is dead and that your father killed him. They have no proof to back it up, but they're checking all of the John Does that were found around the time Loretta Maxwell was killed. They've narrowed it down to a few and are going to see if any of those John Does could be Daniel Cummings."

"So, how did he get here? To New Jersey? Why did my mom marry him?"

Detective Marshall turned a page in the file in front of him. "He said he came to start a new life, to leave the past behind. He wanted to be a new person, that's what he told me. He went to community college, Rutgers University, and business school. He did that all on his own under the name of Daniel Cummings."

"My mom met him in business school," I said feebly.

"He said, and I think I believe him, that while he was married to your mother, he committed no crimes. He was just a typical, hardworking father and husband."

"There's nothing typical about him," I muttered.

"No, there's not." Detective Marshall sighed and put down the documents he'd been holding. "I think he tried to put his past behind him and focused on being Daniel Cummings, husband to Olivia and father to Ellie."

That statement pierced the hard exterior I'd been trying to hold up, the strong person I'd been trying to portray.

"From studying the crimes he committed, I think he wanted a different life. He wanted to be someone else and killed simply to get rid of those who stood in his way. He killed Loretta Maxwell because she got in his way of getting money. He killed Daniel Cummings to get an identity. He killed Joe Collins because he was going to expose him."

The detective paused, and I hated him for it. He told me about those murders, but not the one I really cared about.

"Then why did he kill my mother?" I spat the words out, accusatory and angry, but I had neither the desire nor energy to apologize for it.

"Your father—Rick Thorton—has confessed to two of the crimes. Joe Collins and your mother. The other two . . . well, we think we can get him on them. The district attorney is working on some offers to get him to plead guilty and to avoid a trial and get all four convictions, if we can. It gets a little complicated, though, because the other two crimes—if he did commit them—happened out of state, so it is out of our jurisdiction, but we're working with the Florida authorities the best we can."

"You didn't answer her question," Aunt Mel said, taking my hand.

"Yes, I know. He was very candid with me, once he finally broke down and admitted he was Rick Thorton. At first, he kept up the charade, but I think in the end, he knew he couldn't get away with it."

"What did he say?"

"Olivia had found out. Joe Collins had sent her a letter telling her everything. Rick had decided he was not going to pay Collins anymore, so Collins threatened to tell Olivia. When Rick called his bluff, Collins wrote Olivia the letter. When Olivia confronted Rick about it, he killed her. He wanted to keep hiding it, keep living as Daniel Cummings, and he thought Olivia would turn him in. So he killed her. He was trying to protect himself and didn't want her to get in his way."

The first thought that came into my mind was "what a waste." His sole purpose in killing her was to cover up his crimes and who he was. And here, six months later, it had all become uncovered. Did his need to protect his lies really override his love for her? All of those kisses, the hugs, the words of praise and kindness, the gifts—those had not seemed fake. They were real, weren't they? But, in the end, all of that was meaningless because all that really mattered to him was covering his lies.

"So that's why he killed her?" I asked, even though that is exactly what he had said.

"Yes, Ellie. Sorry to be the one to tell you this."

I nodded, trying to contain tears I surmised were only the first that would be shed over this revelation. Aunt Mel rose from her chair and knelt down next to me, draping her arms around me.

"Oh, El," she began but didn't finish. Her tears started quietly but quickly erupted into sobbing, and she pressed her face into my shoulder. I put my arms around her. It was her sister, someone she'd known her whole life, and now she knew the senseless cause of her death.

A few minutes passed as Aunt Mel and I held each other and attempted to control our tears. Aunt Mel put both hands on my face and forced a smile through teary eyes.

"We're going to be okay. Okay?" she said, probably for both of our sakes.

I attempted a feeble nod, but more tears escaped down my cheeks and onto her hands.

"We have each other. We have my sister, Julia. Olivia is looking down at us, and she's happy we have each other. We'll take care of you, El. I'll take care of you, and you'll be okay."

I nodded again, a little more strongly this time. I thought about Aunt Mel's statement—Mom looking down at us, and immediately I thought of the huaca. I wanted to share it with Aunt Mel so that she could see her sister again, but I knew it wasn't the time to think about it. I pushed the thought aside and nodded again, decisively and strongly, for Mel. "Okay," I said, rising from my chair.

She rose from her kneeling position beside me and wrapped her arm around my waist. Gabe was right behind me, and I thought about the tragedies he'd faced in his life. His father jumping off a parking garage, his grandmother dying, and having to take care of his mentally ill mother—all of those terrible events had dominated the greater part of his life. He was strong, independent, and loyal. His presence in my life was a miracle. He could perhaps help me through the months ahead.

NINETEEN

I STILL WASN'T SURE IF I SHOULD HAVE come, but I guessed I was looking for closure, whatever that meant. Just one of those clichés that I was growing increasingly less fond of. How do you find closure when your father killed your mother? There is no closure—that fact will always be there, haunting me. I would think about it in every memory I had of him. I would be reminded every time I visited my mother.

I thought I would find closure after the arrest or at the sentencing, once everything had been made clear. But there still remained a deep well, a hole in my soul that would never be closed.

The guard ushered me to a booth, and I sat with the phone in my hand, waiting for him. I wanted to take my eyes off him as he walked toward me, but I forced myself to watch him. I was not going to let fear of him take away the last bit of control available to me at the moment. He looked so different to me now—a prison uniform, prison haircut, and angry eyes, so void of the love they once feigned for me.

He held the phone to his ear and nodded at me.

"Hi," I said. Why had I come? I was tempted to run out and never look back, but that was the fear again—the fear of him. I would not let it control me. I was here for something; I didn't know what, but I wasn't going to leave until I had it.

"Hi, Ellie. I'm glad you came."

"I'm still not sure why I'm here."

"I'm still your father, Ellie. Nothing's going to change that. Even though I'm in here, I still want us to have a relationship."

I shook my head. "No. I'm here to say good-bye."

He squeezed his lips together and shook his head. "No, don't, Ellie. I'm sorry, but you can't begin to understand."

"Understand? What am I supposed to understand?"

"Ellie, you were born with everything. You've always had everything. You don't know what it's like to have nothing. I was born with nothing. My mother was hooked on drugs. She cared more about drugs than her own kid. I had to make my own way in life. I couldn't rely on her. You had the best mother in the world. You can't know how it was for me."

"*Had*. I *had* the best mother. Because of you, I don't have her anymore."

"I know, Ellie. And I'm sorry. But she was going to ruin everything for me, everything that I worked so hard to build. I couldn't let her destroy me."

"So you killed her, just like you killed everyone else that got in your way."

"Everything that I am I made myself, Ellie. I had nothing. My mother gave me nothing. I had to re-create myself, put myself through college and business school. I worked hard all my life to get where I was, and now look at me." He waved his arms around at his surroundings. "Look where I am. I ended up in the same place."

"You put yourself here. No one else did."

"I know, Ellie. But, please, just don't say good-bye. You're all I have left. I've lost everything. I'd like to at least think I did something right by you. You're an amazing young woman, and I had a piece in that."

My eyes started to sting. Thoughts of sliced cucumbers and shredded zucchini abounded in my mind. The small, simple things that he'd done for me throughout my life. Those simple actions, born out of love for me, would follow me wherever I went. They were woven into who I was and would never leave me. But that didn't mean I had to leave him in my life. I couldn't sit here, week after week or month after month, visiting Rick Thorton, a stranger who had killed my mom. The man who was my father, Daniel Cummings, died the same night she did. The man who raised me and loved me died with her. The man I'd been living with for the past six months was a stranger to me, who lied and hid, and I owed him nothing.

"You're the one who told me that if someone hurts you, you have to cut him off."

"No, Ellie."

"I'm sorry, but I can't come visit you. I have to make my own life now and figure out how to live with this for the rest of my life."

"Will you at least write to me? Tell me how you're doing and what you're doing."

"I don't know."

"You mean I'm not even going to know where you're going to college. Nothing?"

I shook my head. "No. I don't know you, Rick Thorton. I'm sorry, but I don't."

"Ellie, wait." I went to put the phone down, but his next words stopped me. "What about Gabe?"

I slowly pulled the phone back up to my ear. "What do you mean?"

He leaned back in his chair; a small smile of satisfaction crossed his face as he continued. "I don't know how he did it or what exactly he did, but I do know Gabe has something. He did something."

I didn't know how to answer that. I quickly thought back to the times I had wanted to share the huaca with him, had wanted to take him there.

"Yeah, it's something. I don't know what it is or how he did it." He studied my face, and I tried not to react. "What is it, El?"

I shrugged.

"How did we get there? To where Olivia was? How does Gabe do it? It's him, right. I know it is."

"I'm not telling you anything."

He shook his head. "You don't have to. But I'm pretty sure he doesn't want anyone else to know. Right?"

I looked away, but he knew me. He could read my face.

"Yeah, that's what I thought. Whatever secret Gabe is keeping. He wants you to keep it, right? He's bewitched you. What is it? Is he a mind reader? What kind of power does he have? Where does it come from?"

I shrugged again, not saying anything.

He laughed. "I can't believe we're sitting here talking about this. I wouldn't believe it if I hadn't seen it for myself, if I hadn't felt that force that took us in and threw us out. I don't know what it is, El. I bet you know more than you're letting on. Tell me, El."

"No."

"Okay, but I'm going to be asking around, then. Ask the

guys around here and the guards. Maybe the local papers will get wind of it. Before you know it, it'll be on *Good Morning, America*, and every reporter, scientist, and nutcase will be knocking down Gabe's door."

"No one's going to believe you."

"Okay. Take your chances then, El."

I wished he would stop calling me El. That wasn't who I was to him anymore.

"What do you say, El? Tell me your little secret, and then it would be our little secret. I won't tell anyone. Promise."

"How could I possibly trust you?"

"Because then we both get what we want. I keep your secret. You keep coming to visit me."

"No," I said and stood up. I didn't hear what he was saying, but I saw the look on his face. He knew I'd give in. I had to protect Gabe's secret and make this deal with the devil, trust that he would keep the secret to get what he wanted. That's how he lived his life—by forcing people to do what he wanted in order to get his way. He always got his way. Even here in prison, he was getting it.

I sat back down and put the phone to my ear again. "What exactly do you want from me?"

"Monthly visits, weekly letters." It was like he'd had it all planned out already. He knew what he'd be asking for before I'd even come.

"If I do that, then you won't tell anyone about what you saw?"

"Tell me what I saw, El."

I hesitated, but it was the only way to keep the secret. "I don't know exactly how it all works. It has something to do with his Inca ancestors. They believe in staying close to the dead, so they have this ritual to go visit them." I didn't want to tell him about the huaca. It was too valuable. I tried to keep it as vague as I could and hoped it would satiate his curiosity.

"How does it work?"

"I told you. I don't know exactly. Some kind of ritual. I don't understand it all."

"I'm not sure I believe you, El."

"If you think I'm lying, then I wonder who I got it from?"

An evil smile crept to his mouth. "It doesn't matter, I guess. You keep visiting me, by the tenth of each month. A letter postmarked by Monday of each week. Your secret goes to the grave with me. I'm not interested in revealing this ritual-thing. It does me more good as a secret than known to the world."

He was so methodical in his cunning and deceit. It was how he lived his life—the only way he knew, I supposed. "And what am I supposed to say in these letters?"

"Humor me. Tell me about school. You know, father-daughter stuff."

"That's a joke."

"It's your choice, El. You want Gabe's secret to stay a secret? You do as I say."

"There really is no choice then."

"I suppose we have a deal," he said.

There wasn't really anything else left to say. If I wanted to keep Gabe's secret, I would have to keep the attachment to Rick Thorton. That was who he was now. When I came to visit him, I would have to ask for Rick Thorton. I was going to have to write him letters, detailing my life. It was what I'd done before—recount my day at dinnertime and tell him what I was feeling. But it would be different now; he was a different man, and it would be done by force, not from love. But Gabe's secret was much too important to trifle with. I knew Rick would keep the secret, if it bought him what he wanted, which was me. Or at least that was what he said he wanted. I wasn't even sure anymore.

"I guess I'll see you next month," he said, smiling. He winked at me and then put the phone down.

I put the phone back and got up. As I walked away, I could see him, through the window. I pulled my eyes away from him, but not out of fear. I no longer feared him. But I couldn't look at him. I think it was pity, perhaps. That was all I had left to feel for him. Fear, love, hurt—I had felt all of those at different times during the last month. Pity was all I had left.

Gabe was waiting for me outside the visiting area. Part of me wanted to tell him everything, but I didn't want him to feel any guilt for the agreement I'd made with Rick. It was how it had to be. No matter how unpleasant visits and pretend letters were going to be, I had to do it. Gabe's secret was too valuable.

He gave me a hug, and we walked out into the cold. He might have sensed that I didn't really want to talk about it. I knew I would have to tell Gabe eventually, but I would wait until it was time for the next visit.

•••••

It was a huge undertaking. Aunt Mel was helping me, and my Aunt Julia had come from Colorado too. How do you dismantle an entire house, filled with every memory of your childhood, and pack it away into boxes? The house was up for sale, and the realtor thought it would go quickly.

We were donating most of the furniture. I really didn't want to profit off such a tragedy. The truck had already come by and picked up one load; they were coming again tomorrow. I was moving in with Aunt Mel in Dunellen, just fifteen minutes away. Westfield High had agreed to let me finish out the school year and attend my senior year, so I would drive to school from Aunt Mel's house every day.

There was a lot of my mom's stuff that I wanted to keep. Every item that belonged to her, to be exact. I was keeping all of her clothes and jewelry. I wanted to keep some of her kitchen items—the silverware she'd special-ordered, the mixing bowls she'd picked up in Soho one day, and the pot holders she'd bought off a street weaver on a trip she took to Guatemala one summer.

We packed up all her books, photo albums, and scrapbooks. Aunt Mel had helped me rent a storage unit to keep a lot of it in.

"What do you want to do with these?" Aunt Mel asked me, holding up a box of ceramic items.

I looked into the box. It was an assortment of small ceramic cups and plates. Among them were the remnants of my old tea set with the pink roses. I carefully picked up a small saucer, turning it over in my hands. It had several chips and had seen better days, but I knew I would be keeping them.

"Mom and I used to play tea party with these."

"Aww," Aunt Mel said. "Grandma gave these to Olivia for Christmas one year. I remember these." She took the saucer from me, fingering the smooth surface. "We played with this set for hours." She looked in the box and examined what was left.

"Will you help me pack them up?"

"Yeah." We sat down on the floor and wrapped them in bubble wrap and packed them away. "Don't put them in storage. You should keep this at the house."

"I was thinking the same thing."

We spent the rest of the day packing up the house, but there were still countless hours left ahead of us. I took a few suitcases with me to Aunt Mel's, and we made plans to come back the next day.

I decided to wait a while before going back to school. I needed time to put things in order, if that was even possible. Gabe brought me homework every day, and I left it piling up, figuring I would get to it one day, or I wouldn't. But he kept bringing it. I guess it just gave him something to do, some way to help. He had come by to help out with the packing too.

Sarah had even come by and helped for a few hours. We weren't exactly friends again. I think we'd silently decided to dissolve the friendship, but there was a history. We would never make lasagna together again, but long-time feelings don't go away as easily as you want them to. Even Sarah could be human through a tragedy like this. We hadn't talked about the superficial things that she found so integral to her daily life. Instead, we'd reminisced about childhood days and remembered the times we'd spent with my mom: running through sprinklers and making frosting-covered sugar cookies. It had been the old Sarah, the old us. I knew at the time it wouldn't last, but I'd savored the simplicity of the moment, knowing at the time that I would pack away the friendship along with everything else to live only as a memory of a time past. I knew that a new life was waiting—not one I'd necessarily wished for, but one I was ready for.

•••••

My room was empty. The movers had taken my furniture and boxes of clothes to Aunt Mel's house. I sat on the carpet in the middle of my room, trying to imagine it as it had been only days before. It had been my whole life. Now it was empty and would belong to someone else. I hadn't thought letting go of my room and my house would be so difficult, but it was all I had left of my life from before. My mother was dead; my best friend was not my best friend anymore. And my father was gone and would never be my father again, despite the continued communication he'd managed to extort from me.

And now my house would go to someone else. I would drive by it again and wonder what it was like inside, who was sitting in the spot where I now sat. Thinking about my future—my senior year, the college years that lay ahead, and Gabe—gave me hope. It helped me feel that loss sometimes led to gain. Despite all I had lost, I had gained something too. I had Gabe. And I had my mother back in a small semblance, and that helped ease the pain, if only a little.

My cell phone rang, and I pulled myself up to go find it. It was in my shoulder bag in the hallway.

"Hello?"

"Hi. Is this Ellie?"

"Yes. Who's this?"

"My name is Leila Reed. I'm an acquaintance of your father's."

The words made me freeze. An acquaintance of my father's. I wondered what other questionable people from his past might be coming into the open now that his true identity had been revealed.

"Ellie?"

"Yes. What do you want?"

"First, I want to say I'm very sorry for what has happened. I just heard about it a few days ago. I knew your father through my fiancé. They worked together on a project earlier this year. I can't imagine what you're going through."

"You're calling from Manhattan. I can tell from your phone number."

"Yes. I run an art gallery, not too far from your

father's favorite café. We used to meet him there for lunch sometimes."

"You and your fiancé?"

"Yes. They still kept in touch and were friends."

"Recent friends. Not from his past, right?"

"No, Ellie. We only knew Daniel Cummings. This is a great surprise to all of us. We're very shocked."

"Oh."

"I'm also calling because your father had told me about your friend, Gabe's mother. He said she was an amazing artist, even though he hadn't personally seen any of the artwork. But you'd told him about it. He said he didn't trust anyone's opinion more than yours, Ellie."

I remembered when he'd said that. He'd said he would call her; it had been Saturday at dinner, the day before everything in my world changed. Her words brought back feelings for my dad that I had wanted to leave behind, feelings I probably would never be able to completely rid myself of. "Oh."

"He gave me your number, and said I should call you to ask you about her, about the art. He said it was your friend's mother, told me he had a feeling this young man would soon move from friend to boyfriend. I hesitated to call you, but Ellie, I feel like I already know you so well. He's told me so much about you. And, well, I finally decided I should call you to find out about this amazing artist. I hope it's okay that I'm calling you."

"Yeah. I mean, it's fine. I'm just a little shocked. It's a little shocking after all I've found out about him."

"I know. And that's partly why I wanted to call you. Whatever he was, whatever he did—and I'm not dismissing it or making less of it because I know they were horrible things that he did—but I know he loved you. He told a lot of lies and lived a lie, but his love for you was never a lie. He loved you."

Any response I could muster got caught in my throat. I thought I'd cried my last tear for him, but there were fresh ones ready to emerge. I pushed them back because I didn't want to display them for someone I'd just met on the phone. My voice cracked as I attempted to respond, so I cleared my throat. "Um, well."

"I'm sorry, Ellie. I don't want to make you uncomfortable. I just thought I owed it to you to tell you that. He called me right after he'd had dinner with you and Gabe."

"That's okay. I just don't know what to say."

"Ellie, I'm sorry. Maybe I shouldn't have called you."

"No, it's good. I'm glad you called."

"If it isn't asking too much, I'd like to take a look at the paintings. Gabe's mother's paintings. What is her name?"

"Susannah de la Cruz."

"That's a beautiful name. My gallery is really small. We don't have a lot of space, but I am looking for new pieces and new artists. Can you tell me a little bit about her?"

"She's amazing and interesting—eccentric maybe. She's somewhat agoraphobic—doesn't leave the house. Gabe is incredible with her. He does everything to take care of her. I'm sorry. I don't know if I should be telling you all of this."

"It's okay. Would it be better if I talked to Gabe?"

"Yes. I'll give you his number. She's a very talented artist—I guess that's what's important. You'll be amazed." I gave Leila Gabe's number. "I'll text him and tell him you'll be calling him."

"That sounds great. Thank you, Ellie. I was unsure about calling you, but I'm glad I did. I know Daniel was very proud of you. I can't begin to imagine what you're feeling right now, but you should know that his love and pride for you were never a lie."

"Thank you," I managed to say before my throat went numb.

"I hope to meet you soon, Ellie. Take care of yourself and please call me if I can ever do anything for you."

"I will. Thank you."

I disconnected the call and texted Gabe. I didn't really feel like talking to anyone at the moment. I needed a quiet minute with my thoughts, thoughts of my dad that I had hoped were long gone. They were still there—thoughts that I doubted would ever leave me.

TWENTY

GABE AND I DROVE INTO THE CITY. Driving into the city is really the last resort; parking is insane, with parking garage rates to match. But we were taking several of Susannah's pieces to show Leila, and it was the best way to bring them. Carting them on the train would have proved difficult.

Susannah had parted easily with all the pieces. Having them out of the house was preferable than facing them to the wall, which had been their status up until now. She hated the paintings. They represented her manic episodes in which all she could do was paint. The process of painting, for her, was therapeutic. It was a need to create something, rather than to wallow in the pain her disease created. For her, it was the process, not the end result, that brought her solace. So, she painted—every day, all day, and into the night. She painted when she wasn't baking or cleaning. The process of creating something was only surpassed by the need to produce order through cleaning.

Gabe found a garage only a few miles from the gallery. We had about ten pieces altogether. Leila had wanted to see a sampling, and it had been difficult for Gabe to narrow it down. He had such a great admiration for his mother's art, and rightfully so. She was extremely talented, and picking only a small sample had been a hard task.

We walked out to the street, holding about half the paintings each, and quickly found a cab. Only in New York City would you have to take a cab from your parked car to your actual destination. The cab driver opened the trunk for us, and we carefully laid the paintings down.

Gabe kept turning around, as if checking the closed trunk would give him any indication as to how the paintings were faring. I squeezed his hand, happy to be the one giving support to him for a change. We were there quickly, and Gabe paid the cab fare.

Leila was exactly what I had expected. She had dark brown straight hair to her shoulders and wore dark rimmed glasses and a black calf-length skirt. She greeted us at the door and held it open for us.

"It's so nice to meet both of you." She shook our hands and motioned for us to come in farther. "Ellie, I just want you to know that your father spoke so highly of you, and I'm really, really sorry about everything. The news was just a real shock to me, and I'm very impressed with you and how you're holding up. And thank you so much for coming in to meet with me."

"Thank you." I still wasn't used to people talking to me about it. I didn't know what I was supposed to say, but I guess maybe they didn't either.

She turned to Gabe. "And I'm very excited to see these pieces. I know very little about the artist and her work, but I have really been looking forward to seeing these."

Gabe handed her a small one first. It was one I hadn't seen before. A little boy looked down at a toy in his hands. It was a small wooden train with one wheel broken off.

"This is you, right?" Leila asked.

He nodded, looking down to the floor. "Yeah, from several years back."

"You have the same profile—probably the same eyes too, if I could see either set of them." She looked at the painting and then toward Gabe's downward eyes.

He lifted his eyes and met hers. "That was one of her firsts."

"Are you sure you want to part with it? It seems like a very special piece, especially it being one of her first and one of you. Is she okay with it?"

"Yeah. She doesn't want any of them. And this one," he said pointing. "This one—it's from a long time ago. A time I don't really want to remember."

She nodded her understanding and then put the canvas down on a long table, picking up the next one. "I'm sure you've put a lot of thought into the pieces you've brought me."

The next one was of a scene from their backyard. There was a rusted lawn chair in the middle of the yard, a deflated soccer ball by its side. To the right of the chair was some broken-down chicken wire that looked like it had been used for a garden at some point, but there was very little semblance of garden left behind.

"Where is this?" she asked Gabe.

"Our backyard."

"I would really like to meet your mother," Leila said, putting the canvas down next to the first one.

"I know. I told her that, but she really doesn't leave the house anymore."

"Do you think she would talk to me on the phone?"

"Maybe. I can ask her."

"Please do. I love these pieces, and I want them. I'm not too worried about being able to build a show without her presence. Not to minimize her condition, but I think it adds to her appeal. It shows in her artwork."

Gabe didn't say anything, and I wondered how he felt about what she had said—how his mom's disorder made her a more appealing artist. I guess it made sense if you thought about artists like Van Gogh.

Leila looked at the rest of the pieces and had a declarative and enthusiastic statement for each of them. She went on to explain her rates, the commission she takes for each piece. Neither Gabe nor I knew the least bit about commission rates for artists, but I didn't sense that he cared. For the past years, these had been taking up space in his mom's room—painful reminders of the way she spends her days.

"So do we just leave these here?" Gabe asked.

"Yes, I'll start with these and make a small display. If there's interest, I'd like to build a show for her work and I'd be interested in seeing more pieces. She has more, right?"

Gabe let out a small laugh. "Yeah. She has a lot more and there are more coming."

"Wonderful!" she said, squeezing his arm. "I have some paperwork for you to look over. I'm going to need her signature on a few of these. Follow me, please."

We followed her into a small closet-sized office and stood by her desk as she explained some of the paperwork. She spent the next forty-five minutes going over details and talking about her plans for Susannah's artwork.

We walked out of the gallery, and Gabe put on his stocking cap. I locked my arm through his and then stuck my hand in my coat pocket. Empty-handed, we decided to walk back to the garage instead of taking a cab.

We'd only walked half a block when light flurries began to slowly fall. As we neared the parking garage, I could tell the snow was beginning to stick, coating the sidewalks lightly. Cars were using their windshield wipers to clean away the slow-falling snow. In New York City, it was almost impossible for a white blanket of snow to remain unscathed even for a moment. Pedestrians, cars, and trucks go over it as quickly as it falls. But it made me hopeful. Despite the quick sullying, maybe the snow did make everything clean again. Gabe pulled me closer and kissed my cold, wet cheek. Today, I chose to believe my mother's optimistic statement.

DISCUSSION QUESTIONS

1. Why does Sarah vacillate between keeping the friendship with Ellie and pushing her away?

2. Does Ellie really want to keep Sarah's friendship or is she just scared of losing someone else in her life?

3. Why does Gabe choose to reveal such a sacred secret to Ellie?

4. How does Susannah's mental illness shape the kind of person Gabe is?

5. Would Ellie have been safe with her dad the rest of her life had his crimes stayed unknown?

6. Does Ellie's dad really love her? Does she believe that he does?

7. What will Gabe say once Ellie reveals to him the arrangement she has made with her father?

8. What kind of growth do you feel Ellie undergoes through the course of the book?

ACKNOWLEDGMENTS

I WOULD FIRST LIKE TO THANK MY mother, Corina Argueta, for inspiring me with the idea for *The Huaca*. You are a great mother, and I admire your lifelong dedication to your family. Claudia and I have inherited our love of writing from you! Thanks to my father, Jose Argueta, for never-ending love and support. You are so generous to everyone around you. Muchas gracias. Los quiero mucho.

Thank you to my best friend and husband, Nolan Mickelson, who talks to everyone about my books. Your continued support and encouragement have made everything possible. I love you, and I thank BYU volleyball for meeting you. A huge thanks goes to my three wonderful boys—Omar, Diego, and Ruben. Being a mom is my favorite thing in the world. My sister, Claudia Armann, has been my lifelong friend. Who knew that all of our creative craziness as young girls would turn us into writers? Thank you for the time spent on reading and critiquing my manuscripts.

Thank you to all of my Mickelson family. I love being a part of this family.

Thank you to everyone at Cedar Fort. Thanks to Abby Volcansek for being my first teen reader and for giving me hope that other teens might enjoy my book too. Your enthusiasm has meant so much to me. Amanda Gignac, I am so glad that we are friends. I think very highly of your opinions and am grateful for your thorough editing. Thank you to Kay Pluta for early feedback on my manuscript and for taking time away from your own writing to read it.

Thanks to my friend Travis Anna Harvey, for letting me borrow your grandmother's beautiful nickname. I am so glad we met freshman year and have stayed friends all of these years.

ABOUT THE AUTHOR

MARCIA MICKELSON WAS BORN IN Guatemala but came to the United States as an infant. She considers herself from New Jersey even though she's lived in three other states. She graduated from Brigham Young University and now resides in south Texas with her husband and three sons. Marcia is the author of *Star Shining Brightly*, *Reasonable Doubt*, and *Pickup Games*. Learn more about Marcia on her website www.marciamickelson.com.

0 26575 11909 1